Linda,
  Fly with me by
Susan Elizabeth Richards

MW01165244

THE EXUMA ENIGMA

Susann Elizabeth Richards

This book is dedicated to Maureen Luther whose support and encouragement is never ending.

EXUMA SONG

Sou-Sou East as fly the crow
To Exuma we will go,
Sail her down, sail her down,
Sail her down to George Town.
Highbourne Cay the first we see
Yellow Bank is on the lee
Harvey Cay is in the moon
Farmers Cay is coming soon.
Now we come to Galliot,
Out in the ocean we must go.
Children's Bay is passing fast
Stocking Island come at last
Nassau gal is far behind,
Georgetown gal is on my mind.
The wiggle and a jiggle and a jamboree,
Great Exuma is the place for me.

Exuma Song
Author unknown
"The Exuma Guide"
by Stephen J. Pavlidis
2009

CHAPTER ONE

Carole brought in the mail; her mind was cluttered with thoughts of the future. Her husband Ted was retiring this week after spending 30 years working for the Post Office, and she was anxious about the change of their routine and on how they might spend their golden years.

Once inside, a manilla envelope caught her eye; it was from her deceased grandfather's brother Leo, an old codger who lived somewhere in the mountains in California where he had spent his life mining gold.

She opened the envelope which contained a deed of 100 acres of beachfront on the Island of Exuma in the Bahama Islands. Bewildered, she went online and did a Goggle search.

When she heard a car door slam, she watched for her husband Ted to enter their home. Carole admired Ted as much as the day they had met. At 65 he still had a full head of hair, although the once sandy colored locks were now a shade of gray, while his hazel eyes still sparkled.

"Hi, handsome, only four more days until your retirement, and then you'll be all mine."

Ted smiled tenderly and gave Carole a kiss on her check. "I hope I can fill that bill; I'm feeling a little remorseful. Seems like I've worked for the Post Office all my life. I think it's getting to me; I know I'm going to miss it, but I do look forward to the freedom of my new life."

"Speaking of the Post Office, you won't believe what I got in the mail today."

Ted intently studied Carole's eyes. "Whatever it is has put a sparkle in your eyes. Tell me!"

"Let's go out on the patio." She took his hand and let him toward their back yard. "I'm not sure how you are going to react."

"Carole, this is a bit too much drama. What on earth are you talking about?"

"Just come with me, and I'll show you."

1

They moved through the sliding glass doors that led to the outside screened-in room. Carole plopped herself down on the soft aqua cushions of the white wicker couch. Beyond them was a small pond that was frequented by a slew of wild fowl.

Ted sat down next to Carole. "Okay, what's this all about?"

"Do you remember me telling you about my Uncle Leo, you know the crotchety old man who lives out in California somewhere up in the mountains around San Bernardino? In its day it was a gold mining town, and my uncle mined gold there. He did quite well at his craft, so good that he was seldom home. So, his wife took their young son, my cousin Scott, and left him. Which left my uncle alone to continue his mining adventures."

"Seems kind selfish of him, don't ya think?"

She nodded. "Yes, I suppose it does. His wife took Scott to Escondido, a city east of San Diego. She provided for him the best she could without the help of my uncle. After he finished high school, Scott moved to San Diego where he fell in love and married a girl with a young son, Brett, whom he adopted. Unfortunately, Scott and his wife became involved in the drug scene which ruined their lives.

"Brett was old enough to be on his own, and he turned out to be a fine young man and has his own business teaching people to fly seaplanes."

"I think I got the picture now; I hope the old dude sent you a nice hunk of gold."

Carole exhaled a big sigh. "Not gold, but something of value."

"For Pete's sake, Carole!" Ted exclaimed with impatience. "What did he send you?"

"It's a deed to 100 acres of land on the Bahama Island of Exuma."

"100 acres of what? Some scrub trees on a mosquito infested island we will never visit?

"No, Ted, be serious. I looked it up online. It's in the southern Bahamas right on the Tropic of Cancer."

"Well, at least it will be warm there."

"Ted, you are being impossible." Carole reached for the envelope sitting on the coffee table in front of them and removed the deed. After scanning the document, Ted seemed more interested. "You know, we have to do more research, and we really need to take a trip there, don't you think?" This time his eyes sparkled as he gave Carole a big hug.

***

Ted and Carole boarded the 19-place Lynx Prop Jet and found their seats. They sat side by side and prepared themselves for takeoff.

The flight took less than 2 hours. When the plane was making its final landing approach, Carole exclaimed, "Look at all those small islands. They seem to be floating in a sea of aqua blue."

Ted grinned. "Looks like a fisherman's paradise; this isn't going to be half bad."

After the plane landed, they descended the stairs leading to the tarmac and found their way to customs. Everything was orderly but slow, but finally they were through. "Carole, which way to the airport lounge? That's where we're to pick up our car."

"It's supposed to be right across the street. We are to contact someone named Felix; he owns the lounge and the car rental business." They hefted their backpacks and headed for the exit.

The lounge was in a good-sized yellow building adjacent to a parking lot filled with compact cars that appeared in sad shape.

Inside the lounge was a small bar. There was no air conditioning, but large fans humming above their heads kept the place cool. Ted approached the bar and got the attention of the bartender. "Hi, my name is Ted Jones, and I'm here to pick up a rental car. I was to contact someone by the name of Felix."

"Yeah, he's here, but he went outside to check on something and should be back in a little while. If you don't mind waiting, I'll go out to get him."

Ted grunted; he was anxious to be on his way, not to hang around a lounge all day. "Well, just give me a draft beer, and my wife will have a Coke."

"Would you like a Budweiser?"

"Sure, anything that's cold."

Ted returned to where Carole sat. His jaw was tight. "Here's a Coke; we have to wait for Felix who is missing, so relax, we may be here for a while."

Carole was confused and not sure of what she was to do next. Curiosity covered her face, and her voice contained a slight tremble. "I should have listened to Kayleigh; I'm not sure I'm up to this type of adventure."

Ted took a sip of his beer and thought about an answer. "Carole, don't buy trouble, it's just a slight delay; after all, we're in the islands. I'm sure things are done at a slower pace here."

After they waited just a short time, the bartender returned. "Felix's on his way. It'll be just a few more minutes."

A black man entered the lounge, and the bartender got his attention and pointed to Ted. The man had a welcoming smile on his face, displaying a jolly disposition which took the edge off Ted's impatience.

"Sorry for the delay. I was out back working. My name is Felix. I understand you are waiting to get a rental car. We only rent compact cars and a few jeeps with four-wheel drive. What did you have in mind?"

"A compact will do. We are here for 10 days. Just want to see the sights. Doubt if we will do anything other than stay on the main roads."

"Let me get the paperwork out of the way, then I'll get you a vehicle. May I have your driver's license?"

"Sure." Ted reached for his wallet and handed him his driver's license. Then he took the last swig of his beer.

Felix returned with the rental agreement, collected a $200.00 deposit, and escorted the couple outside. They threw their backpacks into the rear seat of the car.

Felix opened the door of the beat up blue compact car for Carole. "Have a seat, madam."

He handed the keys to Ted. "Don't forget to drive on the left side of the road. Where are you staying?"

"It's a place called the Peace and Plenty in George Town. How do we get there?"

"Just take this road in front of us; it run south. You'll reach George Town in 10 miles. Your hotel will be a coral building on your left as you start to approach the center of town. It overlooks the water. It's nice location. Enjoy."

"Thanks! See you in 10 days."

Ted drove the small blue car onto the Queen's Highway. The road was in fairly good shape with a few potholes that he could easily avoid. The highway ran along the eastern side of the island. Carole was enthralled with quick glimpses of the ocean and sandy beaches. The area was sparsely developed, and the other side of the road was bordered by lush vegetation.

"Ted, this place is so laid back; it'll be easy to relax here."

Carole's contentment was disturbed when she felt a warm blast of air over her feet. She looked down to see a hole in the floorboard about the size of a softball between her feet and the gas pedal.

"Ted, look down! I can clearly see the road pass under the car. Did you see that hole before?"

He nodded. "Yes, but it doesn't interfere with my driving."

"Why didn't you stop and return this rattletrap and trade it for something without a hole in the floor?"

"Carole, I think you're overreacting. The car runs fine. If we go back, there's no guarantee the next car will be any better. We're almost in George Town, so please look for our hotel."

Carole pouted and focused on the buildings ahead.

Ted slowed the car as they entered the city limits.

"That's it! It's on our left, and the parking lot is right there."

Ted swerved into the parking lot. The hotel was a coral building surrounded by colorful flowers.

Carole's mood lifted, and she smiled. "What a pretty sight. Oh, I love it. The pool looks inviting, and we are overlooking the harbor."

They grabbed their backpacks and went inside to register. The staff were friendly, and after the check-in was over, they were escorted to their room.

Carole scanned the interior. "I like the room size. The white wicker furniture is like what we have on our patio, and the bedroom and bath are nice and clean. Look, we even have a balcony." She opened the sliding door, and they both went out. A fresh sea breeze came from the water.

Ted breathed in the salty air. "I think that's Stocking Island over there; they are supposed to have a fun type of restaurant, and this place offers free boat rides to their customers."

Carole was excited. "What do you say, Ted, let's go."

"You mean now? Carole, I think it would be better to get over to the Government House to check out the location of the property your Uncle Leo gave you. Get the deed. We can go to Stocking Island afterward."

Carole grabbed the envelope containing a copy of the deed from her backpack and headed back downstairs. The girl at the front desk gave them directions to the Government House which turned out to be just a short walk from the hotel.

The Government Building was a grandiose pink and white structure. They entered through the massive front door and stopped at the information desk. A young black girl with mesmerizing blue eyes greeted them. A tag on her blouse indicated her name was Diane.

Carole showed the deed to the girl. "I just received this deed for property somewhere on this island, and I was hoping someone here could give us further information."

"You're in luck, our property manager is in his office. I'll notify him. Please have a seat."

"Thank you." They both sat in chairs adjacent to the counter. Carole fidgeted about in her chair, while Ted picked up a magazine and thumbed through it.

Diane returned. "Mr. Nichols will see you now. Follow me." The office door was open, and they entered a spacious room with a view of the harbor. A distinguished looking middle-aged man dressed in a blue seersucker suit arose from his seat at a large ornate desk and extended his hand.

"Welcome to Exuma. I understand you have a deed to some property here."

Carole still had a tiny bit of anxiety. "My name is Carole Kelsall Jones, and this is my husband, Ted. We are here to investigate the property my Uncle Leo Kelsall recently gave to us." She handed him the deed.

"Well, my dear, the Kelsall name is well known in these parts. They helped settle Exuma back in the 1770s. They were loyalists from the colonies, and because they were loyal to the crown, the magistrate of Devonshire, England, granted them 900 plus acres of land. When John Kelsall died, he left the property to his children with the stipulation that the property be passed on to their descendants. So, you may be eligible for more than the 100 acres in this deed."

"That's unexpected news, as I just split our property up to include my daughter and my nephew. My husband and I just retired, and this would be an ideal way to begin our new life. Where can we find the property?"

"This land is on the island of Little Exuma. It's about 20 miles south of here. Your plot is at the tip of the island which may cause you a problem because there is no navigable road in that area. I'm sure you could find someone to take you there—you'll need a 4 wheel to get that far south. You might consider visiting the Hermitage House

6

in Williamstown, a good place to start. It is the original homestead of the Kelsall family's plantation. The main house is still standing after all these years. I will have my secretary provide you with a map of the area, and while she's at it, she can make copies of these deeds to file on your behalf. If you have any more questions, please feel free to pay me a visit, and welcome to our lovely island."

Carole was relieved at the smoothness of the conversation. "Thank you," she smiled. "I'm so excited."

Ted smiled and escorted Carole out of the building. Armed with the map, they returned to the hotel to retrieve their car; then they headed south on the Queen's Highway for about twenty-five miles. They crossed a bridge at Ferry and were officially on Little Exuma and a short drive to Williamstown.

Ted parked the car near the old plantation. "There's the house. Do you want to explore it?"

"No, not now; let's see how close we can get to the property. From looking at this map, it's only about three miles to the end of the island."

Ted hesitated. "But Mr. Nichols said we should use a four-wheel drive. I don't want to get stuck."

"Come on, Ted, I want to see our property. A few more scratches aren't going to hurt this heap."

"Alright, Carole, if that's what you want, let's go."

The paved road gave way to a dirt road which was very rutty and rough. Ted banged and swerved the car along until he knew it was time to stop.

"We better walk the rest of the way. It can't be that far."

The terrain was sparsely overgrown with vegetation. A few tall pines blocked their way, but they maneuvered between them before emerging into a clearing.

Carole became ecstatic. "Oh, Ted, look!"

A large crescent beach lay before them, the white sand caressed by a beautiful sparkling, iridescent sea.

"This is spectacular; we have our own paradise. I can't believe my eyes! Look over there—that looks like a line of reefs just offshore."

"I bet it's loaded with fish. Yes, Carole, this is a perfect spot. Let's take a walk."

7

They kicked off their sandals. The snow-white sand felt so soft and warm on their feet.

"This is a perfect place to build our retirement home," Ted noted.

"Yes, but, Ted, it is a little too remote for me. Maybe we should be closer to Williamstown."

"Don't be silly. We'll fix the road and buy a boat. Then we can go anywhere from here."

"Speaking of boats, there's a blue and white sailboat anchored offshore up ahead of us."

The closer they got they were able to recognize a young couple camped on the beach by the sailboat. When they approached, the couple rose to greet them. "Isn't it beautiful here? We don't usually see people this far from civilization. What brings you here?" The young woman spoke with a slight lisp. Her dark blonde hair caressed her shoulders; she had wide brown eyes and a warm grin.

"Yes, we were just discussing that very fact. You seem to have a British accent; are you from England?'

"Yes, I'm Kate, and this is my husband, Lance."

Lance was a handsome man with dark hair. His smile and kind eyes reflected a happy-go-lucky attitude, and he was more than willing to discuss their travels. "We traveled to Nassau from Liverpool and picked up this 27-foot Oday sailboat. It needed some detailing, but I'm a skilled carpenter, so it was an easy fix for me."

Ted laughed. "I was going to ask if you sailed that boat across the pond but knew better. How'd you pick this spot?"

"We loaded ourselves and the boat on the mail boat which dropped us off in George Town, and we sailed our way down the coast to this spot."

Carole grinned. "How great, I don't sail or snorkel or know how to use a Kayak, but when we move here, I am going to try to learn."

Kate asked, "Move here? Like on Exuma?"

"No," Carole explained. "Right here on Little Exuma. We just inherited this property."

"Really, are you sure?"

"Why, yes, don't you believe me?"

"It's not that, but just yesterday two men in a power boat stopped here and told us to leave because they were going to develop this area. They went so far as to threaten us. They looked like real tough men, the kind to avoid."

"But you're still here?"

"Yes, it's so beautiful, isolated, and away from the busy hustle and bustle, but if they return, we may have to find another area, at least until we know what's going on. I'm sure there are many lovely places around. We'll most probably move closer to Williamstown."

"I'll tell you what's happening," Ted said. "I'm going back to Mr. Nichols at the Government Building and file a complaint."

Carole placed her arm around Ted. "Please settle down, dear. There must be some explanation. They could have gotten confused on the location of their property. We better go now; you said we could explore that Hermitage House." Looking back at the couple, she said, "It's been nice talking with you. As far as we're concerned, you are welcome to camp here, just please be careful if those men come back."

***

They returned to their car, which Ted turned around, and they bumped their way back to the paved road which ran along a large salt pond. Looking at the rear-view mirror, something caught his eye, and his gaze became intense. He brought the car to a halt. "Carole, get out of the car right now!"

She looked at his face and threw the door open. "What's wrong?"

"I'll tell you later, it's only a short walk to the ruins. I'll meet you there. Now get going."

Carole couldn't find the words to speak and was petrified—what could be wrong? Her heart beat fast as she followed Ted's instructions. She didn't even look back as his instructions had been forceful enough to frighten her. She began to run toward the ruins.

Ted got of the car and opened the back door. Above the back seat were large brown scorpions scrambling along the rear window. Frantically he looked around for something to rid them from the car. Thoughts rushed through his mind; there must be something in the trunk he could use. He moved to the rear of the car and bent down to open the trunk.

Something cast a dark shadow over him, and as he started to turn, he felt something sharp hit his head. He fell to the ground and blacked out.

***

Carole finally stopped and looked back, but she could no longer see Ted or the rental car, so she continued to walk until she saw the remains of the Hermitage House perched on a hill ahead. Now that

9

she had reached her goal, she took time to reflect on Ted's reaction. What could have been in the car that upset Ted to such a degree, and where was he? Why hadn't he joined her like he said he would? What should she do? Then it hit her; she was all alone in this strange place.

"Ted, where are you?" she yelled. "Don't leave me here all alone!" The beat of her heart accelerated into palpitations, and her knees went weak. Sweat poured from her brow, and she started to tremble. "Ted, answer me, please!" She looked around, not knowing if she should return to where she'd left him, but no, she couldn't do that. Ted would say she was overreacting. Besides, he said he would meet her at the ruins.

She tried to calm herself; her stomach was upset, but her chest pain had subsided. Looking ahead, she tramped up the hill. Turning sideward she saw a splendid view of the ocean. What a perfect spot for a house—no wonder the Kelsalls had chosen this spot to settle.

When she approached the old structure, she stopped and turned back from the hilltop, looking at the road for any glimpse of Ted. The road was deserted. She turned back to the old mansion. It looked safe enough.

"I'm going inside," she said out loud, her voice edged with cautious bravado.

Carole stepped through the front door which led into a large room. She was intrigued by the vastness of the plantation house and wandered from room to room; finally, she reached the kitchen and began searching for artifacts like kitchenware. Hoping to find a spoon or a pan, she rustled through the debris.

Suddenly she felt a strange white aura overtake her body. An image came into sharp focus—a vivid image of a tomb.

"What the—?" She blinked but the image remained. She had to be delusional! It was the heat, or the effect of her rapid heartbeat. And where was Ted? Why hadn't he shown up already?

A wave of desperation descended on her. "Where are you, Ted?" She had to go back and check on him. Something dreadful may have happened to him. She ran to the nearest door which led out to the rear yard.

There in front of her was the tomb she had just seen in the image that had flashed before her in the kitchen. Her stomach churned and perspiration dripped off her forehead. She had to find the road that led to the salt pond, but she was disoriented.

She ran past the tomb and stumbled into a hole, then tumbled face first to the ground. When she tried to get up, she felt two large hands wrap around her throat.

CHAPTER TWO

Kayleigh put the number Carole had given her into her cell phone and waited for someone to answer. She questioned her role in this matter, feeling the task was dumped on her by her mother.

She jumped when a loud voice spoke. "Kelsall's Sea Plane Base, how can I help you?"

"Hi, my name is Kayleigh Jones, and I'd like to speak with Brett Kelsall."

"Speaking. If you are interested in taking a sea plane flying lesson, be prepared to wait awhile, we're mighty busy now."

She didn't know why, but the sound of his voice intrigued her. "No," she laughed," no, that's not why I called, besides I'm an airline stewardess. I don't fly planes, but I need to talk to you about a personal matter."

"Who are you again? K Lee something, it sounds Asian, and you want to talk to me about something personal. Come on, lady. What is this about?"

Kayleigh realized she'd better not beat around the bush. "Please excuse my inquisition, but this is an important matter. I am Carole Kelsall's daughter. My dad is Ted Jones. My mother's father George was your grandfather Leo's brother. Uncle George died a couple of years ago after having a stroke."

"Okay, that clarifies a lot. I know Uncle Ted, he's a cool guy. He used to play ball with me and tell me stories. I didn't see Aunt Carole much; guess she was always busy."

"That could be because she was taking care of me."

"Could be, but I haven't seen my gramps since my father died from a drug overdose. That didn't set well with the old man, and he blamed my mom for his death. She had it rough and died the same way. By then I was old enough to be on my own and, believe me, I don't do drugs."

Kayleigh listened to his story as she idly watched two black and white ducks swimming in the lake behind her apartment.

"So why the call, did Gramps die?"

"No, I understand he's still alive and living in some mountain town in California."

Brett sighed. "Yup, it's Big Bear City, which is a nice little town. Are you ever going to get around to why you called me?".

Kayleigh was confused on what to say next; she couldn't figure out the tone of his voice but sensed he seemed to have a mischievous manner. She was curious to find out more. "Yes, of course, my point is that Uncle Leo, sorry I meant to say your grandfather just sent my mom a deed for 100 acres of prime land on the Bahama island of Exuma."

She paused and waited for a response. Getting none, she continued, "My mom has split the property into three parcels. 50 acres for her and my dad, and she divided the other 50 acres between you and me. My folks are there now checking things out. I need to get your address, so I can mail you a copy of the deed."

"Sure, that'll be fine. Hey, K Lee, hold on a minute, one of my students just walked in. I won't be long, so just hang on."

While she waited, she watched the black and white ducks start to climb out of the pond and walk on her lawn, heading for the back door. It was her habit to feed them, but she was busy with her phone call and had forgotten to put their food out.

"Hi, are you still there?"

"Yes, I'm watching Donald and Daisy waddle up to my backdoor."

"Huh?"

"They are wild ducks that are looking for a handout."

"You know you shouldn't feed them, but that's your business. You wanted my address, right? Well, here it is: Kelsall's Sea Plane Base, P.O. Box 597609, Salton City, California, 92275. I can't quite figure out where I fit in this equation."

"I guess Mom just wanted to keep the property in the family; it seems that somewhere around 1780 a family of Kelsalls settled on Exuma and developed a cotton plantation. I don't think it's anything other than that. Thanks for your address. I'll send you a copy of the deed tomorrow."

"Wait, before you go, don't forget to let me know what your folks find out about the island. It might be fun to go there together and check our property." His voice turned enthusiastic. "We're Kelsalls; we should check out our history. What do you say?"

Kayleigh felt a tinge of panic. "I'll have to think about that. I might not be able to get away—my boyfriend Lou is the jealous type."

"Be serious, girl, I'm not a serial killer. I'm your cousin."

"Second cousin," she noted. "Okay, Brett, I'll keep that in mind, and I will get back to you. I must go now."

"Thanks for the news, K. Lee. I think I'd better go check on Gramps; I just hope he'll agree to see me, it's been so long. I'd like to make amends with him. Take care."

"Bye, Brett." Kayleigh hung up the phone. She needed time to digest what had just happened. She was experiencing an array of mixed feelings. She sensed she was fighting an intense desire to meet him, but she was also feeling a bit of guilt that going on a trip with a guy, any guy, even a distant cousin, might be betraying Lou.

Crazy thoughts buzzed around in her head as she remembered the warm timbre of Brett's voice when he suggested visiting Exuma. Then the squawking of the ducks brought her back to reality.

"Oh, sorry, I forgot about you two." She went to her pantry, grabbed a sack of grain, then went back outside to feed the ducks.

CHAPTER THREE

Brett couldn't stop thinking about the phone call from Kayleigh. In fact, he had trouble concentrating while teaching a new pilot with his seaplane instructions. By the end of the day, he had decided to fly up to Big Bear City to visit his grandfather.

The next morning, he cancelled all the scheduled sea plane instructions, stating he had an urgent need to see his elderly grandfather. He packed his piper cub with a few of his personal provisions and headed to Big Bear Lake. He calculated the flight would take him less than an hour. It was only about 100 miles by air. He didn't have to take his high powered L65 Sea bear Amphibian plane with twin Rotax turbo engines for such a short hop. His smaller seaplane would do the trick.

He was in the air by late morning, eager to arrive just before noon, anticipating taking his grandfather out to lunch. He cruised over the desert then climbed up to 8500 feet which was the altitude of the lake. Once there he circled over the lake looking for his grandfather's cabin. After spotting it, he flew over the cabin, landed his plane on the water, and taxied it to a sandy spot not far from his grandfather's place.

The noise of a low flying plane buzzing his house disturbed Leo Kelsall. He glanced out his front window. "The nerve of that pilot, has he no respect for others?" Leo put on his boots, grabbed his six gun and left his place in a huff. He walked toward the seaplane where the pilot was anchoring the craft. "Hey, mister what's wrong with you? This is a residential neighborhood. Get out of here now!"

Brett looked up to find the old man still ranting. "Hey, wise guy, what's the meaning of buzzing my place? Get your rig out of here!"

Brett hesitated, then smiled. "Hi, Gramps, remember me?"

Leo frowned, then squinted as he tried to recognize the pilot. "Gramps? Don't you have any respect. I ain't got no grandkids; who are you?"

"I'm Brett, and I am your grandson."

16

Leo's eyes scanned Brett's face. When he realized who he was, he choked up with a lump in his throat. "You're my Scottie's boy, aren't you? What the hell are you doing here?"

Brett approached Leo with his hand extended. "It's been a long while, hasn't it? Sorry it took me so long to visit." Brett looked at the gun in Leo's hand. "I really don't think you're going to need that."

"Well, you ain't getting any of my gold if that's what you're after."

"No, Gramps, I just want to take you to lunch."

"Huh, how come?"

"I wanted to tell you that Aunt Carole just split some of the property on the deed for the Exuma land with me and her daughter Kayleigh." He finally knew her real name from the back of the envelope containing his copy of the deed.

"Well, I'll be damned. That was mighty nice of her. Did she say why?"

"Apparently she and Uncle Ted have just retired, and she felt 100 acres was too much for them, and she wants to keep the land in the family."

Leo looked at Brett, thinking he should kick him out, but decided to hear what he had to say. "Okay, let's go to the Bears Den, they have good food, and I'd like to know what's on your mind. Come with me while I get the keys to my truck."

The truck was in the driveway outside of Leo's cabin. "Wait here." He held the gun up. "I need to get rid of this, and I'll be right back."

Brett glanced around the lake and at the canopy of tall pine trees that blanketed the mountain side. It was such a contrast to the desert cactus and tumbleweeds that covered the landscape just 100 miles away.

Leo returned, and they climbed into a shiny new silver Dodge Ram. "This is a nice ride, Gramps."

"Yep, it is. I need something reliable to drive up here in the winter."

The restaurant was in the center of town, which was busy with traffic. They found a parking place and went inside. They sat and discussed many previously unaddressed issues about Brett's parents. While they talked, Brett began to feel that Leo was starting to warm up to him.

17

Leo surprised Brett by revealing a secret. "Well, this may come as a surprise to you, but I think I have another child out there somewhere. After your grandmother left me and took Scottie away, I met this gorgeous woman. She knocked me off my feet, but there was no way I was going to get married again. Gold mining is my passion, and no damn woman was going to take me from it. She was a pushy one and, in the beginning, I really liked her until I got the feeling she was after my gold, so, I called it quits. But she persisted, and I weakened. A few months later she tells me she's pregnant. So, I told her to leave."

"Why'd you do that, Gramps?"

"Because she deceived me, the lying bitch. Her name was Connie Marino, Mondello or maybe Magnano, something like that, so if she really was pregnant there could be an Italian stallion or princess stopping by to see me someday, but trust me, they ain't getting a dime from me."

"Well, I'm not here to ask you for anything. I just thought I should keep in touch. You were so good to me when I was young, and Aunt Carole made me think about that. She and Uncle Ted are in Exuma now. Kayleigh and I are planning to check out our land when we get the time. So, thank you for making that happen."

"Kid, I hope that you get to enjoy it. I never went there, just inherited the deed from my dad and put it aside while I mined gold. I didn't have the interest or the time. I had a sick spell last month and started to think about the deed. That's when I made up my mind to pass it on before it was too late."

"Well, who knows, Gramps, maybe someday I'll take you there, but I better get back now. I have a business to run."

They returned to the cabin, and Brett headed for the lake. He powered the plane up and took off, circled around the lake, then buzzed Leo's house again, tipping the wings of his plane as he passed over. In the cockpit Brett's mind was jumbled with thoughts about the incredible life Leo must have lived.

*"Be scared. You can't help that. But don't be afraid.
Courage from hearts and not from numbers grow."*
John Dryden

CHAPTER FOUR

When Carole regained consciousness, she was surrounded by darkness. Her neck was painful, and she placed her hands around it, gently massaging her warm skin. She was relieved when she couldn't find any open wounds. Then reality set in as she remembered someone trying to strangle her. She was petrified and couldn't move. Where was she? It felt damp and smelled odd, kind of musty, but there was some other smell she couldn't place. She moved slightly and realized she was laying on a pile of sticks. She closed her eyes with the hope that it was all a bad dream and fell back to sleep.

When she awoke again a tiny ray of the misty morning light shone a small beam on her face, warming her. More aware of her surroundings, she moved her head around only to discover she was inside a tomb.

She shrieked, "Oh, no, it can't be! She moved again and realized that she was lying on someone's bones.

She began to tremble and felt the rise of sheer panic in her throat. "Help! Someone, please help me. Please! I beg you, help me! Ted, where are you?" She reached under her body, grabbed a long bone, and started to hit the cover above her. "Get me out of here!" She pleaded, "I'm not dead!"

***

Kate and Lance were enjoying an early morning swim when the same two men who had threatened them returned. This time they were armed, and they pointed their weapons at the two of them.

The tall one spoke first. "What the hell are you two still doing here? We told you to leave yesterday; seems you don't listen when we talk nice. Lenny and I don't like it when people don't listen to us. And that usually means they must be taught a lesson for not taking us seriously. So, if you want to live to see another day, you need to leave this place. We will wait here while you get all your stuff on that pitiful boat, and you sail away."

Vinny kept the barrel of his assault rifle pointed at the couple, while Lenny beached their boat and got out, walked over to Lance and twisted his arm up his back, then placed his pistol to Lance's head. "Now, little lady, you will break up your camp and put your stuff on the boat or your man here will regret he ever saw you."

Kate had no choice. Tears streamed down her cheeks as she disassembled the tent and rushed around to gather their other belongings. When she finished removing everything from the beach, she asked, "Does that satisfy you?"

From his place on the power boat, Vinny spoke. "Now you two get out and don't return. Big Gina don't coddle to trespassers. Next time we won't be so nice."

Lenny released his hold on Lance, who ran to Kate's side and embraced her.

Vinny fired bullets into the sand a few feet away from the couple. "There's no need for kissy, kissy. Get your asses out of here!"

The couple scrambled aboard the cluttered sailboat. Kate hauled the anchor, while Lance started the engine. "Kate, don't bother with the sails for now." Lance pointed the boat toward Williamstown and left the two wild men behind. He was relieved they made it out alive.

"Kate, we'll find another spot, there are many beautiful areas around."

Kate nodded; she hadn't spoken a word since they left the beach.

Lance was concerned. "Honey, are you okay?"

"Blimey no. I'm scared shitless! I've never encountered anything so frightening in my whole life. How do we know they won't come back for us? They know what our boat looks like, they or the Big Gina character they spoke of could seek us out and kill us."

Lance reached out to comfort her. "But they didn't kill us when they had the chance. We are out of their way. I don't think we mean that much to them. They were so adamant on removing us from that spot. I'm sure they're up to something unscrupulous. Let's just anchor around Williamstown. It's a small village with a few stores. I don't think those thugs will bother us again. It will give us time to calm down and investigate other sites."

They began to feel more at ease as the day progressed. "Kate, let's take advantage of the warm breeze."

"Yes, let's do. I'll move some of this equipment out of the way and hoist the sails."

"When we get closer to Williamstown, we need to look for a stone beacon. There's a nice place to anchor there."

"You're right, Lance, I read about that beacon. It was built 200 years ago to guide merchants as far away as Nova Scotia who came to purchase salt from the huge salt pond here."

By midday they had reached their destination and anchored their sailboat just offshore. "Look, Kate, what does that marker say?"

Kate moved closer to the marker on the beach. "It says this is the spot where the Tropic of Cancer crosses the island. How cool is that?"

They pitched their tent and settled into their new camp. But Lance was not ready to relax just yet. "Let's take a walk up to the old ruins on the top of the hill, then go see what there is in town. There's supposed to be a pub there. We should get a pint and relax."

***

Carole had exhausted herself with all her screams for help and lay silent in the dark eerie tomb when she was once again engulfed by an aura. "Oh, no! Not again."

Just as she spoke, she saw a vision of Ted. He was bound to a tree. "Teddy, where are you? No wonder you didn't meet me. How can I find you before they kill me?"

She couldn't relax, but she lay still waiting for her destiny, when she heard voices. Hope and fear waged a war in her mind. Would she be saved, or would her life be soon over? *Oh God,* she prayed. *Please protect me. Don't let them kill me.*

CHAPTER FIVE

The voices grew louder as they approached the tomb, then the familiar sound of their spoken dialect excited her... could it be the young couple they'd met on the beach? She picked up the bone and knocked it hard on the tomb's cover. "Help me! Someone please help me! I'm in the tomb!"

Lance and Kate were amazed at the condition of the building's foundation. "Kate, whoever build this house knew what they were doing; it's built like a castle."

"Yes, it is a strong structure, but I can feel something eerie in here. I don't know what it is, but it makes my skin crawl. Let's explore the other side."

They wandered around but stopped short when they heard a muffled voice begging for help. "Kate, did you hear that? Where is it coming from? Someone's in trouble."

Their eyes scanned the perimeter of the grounds, listening intently for a clue to where the voice was coming from.

Kate shouted, "Where are you? How can we help?"

Carole was desperate but now hope surged through her. She took hold of the bone with both hands and pounded it on the tomb's lid as hard as she could. "I'm here in the tomb, and I can't escape. Please help me!" Her feelings of intense loneness had vanished for the moment.

"Someone's in the tomb, look over there!" Lance said.

"Oh, Lance, how macabre. Has someone risen from the dead?"

"Don't be absurd. Someone's in there; we must help."

They ran toward the tomb, and through the small opening they spoke to the prisoner inside. "We're here, and we will get you free."

Lance pushed the tomb's lid, but it hardly moved. Kate encouraged him. "Try harder, this is a matter of life and death."

"Kate, get over here by my side and on the count of three, push with all your might."

"I'm ready."

"1,2,3! Push!"

To their astonishment the tomb's lid moved. "Let's try again, push!"

This time the cover slid enough to allow them to see inside. Carole's face was visible. "Lance, it's the woman we met on the beach."

Lance peered down at Carole. "Don't lose faith, we will get you out of there."

They placed their hands on the lid, and with the weight of their bodies behind them, they shoved it. This time it slid more, giving Carole room enough to slither herself upward.

Lance grabbed her arms and lifted her out of the tomb. Carole clung to him. Tears covered her face, but her body was so rigid it wouldn't bend.

Lance held her and let her cry.

"You're my hero," Carole said through the tears streaming down her face.

Lance looked at Kate. "Perhaps you could help me, dear."

Kate placed her arms around Carole. "You're safe now, we're here to help you."

Carole stepped away from Lance and grabbed Kate's hands. "It's been horrible, please don't leave me!"

"We won't; you're safe now. What on earth happened to you—how did you get inside … that?" Kate pointed to the tomb.

"I'm not really sure. Ted is gone, but I know he is alive, because I saw him in an image."

"An image?" Kate looked at Lance, who just rolled his eyes. "What type of image?"

"It's the strangest thing. When I was in the old house, I saw an image of a tomb. I hadn't seen the tomb before, but there it was, an image as clear as day. Then I ended up inside it, and while I was inside the tomb, I saw an image of Ted."

"Carole, I think this whole affair has you a little off balance," Kate said in a gentle tone.

"Oh, please, you must believe me because it's true. I must find Ted. The last time I saw him he was at the salt pond. He was upset about something in the car, and told me I had to get out, and I was to meet him here, but he never came. I didn't understand why until I saw the image. Now I must go back there and find him."

"But Carole, you can't do that. We met those two men we told you about again today, and they nearly shot us with a high-powered rifle. We've got to get out of here."

"Kate's right," Lance said. "We need to leave now." He stared intently at his wife. "You and I have just become involved in someone else's trouble. And you, too, Carole. So, let's go before we are all dead."

Carole looked deep into Kate's eyes. "Lance is right, but I need to find my husband."

Kate released her hold on Carole. "I'm sorry, and I understand. Just, please be careful."

Carole turned around. "Which way is the road? I'm all mixed up." Her steps were wobbly, and she stumbled. "I need to rest a bit, then I'll be okay. You two run along."

Kate looked at Lance. "We cannot abandon this woman; we must help her. We mustn't cast a blind eye to her needs. But right now, Carole, you need to drink and eat something. Then you'll feel better and be better equipped to find your husband. Come with us."

The two English sailors helped Carole down the hill to their sailboat. Kate gave Carole some water and a snack. After eating, she regained a modicum of her energy, but her impatience to find Ted was just beneath the surface of her mind.

"Please, I beg of you, please just take a walk with me to the salt pond. That's all I ask; then you can go your own way."

Kate stared at Carole before responding. "Yes, I'll go with you. The pond is just beyond that beacon." She offered Carole her hand. "Come with me." She turned to Lance. "I'll be right back."

Lance opened his mouth as if to argue but then seemed to change his mind. Instead, he nodded his head and from his seat on the boat, watched the women walk away.

CHAPTER SIX

Lance sat on his sailboat with his feet upon the rails and brooded about the events of the last two days. Tugging at his chin, he wondered how the heck he and Kate had gotten involved in this misadventure? He knew for certain that the two men were evil and malicious. So, what was he thinking, letting Kate go off without him? The two women could be in some serious danger. He went into the ship's galley in search of a weapon.

Kate and Carole rambled around the salt pond. "This is the area where we parked the car, but it's gone. How could that be?"

"Carole, he must have driven it somewhere else."

"NO! he wouldn't leave me. I know him." Her face drained of all color. "You don't know my husband. He is not the kind who doesn't keep his word. Someone must have stolen it."

Kate was having a hard time keeping her composure. "Carole, get a grip! I didn't mean to upset you. You said you saw an image of Ted. Tell me exactly what you saw, every detail."

"Let me think, it's kind of blurry now, but he looked like he was bound to a tree."

"The only trees are those by the road that leads into the interior of the island. They line the side of the road. We better hustle; we shouldn't be alone like this for long."

When they approached the tree line, Carole hollered, "Ted, we're here for you. Can you hear me?"

Kate felt like shrinking into the brush. "Oh, lordly."

Hearing no reply, Carole tried again. "Ted, we are here, where are you?"

Suddenly they heard a brief rustle of something from within the thicket of trees. Carole looked at Kate. "I'm not sure now, what if it's the men?"

"Well, then we're doomed, but it may be Ted, and here we are, so let's find out."

They trudged through the thorny branches that seemed to reach out to scratch them. A large tree grew a few steps away. Ted's body

25

was bound, and his mouth gagged, but his legs were free from restraints. Carole ran to him and touched his matted hair and then caressed the stubble on his cheeks. "Darling, I'm so sorry, this has been a nightmare." Ted's eyes welled up with tears. "Thank God you're safe now."

Kate tried to release the knotted ropes but couldn't untie them. But she did manage to remove the gag fastened around his bruised head. She franticly searched for something to help her loosen the knots on the ropes. Finding nothing she looked though the bushes and saw someone walking up the road. She snuck through the brush, taking care not to make any unnecessary noise. She was relieved to see Lance and called out to him. "We're over here." She ran to meet him and led him to Ted.

Lance used the filet knife he had brought as protection and slit the ropes. Ted nearly collapsed, but the two British sailors held him upright.

"Don't try to talk," Lance told Ted. "Let's just focus on getting away from here." Together the four returned to the sailboat.

Carole cleansed Ted's wounds while Kate cooked a meal. It gave Lance time to analyze the situation. "Ted, we all must leave this place. Staying here is not an option. It isn't safe for any of us. Those men will stop at nothing to eliminate you and Carole. They want your land, and unfortunately you are in their way. Nothing can change that. You have a bullseye on your back. And don't expect the government to help you, they won't."

Ted spoke up, his voice raspy. "Well, we will get on the next plane and go home."

"On the surface, that sounds like the logical choice. I know you just want to forget the whole episode. But these men are villains, and they will track you down and eliminate you before you reach the plane." Lance paused. "The best thing you can do is disappear."

"Disappear? How can we do that?"

Ted and Carole stared at Lance and then at one another.

"I have an idea," Lance said. "But let's eat before I explain."

CHAPTER SEVEN

Kayleigh sat next to Lou, her pilot boyfriend, in the crew lounge of the Rio de Janeiro-Galego International Airport. They were waiting for the cruise ship passengers to board the chartered jet on its return flight to Miami, Florida.

To get his undivided attention, Kayleigh placed her hands over Lou's. "Lou, I'm worried about my parents; they were supposed to have returned to Florida five days ago. I haven't heard a word from my mother, which is not like her. I don't want to panic, but I have a bad feeling that something went wrong."

"Have you called her?"

"Of course, I have. I've tried a few times when they first arrived there, and every day since they failed to return. Her phone doesn't ring, there is no voice mail message, not even a full mailbox notification. Nothing at all."

"How about the police?"

"They haven't got a clue and don't seem to want to get involved. I also called the hotel where they planned to stay, and they told me they checked in, then went for a ride but never returned."

"Sounds strange; maybe they didn't like the place and found one they liked better."

"That's a point, but I must find out for myself, so I'm going to need to take some time off, and I'd really like for you to go with me. I don't think I should go alone."

"Kayleigh, you know I can't go. I'm on the schedule to fly. I can't jeopardize my job. But you're right, you shouldn't go alone. Don't you have a girlfriend who would go with you? How about Patty, you and she are pretty tight."

"No, I couldn't ask her to put herself in possible danger. Lou, I need you to help me find my parents. There are other pilots who could take your flights for a week."

"Sorry, Kayleigh, it's not that simple."

Kayleigh felt rejection surge through her, and she withdrew her hands. "I thought you love me, but I'm beginning to think that's a bunch of B.S. You just keep me around for your convenience. But that's okay. I'll find a way. Thanks for nothing."

Kayleigh stood up. "I need to think. I'm sure you're not interested in my inconsequential chatter."

Lou shrugged his shoulders. "Have it your way."

Kayleigh walked to the other side of the room and stood in front of the windows overlooking the runway. How could he be so cold? They'd been committed to each other for over three years. He'd just shown his true colors, she thought. He only likes her when he's having things his way. Well, that wasn't going to work for her anymore.

***

"Kelsall's Sea Plane Base."

"Hi, Brett, this is Kayleigh."

"Kayleigh, it's nice to hear from you."

"Brett, I need to go to Exuma right away. Is there any way you could go with me?"

"Gee, Kayleigh, that's short notice. I'm booked solid with sea plane flight instructions. What's the rush?"

"My folks never returned, and I'm worried sick. I've tried to contact them but haven't been able to. I called the police and the hotel where they were to stay, but no one knows anything about their whereabouts. I'm afraid something is drastically wrong."

She anxiously waited for his reply, but there was only silence which she found maddening. She held her cell phone up and looked at its face to make sure they were still connected. What's going on? Unable to wait a moment longer, she asked, "Brett! Are you still there?"

"Yeah, I'm here. I'm trying to figure out what I need to do. I have a personal motto to never dismiss a gut feeling."

"So, what does that mean?"

"I'll go with you, just give me a day, and I'll get back to you."

Kayleigh sighed. "Thank you. I needed to hear that."

***

Lance and Kate invited Ted and Carole on their sailboat, and he sailed from Little Exuma to George Town. He docked at the town wharf and helped Ted and Carole off the boat. "Follow me, we're going to rent you a houseboat and take it some place north of here.

28

Preferably in an area that doesn't get too much boat traffic. You can relax there until the threat to your lives goes away."

Carole was weary of the plan, but the thought of being locked in a tomb still frightened her and being anywhere but in George Town seemed inviting. "The sooner we leave here the better."

The houseboat rental facility was a short distance south of the wharf in Kidd Cove. They made a quick dash there.

The manager showed them the boats; he rented two different sizes. The 35-foot ones had one bedroom while the 43-foot had two.

Ted said, "We don't need anything larger than the 35-foot boat."

Carole was impressed. "They're so colorful and roomy with everything we would ever need on board; it has air, hot and cold running water and a spacious kitchen."

The negotiations went quickly. Lance told Ted, "I'll pay the rental fee, that way no one can trace it to you. When the threat to harm you has passed, you can reimburse me."

Ted shook his hand. "Thanks."

The manager helped them aboard. "Remember, you can call me on the marine radio with any concerns."

Lance drove the houseboat to a safe secluded marina, and Kate followed them in the sailboat.

*"You'll never do a whole lot unless you're brave
enough to try."*
Dolly Parton

CHAPTER EIGHT

Kayleigh strode back and forth as she awaited Brett's arrival at Miami's Sea Plane Base. She noted that it wasn't a very busy place; in fact, there hadn't been one seaplane land since her arrival. She recalled how the place had buzzed with activity when Chalks Airline used the base to transport fishermen and divers to and from the island of Bimini two or three times a day.

Gazing upward she searched the sky for a seaplane. Finally, she spotted what looked like a white dragon fly in the distance heading her way. When she saw the white pontoons hanging below the fuselage, she felt her heart pound. Excited now, she whispered, "This has to be Brett."

The four-place Sea Bear Amphibian circled above her, then with a precise maneuver, it splashed down in the water and motored up on the ramp. The noise from the twin engines ceased, and the seaplane's back hatch swung open. The pilot looked at Kayleigh. "I'm here to pick up a passenger named Kayleigh Jones."

"Hi, Brett, that's me."

He climbed out of the hatch and down the spine of the plane which served as a walkway and sauntered to her side. He extended his hand. "Glad to meet you, cousin. The Kelsall genes fit you well."

Kayleigh felt her face redden. What an unusual way to pay a compliment. Her eyes fluttered, and she grinned up at him which gave her opportunity to give him a once over. His straw-colored wavy hair was unruly and a bit too long. His clothes were casual, almost sloppy, but were clean. Certainly, he didn't have the polished look of Lou, but his body was tall and lean and his grip strong.

"Glad to meet you, Brett. I can't thank you enough for agreeing to accompany me to Exuma."

"It took a lot of concentration and coordination to move everyone around. Bottom line, I got it done. Now for our journey, but first I must top my tanks off, then we can embark on our unpredictable adventure."

30

"Your plane is larger than what I imagined, although I've never paid much attention to sea planes, as I'm always aboard jets."

"Well, she's not what I use to teach my students, that's a Piper Cub. But this one, she's my special gal, and she flies like a dream. I've taken her to Lake Havasu, Lake Mead, and Catalina Island, but this is her longest journey. You'll see, she's simply amazing."

"I'm ready; where can I stow my gear?"

"Here, give me your stuff." Brett took hold of her backpack and escorted Kayleigh over to the plane and opened the hatch, climbed in, and put her belongings in the seat behind his.

"Hop in," he said and helped her into the cockpit. "After I put gas in the tanks, we'll be off. We should be there in a couple of hours."

***

The plane buzzed above the sea, moving at 138 miles an hour. Brett had set the attitude at 7000 feet to give Kayleigh a better view of the sights below, and she was captivated by the brilliant sights as the blue sky meshed into the deeper blue sea which was sprinkled with many small islands. The cays were surrounded by white sand and multiple shades of translucent turquoise.

"Brett, this is remarkable. I hope we don't run into any turbulence that would spoil a perfect day like this."

"Don't fret, I checked the weather earlier, and it looks like an ideal day to fly. Tell me, have you decided on an agenda for finding your folks once we arrive in Georgetown?"

"Frist thing we should do is to stop at the hotel where they planned to stay. Oh! Did you bring a copy of your deed? I forgot to remind you."

"Not to worry, it's packed away with my passport. We'll need to go through customs before doing anything else."

"Good! After the hotel we better check with the local authorities and make sure they filed the missing persons alert I told them about. Next a visit to the courthouse for the property location. What else? Do you think we'll need a car?"

"I'm not sure. I'd like to use the plane as much as possible. We'll have to see what's involved."

***

Gina Marino, at 57 years old, was a tall well-endowed woman whose physical effect was intimidating. She marched up the steps of the Government house in Georgetown with the intent to be heard, then entered the building and hovered over the young woman at the reception desk. The girl, Diane, looked at the hardness in Gina's face and swallowed, asking, "May I help you?"

"I'm here to claim what is rightfully mine."

"Diane squirmed in her chair. "I'm sorry, I'm not sure what you wish me to assist you with."

"Look, girly, I'm Gina Marino, and I'm a direct descendent of the Kelsall family and the next in line to inherit the Kelsall property, but I hear someone else has been marauding around here claiming my land and that must stop, or I'll call my boys to kick ass. So, I demand to see whoever the hell is in charge to rectify this situation."

Diane's beautiful blue eyes were as wide as saucers. "Just a minute, madam, I'll see if I can find someone to assist you." She dialed a number and waited, diverting her eyes away from the woman in front of her. "Yes, Mr. Nichols, there is a woman here who would like to speak with you." She hesitated, her voice trembling before she responded. "Sir, I don't think that will work." She placed the phone down, glancing up at Gina, then stood. "Please follow me."

She walked as fast as her legs would carry her and knocked on Mr. Nichols' door. Within a moment the door swung open. "Mr. Nichols, this is…"

"I'll take it from here." Gina shoved Diane out of the way and swept into the office.

"Wait one minute, what's this all about?" Mr. Nichols sputtered.

"What's it about is my property, that's what. Seems someone is going around claiming she owns my land, which is a complete lie. It is my land, and you gotta fix that."

Mr. Nichols tried to be diplomatic and quell the disturbance in his office. "Please come in and take a seat. I didn't get your name, or the type of property involved. Do you have a deed to show the authenticity of your claim?"

Gina stomped over to a chair by the desk and sat down. "Mr. Whoever you are, I'm Gina Marino. Mr. Leo Kelsall is my father. He's some demented old fart that doesn't know what the hell he's doing, and he gave my deed to some idiot who doesn't have the know-how on what to do to invest it wisely. My mama Connie was a beautiful woman in her youth, and she had an affair with the old turd and got herself pregnant. So, here I am, and you'll have to deal with *me*." She leaned over his desk, a movement that showed off her cleavage. "If you treat me right, I can make you a wealthy man." She gave him a meaningful smile that made her seem attractive until she stood up straight and shot a malevolent look his way. "A deed is all I need, huh? Just a worthless piece of paper?"

"Tell me, Miss Marino, that's your legal name, right? If your father is a Kelsall, why don't you use Kelsall as your last name?"

"Because the dirtbag kicked my mama out and never married her."

"I'm sorry, Miss Marino, but to use your words, without that worthless piece of paper, you have no legal right to make a claim on that land, and I won't be bribed by your claim that you can make me rich. So, please leave my office now."

"You wait a damn minute, I'm not finished. I need to have that shore front property in Little Exuma, because I'm gonna build the biggest gambling casino in the world, right here. It will be more overwhelming than Atlantis. The people on this island will benefit from it. There will jobs for everyone, and you, if you play your cards right, will become a rich man."

"The property you refer to has legal owners who have a certified deed. If you wish to purchase that land from them, you will have to negotiate that with them."

"Negotiation is not necessary because I am the rightful owner, being a direct offspring of the eldest Kelsall. And you'll be sorry for not helping me—you don't know who you're dealing with. I have ways of getting my way, getting what is mine. Beware, if you value your life and the lives of your children, you'll want to reconsider your decision."

"Miss, please leave my office now. I've had enough, or I'll have you arrested for threatening me and my children."

A knock on the door interrupted their conversation. Within a second the door was open, and two security guards entered the room. They approached Gina. She turned and shoved them aside. "Keep your fricking hands off me. If you touch me that will be the last time, you'll touch anyone. Get out of my way. I'm leaving." She turned back toward Mr. Nichols. "Mark my words—you'll be sorry for your decision." She stalked out of the office.

CHAPTER NINE

Brett started the final decent into Exuma International Airport. He looked at Kayleigh. "I don't want to startle you, but I'm going to lower my landing gear, so don't panic when you hear them drop."

Kayleigh sat up straight. "Oh, darn, I wanted us to land in the water."

"Don't worry, there will be plenty of time for those landings, but we need to go through customs; besides, I have a gun I have to register."

The plane approached the runway, and for a moment Kayleigh felt fearful and she grabbed the arms of her seat, but she kept her emotions well contained. When the plane contacted the ground, a smile spread across her face. "That was so smooth."

"Told you she's a special gal."

Brett moved the plane off the runway. "We got to get this over so we can get on with our adventure." He jumped out of the plane and found a customs agent who searched the plane, and when he completed his inspection, he stamped their passports. "Welcome to our beautiful island; you're good to go. If you care to stretch your legs and get a bite to eat, there is a lounge across the street."

Brett's wide eyes took in Kayleigh's beauty. "What do you think, would you like to do that?" There was nothing more he'd like to do than stare at her lovely face.

"Sure, sounds good. I'd like to freshen up a bit."

They entered the lounge and found a table, ordered drinks and a snack. Kayleigh sipped her lemonade and took a bite of a conch fritter. Then she held up a folded brochure. "I found this map of the Georgetown area over there. It might come in handy."

"Good, let's see if we can find the hotel."

***

The seaplane skimmed over the shoreline at an altitude of 1500 feet. "What a view!" Kaleigh exclaimed. "I'm in envy of the birds. Look at the water. I can't get over how the water changes its texture

34

and color. This is unbelievable. I can't wait to find our very own piece of paradise. Oh, look! That ray just came flying out from below the sand. What an incredible sight."

"They're coming up to say hello." Brett laughed. "I think the noise of the plane's motors or the vibration from our engines may startle them. Look down—I think I see that large building we were hoping to locate because it's close to the hotel. Hold on, I'm going to put her down alongside it."

The plane glided slowly down until the sponsons skipped upon the water. Turning his head toward Kayleigh, his smile reached out to her. "How was that landing?"

"Fabulous. How cool. Where to now?"

"The hotel; it's not far from here." Brett guided his plane slowly past the Government building.

"There it is! It's up ahead, and it has a sandy beach."

"Okay, there's nothing in our way, so I'll beach it." The plane scooted up on the beach and Brett cut the engines. "Let's get out and see what we they can tell us about your folks."

As they did, a group of people surrounded the plane. One of the men approached Brett and asked, "Hey mom, what ya doing that for? You got trouble?"

"No, don't worry, we are fine. Just need to find out a few things."

Brett reached for Kayleigh's hand. "Let's go." They walked on a path surrounded by palm trees, crotons, and bougainvillea, and headed toward the coral two-story building.

Kayleigh's eyes glistened. "Brett, it sure is pretty here."

They reached the hotel and entered the lobby. The tile floors, rattan furniture and panoramic view of the harbor was impressive. At the front desk they introduced themselves to the clerk. "Hi, I'm Kayleigh Jones, and this my cousin Brett Kelsall; my parents Ted and Carole Jones were to have booked a room here. I haven't heard from them in over three weeks. We are in George Town to see if we can locate them, and I was hoping you can brief me on their stay here."

The girl at the desk knew immediately who they were talking about. "We, like you, are puzzled about their strange departure. We have stored their belongings, and their car is still in our parking lot. I was going to call Felix, the rental car agent, but hesitated in hopes that they would return. Their car just appeared a few days after they went missing. That was the last we spoke with them. They were on their way to the Government Building to discover the location of land they had acquired. Carole had her deed in her hand when they left here."

"Tell me," Kayleigh asked, "did they indicate any type of distress when they were here?"

"No, none. They seemed happy with our accommodations and were looking forward to their stay. They just seemed to be in a hurry to discover the location of their property. They left quite happy, even excited. That was the last time I saw them."

Brett moved closer to the desk. "We would like to stay here for a few days; do you have anything with two separate bedrooms?"

The woman eyed the couple with a slight smile. "Why, yes, we have a suite. Will that work?"

"Sure. What about my plane?"

"Your plane?"

"Yes, it's sitting on your beach right now. If you look out your window you can get glimpse of it."

The woman shrugged her shoulders. "That's a new one on me. It can't stay there. The beach is for the use of our guests. We do have a dock where we keep our boat which we use to transport people to our restaurant on Stocking Island. You could move it by the dock."

"What if I anchored it offshore? Would that work?"

"I don't see any problem with that idea. Go ahead, and I'll check with the manager and let you know if there's a problem."

***

Brett and Kayleigh entered the Government Building. It was an impressive old-style structure modeled after the architect of the Government Buildings in Nassau, and it housed many government services, including the police, post office, customs and immigration, and the commissioner's offices. They approached the information desk and spoke to an attractive young girl whose name card read Diane.

Kayleigh held up her copy of the deed. "I would like to speak to someone who could help me identify the location of this property."

Diane looked at the deed, then back to Kayleigh with skepticism. "Are you certain this is authentic?"

"Yes, why wouldn't it be?"

"Because you are the third person in the last few weeks that has claimed to own this property, which is highly unusual."

Kayleigh turned to Brett. "This is my cousin, Brett, and he has his own deed, too."

Diane shook her head and practically rolled her eyes. "Please have a seat. I need to speak to our property appraiser in person. This is becoming too bizarre."

"Oh, please wait, before you go, tell him I am the daughter of Mr. and Mrs. Ted Jones, a couple who were here about three weeks ago, and now they are missing."

"Really? Last week we had the daughter of a Mr. Leo Kelsall. What's going on, a family feud?" She left without waiting for an answer.

Kayleigh and Brett sank into the cushions of two comfortable wing chairs. "What was that all about?"

"Kayleigh, it seems there is another person here claiming the land. I don't want to be an alarmist, but maybe that has something to do with your parents disappearing."

"Brett, don't go there!"

"But Kayleigh, you gotta go with your gut, and my gut just kicked in."

Their conversation was disrupted when Diane returned. "I'm sorry, Mr. Nichols has no time available to discuss the matter with you today. I'll be glad to make an appointment for you to meet with him later in the week."

"I guess we'll have to do that if we are to find anything out." They followed her to the desk where she wrote out an appointment card.

"Could you give us some directions to where the property is located?" Kayleigh asked.

Diane shrugged her shoulders. "All I can tell you is that Mr. and Mrs. Jones's property is located on Little Exuma." She handed her a map of the area.

CHAPTER TEN

Brett and Kayleigh decided to check out their suite before starting their exploration for their land. They relaxed on the outdoor terrace of the Peace and Plenty and listened to reggae music while sipping cocktails. A soft moist wind brushed their faces.

"It's so good to relax; we had a busy day." Kayleigh smiled at Brett.

"I'd say so. It was more than I expected, but it's nice to spend it with such a special companion."

He was sweet, Kayleigh thought. Lou would never compliment her in such a manner. It was always about what he did, where he'd gone, who he'd been with. "What a nice thing for you to say. Just look all around us; this place has so much history. I love this wall behind us, the way it's lined with lanterns, rudders, and anchors, all of which have their own story. The staff told me of the building's history while I waited for you to arrive."

Brett smiled. "Hold that thought. I'm going to get myself another beer; would you care for something else?"

"Sure, another white wine will do." Kayleigh was captivated by his intent to listen to what she had to say. She watched him as he returned with her wine and admired his firm body and his shaggy blond locks. Even his casual manner was beginning to grow on her.

"Here you go." He placed the glass of wine on the table and took a sip of his beer. "Now tell me about the Peace and Plenty."

Kayleigh kept her eyes focused on his face. "This two-story building was named after a ship that transported Lord John Rolle's many slaves to Exuma from his plantation in the Carolinas in the late 1700s. He was a loyalist who relocated here. His slaves were bought and sold on this site. Later, after slavery was thankfully abolished, the building was used as a sponge warehouse, probably around the early 1900s. Following that, it was the home of a prominent family. Then in the 1940s, it was converted into a hotel."

Brett placed his hand on hers and smiled. "I can tell that you love history; I do, too."

Kayleigh felt an awkward urge to move her hand but changed her mind when she felt the warmth of his hand encompassing her own. "Brett, you seem to be such a caring individual. I'm curious why aren't you married or at least have a girlfriend."

She felt his hand tighten, and then he removed it, took a sip of his beer, moved his hand under his chin and waited a moment. "Well, to clarify your thoughts, I am a single guy. A while back I met a nice girl in San Diego. We were very compatible and got along great. The only drawback was that we were dealing with a long-distance relationship, and to rectify that she moved in with me at my place near the seaplane base at the Salton Sea. She got herself a job, and things were going well, but eventually she became sullen. I could tell she missed the city life, and one day she told me she was leaving. I couldn't leave the business I worked so hard to build, so I let her go. End of story. She broke my heart, so now I just focus on my business."

Kayleigh sighed. Looking into his sad eyes she felt guilty for bringing up the subject. "Oh, Brett, I'm so sorry."

"Don't be, it's okay. My heart mended," he added with a rueful smile. He looked past her toward the harbor then pointed at the island across the water. "I hear that the Chat and Chill restaurant over there is a fun place; maybe we should check it out tomorrow, but first I want to take a plane ride over Little Exuma. I'd like to get the lay of the land and see what it has to offer."

"Yes, I'm eager to know what kind of property we have inherited."

"Kayleigh don't put your expectations too high. From my meager research, there doesn't seem to be much land development there."

"Well, we'll find out tomorrow, won't we?"

"Yes, we will. Right now, though, I'm getting hungry, how about you? Let's go inside and see what they're serving."

"Sounds good. My stomach is growling."

***

Lance and Kate sat on the soft warm sand just beyond where their sailboat was anchored in a bay off Stocking Island. They were having a beer and eating hamburgers they'd purchased at the Chat and Chill open-air restaurant. "Kate, I think Ted and Carol will be safe where they are anchored now. They are far enough away from here not to cause suspicion from those mafia type thugs."

"I hope we did the right thing for them," Kate sighed. "I'm not sure they'll be able to survive on that island all by themselves."

"Don't be silly; they'll be okay, and they will continue with their lives when the crisis is over. Besides, I don't want to have any part of their calamity. Those men are extremely dangerous, and I want to live to see another day. As far as I'm concerned, we have never met them, nor do we know anything about their disappearance. And Kate, I expect you will do the same. So, let's put all that behind us and enjoy this island paradise."

"Security is mostly a superstition. It does not exist in nature, nor do the children of men as a whole experience it. Avoiding danger is no safer in the long run than outright exposure. Life is either a daring adventure or nothing."
Helen Keller

CHAPTER ELEVEN

Brett woke up early and threw on a pair of shorts and a t-shirt before checking on Kayleigh who was sound asleep in the other bedroom. He left her a note on the table then went to check on his plane.

He slipped off his sandals and walked through the shallow water to where his plane was anchored. He climbed into the cockpit and made a thorough inspection of his equipment. Satisfied, he went back to the hotel and enjoyed his breakfast. Before leaving he got some muffins and a cup of coffee to go.

He opened the door to the suite and was amazed by the dazzling rays of sunshine that brightened the room. Through the open sliding door, he saw Kayleigh standing on the balcony. She looked up when she heard him enter. "Hi there, how'd you sleep?"

A broad smile swept over her face. "Good morning, Brett, I slept like a baby."

He glanced at her and admired the way she looked, her cheeks already tinged with pink from the sun. "I picked up some coffee and muffins if you're interested."

"That's great, thanks. How'd the plane inspection go?"

"She's all set to go whenever you are."

***

Brett and Kayleigh boarded his seaplane. He took off and circled over Stocking Island before heading south, skimming over the shoreline.

"Look at all those sandy islands!" Kayleigh said. "I love this view. It's so nice, isn't it?"

"Yes, but I'm not crazy about all the reefs that pepper the water around the islands; they could tear my plane's sponsons to bits if I'm not careful when we land. The good thing is that the water is so clear that I can see the nasty hazards."

Within minutes they were flying over Little Exuma. "Brett, there is the small bridge that connects the two islands. There's so much to see! There's the ruins and the salt pond next to it; beyond that there is a road, but you can see where the asphalt comes to an end and changes to dirt."

They cruised over the center of the island which was scattered with overgrown scrub bushes, small trees, and some large pine trees. He circled his plane over the west side of the island than back toward the calmer lee side. At the end of the island there was a large rock formation which rose from a beautiful long crescent beach. "I'm going to put her down just past those rocks but far enough away from the reefs to the west."

The plane splashed gently down, skirting around the frothy waves that were breaking along the reefs.

Kayleigh's eyes were warm with admiration. "You are a master pilot; that was amazing."

"I've had a lot of practice; now let's get out and get our feet wet." They jumped down into the shallow warm water and walked over to the powdery white pristine beach which seemed to stretch for miles.

"Brett, this is magnificent! I feel like I'm lost in paradise. Look, for as far as you can see not another footprint on the beach."

"Just ours, and they will be gone with the next high tide."

"Do you think that this could be where our property is?"

"Kayleigh, I have no idea where it is. We could own 10 acres of that undeveloped land we just flew over or maybe some spot on the other side of the island; we'll find out when we meet with the property appraiser."

"Oh, Brett, I hope it's right here—it's so gorgeous."

"I agree. It sure would be nice to wake up each morning right here. What do you say, let's take a walk up the hill by those rocks and see what the view is like from there?" They spent the better part of the morning wandering along the beach collecting shells and admiring the clear blue water.

"I'd like to go by that old building up by the salt pond and see what's there. Are you game?" Brett finally asked.

"Huh, oh sure. I was enjoying the fantasies in my own little world." She grinned, and her eyes took on a childlike glow.

It was just a short hop by plane. Seeing the beacon, Brett set his plane down just offshore and ran his plane up on the beach. "She'll be okay here while we check out the ruins. When we're done, maybe we could get some lunch in town and talk to the locals."

It was a short hike up the hill to the building. They entered though the opening that once was a doorway and stumbled around inside the old building.

Brett wandered into another room. "Kayleigh, there's not much here, but whoever built this place must have been a master mason."

"Brett!" Kayleigh's voice had the sound of alarm. "Please help me! Something's happening to me. Help!"

"What is it, Kayleigh?" He hurried to the room where she stood in the center. A faint glow surrounding her body. Brett ran to her side and placed his hands on her shoulders. He saw that her eyes were glazed over. "Kayleigh, are you alright?"

"No, Brett, I'm not." She blinked, and her eyes refocused. "I don't know what happened—something overcame me, did you see it?"

"All I saw was a light illuminating your body."

She was shaking. "I had a vision."

Brett stepped forward, taking her in his arms. "Tell me what you saw."

"It seemed so mystical, but I don't get it. It was an image of a blue and white sailboat."

"That's weird."

"Tell me about it! What could it mean?"

"I don't know; it could be a sign or maybe a warning. Let's get out of here!"

Kayleigh was grateful that Brett seemed to believe her. Lou would have scoffed at her assertion that she'd had a vision, much less comfort her.

Brett took her hand in his and gently led her out of the building and back to the plane.

***

They were flying back toward George Town, but before Brett made his descent to land, he circled over Stocking Island.

Suddenly Kayleigh shouted. "Brett, there's the sailboat! The one I saw in my vision looked just like that!" She held a hand to her forehead. "Oh, no, what's happening to me?"

"Hold on, I'm turning around." He skimmed over Stocking Island, descending just above a small bay where he motored up on the shore. "We've got to find out who owns that boat. Come on, don't be afraid."

They walked over to the sailboat where Brett yelled, "Hello! Anybody home?" There was no reply. "Let's go to the bar." He pointed to the outdoor bar and grill. "Bartenders know everybody."

They made their way to the bar. The room was partially full, and the bartender had a scowl on his face when he came over. "You're the clown who just buzzed us, aren't you? If you ever do that again I'm going to have you arrested. Now get the hell out of here!"

"Wait, please, we need to find out who owns that sailboat out there. The blue and white one anchored by the bay. It's important, and I am sorry about my approach. I won't let that happen again."

"That's better, cowboy. Who wants to know?"

"I'm Brett Kelsall, and this is my cousin Kayleigh. We are looking for her parents who were vacationing here, but they failed to return home; we are trying to find out what happened to them and have reason to believe that the people on the sailboat may be able to help us find them.".

"You say you're a Kelsall; that's interesting. That family has quite a history in this area. The folks on the blue and white sailboat are British, and they have been here for a few days now. They're nice enough, but I think they took off in their dinghy early this morning. They haven't been around all day. Do you want me to tell them you are looking for them?"

"No, thanks, we'll come back. We are staying at the Peace and Plenty."

They walked back by the sailboat. "Kayleigh, if you want to take the water taxi back to the hotel, it's okay. I'd like to stay a little longer."

Her eyes filled with tears. "Brett, I'm not sure that this is the sailboat I saw in the image. It all happened so fast. I'm so confused. I wish I never came here."

CHAPTER TWELVE

The Exuma Island chain is 130 miles long and 72 square miles in area. There are four distinct areas, the northern, the Exuma Park, the central and southern Exumas.

Ted sat on the front deck of a 35-foot houseboat docked at a secluded marina on Cave Cay in the central Exumas. Carole opened the side door and joined him on the bench seat located on the bow. "That young British couple was so thoughtful. I don't know what we would have done without their help."

"Dear, without their help, we wouldn't be here to talk about it."

"Yes, that's true, but I'm not sure we should be here like this. I feel so isolated. What if those men find us here? I don't understand how you can be so complacent—it's like you have no sense of fear."

"Carole, we have a month's supply of provisions, and this island is out of the way for most boat traffic; besides, it's for sale. Most boaters would skip it and head for some other island with more amenities. We're only a few days away from George Town. If you wish, we could head north, but I'm not prepared to navigate through these waters."

"Well, Ted, I'm afraid of all this. I miss Kayleigh, and she must be beside herself with worry about us."

Ted turned to Carole and placed his arm over her shoulders. "Kayleigh and her boyfriend pilot Lou are traveling all over the world. She doesn't have time to worry about us. We need to stay away from George Town and let those damn thugs have their way. Like Lance said, we need to disappear, and we have done that. Look all around at the beauty of the island. The marine dock master has told me we can use their skiff any time we want to go fishing or explore the grotto and the beaches."

Carole melted into Ted's embrace. "It's not that I'm not grateful for their help and how they rescued us. I'm just mad that all this happened to us, but you're right, it's not such a bad place to hide."

***

Brett and Kayleigh returned to the Peace and Plenty. But Kayleigh was still shaken from her earlier experience. Brett kept trying to figure out the best way to help her, but not having experienced the phenomena himself challenged his approach.

They walked through the lobby when a woman behind the registration desk called, "Mr. Kelsall."

Brett stopped, turned to see the woman.

"Sir, I have a message for you from Mr. Nichols."

"Great! What did he have to say?"

She handed him an envelope. "It's right here, that nice young girl at the Government Building delivered it earlier today."

"Thank you."

"You're welcome. I hope that you are enjoying our lovely island."

He forced a fake smile. "Yes, ma'am."

He returned to Kayleigh's side and opened the envelope and read it. "He says he'll meet with us at 10 a.m. tomorrow."

"I was wondering if he would after what that girl said to us about how another person is interested in our land."

"Well, it's good news. Now let's take a walk around the town; maybe we can discover a quiet spot down by the Harbor."

"Brett, you go, I'm going to the room. I'm not in the mood to socialize."

He shrugged. "Awe, come on, Kayleigh, the walk will do us both good."

She stood still and looked up to him with sad eyes. He shook off a helpless feeling, then placed his hands on her face and looked deep into her chocolate brown eyes. "Kayleigh, we are here to find your parents. Running away will not change anything."

His gesture of affection was met with a weak smile. "You're right."

"That's better. Let's go."

They took a casual stroll toward the center of town. Brett was hoping Kayleigh would unwind a bit and rid herself of all the pent-up anxiety she was holding inside.

"George Town seems to have a decent number of stores and services."

"Right, Brett, the town does seem to have a charm of its own. Look, there's a dive shop across the street and a hardware store next to it."

The foot traffic was light, and they easily made it to the center of town and passed a straw market by a park. "Before we leave, I need to stop in there and get some gifts for my friends."

"Look over there," Brett said. "The Two Turtles restaurant sign says live music every Friday, what do you say? Should we check it out?"

Kayleigh was still guarded. "I don't know, but it sounds good, and I love to dance."

They passed the Exuma market and headed down a strip of land that separates Elizabeth Harbor from Kidd Cove.

"Kayleigh, would you like to stop for a cocktail?"

She looked at him with a sly smile. "That may help my doldrums."

"That two story building has a restaurant on the second level that looks interesting. Let's see what's there."

They climbed the stairs, opened the door, and sat down at a table that overlooked the cove and ordered drinks.

Brett scanned the cove. "There are a good number of sailboats anchored out there and a dock full of colorful houseboats." The server returned with their drinks. "Thanks, dude. What's up with the fancy decorations on those houseboats?"

"Oh, those, the guy that rents them just gussied them up for fun. They're rentals, and the marina maintains moorings around the area for their private use."

"Before you go, can we see a menu?"

"Sure, I'll be right back."

The water in the cove had a soothing effect, and pink clouds of twilight that lit up the sky seemed to ease Kayleigh's anxiety. She looked at Brett, and he noticed how her eyes reflected contentment. "Thanks, Brett, I needed this."

***

The next morning, they arrived at the Government Building at 10 a.m. and checked in. "Hi, Diane, we're here for our appointment with Mr. Nichols."

She flashed a cheerful smile at them. "Yes, Mr. Kelsall and Miss Jones. He is expecting you, please follow me."

The door to his office was open, and hearing them approach, he looked up. "Welcome, folks, please come in and have a seat. Would you like some coffee or tea?"

Kayleigh shook her head. "No, we just had breakfast at the hotel. Mr. Nichols, I'm not sure if you know that my parents have gone missing? I've reported it to the local police, but I need to follow up with them. We've been busy checking out the area. We have brought copies of the deeds to our property for you to review. Please look at them."

He reached over his desk and took them from her. "Everything is in order and quite legal. This land is in the same area as your parents' property."

"Yes, they split the parcel up between the four of us. Mom said she needed to keep it in the family, and she felt that their100 acres was too much for them."

"This land encompasses the southern tip of Little Exuma. It is a prime location as it includes a section of the most beautiful beach on the island."

Kayleigh felt her heart skip a beat while she digested the information. "Excuse me, I have to catch my breath. Brett and I were there yesterday, and yes, it is a breathtaking area."

"Excuse me, how did you know this was your land?"

"Oh, we didn't know it at the time. We just took a ride over the area in Brett's seaplane."

"Oh, you're the one who splashed the plane down outside my window." Kayleigh noted his eyes had a look of envy. "That's quite a seaplane you got, Brett!"

"Yes, sir, she's an amazing ride."

"Did you happen to fly over the salt pond on your exploration?"

"Yes, it's close to that old building. What about it?"

"I just wanted to mention that the Kelsall family built the tall beacon on that high hill to guide ships coming to pick up salt. That is one of the finest natural salt lakes in all the Exumas. After their cotton plantation failed because of the poor soil, the Kelsall's exported the salt to the U.S., Canada, and even the Queen of England got a yearly supply."

Brett had a playful grin. "Our kin folks were quite a resourceful clan."

Mr. Nichols' face lost its grin, and he locked his eyes on theirs. "I have some disturbing news for the both of you. A woman forced her way into my office two days ago. She identified herself as Gina Marino and claimed she has priority over all the Kelsall land in the Exuma Islands because Leo Kelsall is her father. She claims by being the eldest in the line of descendants, she can claim all the Kelsall land she wants."

Kayleigh practically shouted. "That can't be true!"

Brett placed his hand on hers. "Please, Kayleigh, listen to what Mr. Nichols has to say." Brett looked up. "Leo Kelsall is my grandfather. His son Scott is my adopted father. Scott Kelsall has passed away, and I'm his sole heir. My grandfather did mention to me that he could possibly be the father of another child as he had an affair with someone named Connie after my grandmother left him. But he said if that person ever materialized, he would never acknowledge him or her as his child."

Mr. Nichols took his time to respond as he considered the information. "I must warn you that this woman could cause a tremendous amount of trouble. She was unable to show me any proof of birth, but she caused a ruckus when I told her she would need legitimate signed credentials to validate her claim."

In a calmer controlled voice, Kayleigh spoke up. "I can prove that she is an imposter because I've checked my DNA though the Ancestry website. I have some distant relatives in Devonshire England, but no one like her ever showed up. So, she is lying through her teeth."

"That's a good sign," Mr. Nichols said. "The only thing that could be a problem is if she shows up with a valid deed to the property."

"I don't think that can happen, as my mother received the deed from my grandfather, and then she split it up between me, Brett and both my parents."

"Well, then, all should be well," Mr. Nichols said with obvious relief.

CHAPTER THIRTEEN

The day cracked open, and the brightest shade of gold filtered through the window. Brett stretched and lay in bed thinking about how the mystical premonition Kayleigh had seen at the Hermitage house had affected her to such a degree. Although she seemed to relax during the walk they had taken, she hadn't shared her inner thoughts or fears about the incident with him. He vowed to make it a priority to talk with the couple on the blue and white sailboat anchored at Stocking Island.

The sound of movement in the other room caused him to jump out of bed and get dressed. He opened his bedroom door and watched Kayleigh as she slid open the door leading to the balcony.

"Good morning."

Hearing his voice caused Kayleigh to jump; a look of surprise flashed across her face. "Oh, hi, isn't it a beautiful morning? I could get use to this."

He marveled at how her lithe body moved in the sunlight as he joined her. Together they took in the sights on the Harbor. "What's on your agenda, Kayleigh?"

"Brett, I really need to talk with the police about any possible leads they may have discovered since I notified them of my parents' disappearance."

He watched her as a sense of sadness and anxiety spread across her face. He reached for her. "Yes, of course, plus we need to stress the importance of finding them."

She backed away. "Look, Brett, maybe it's not such a good idea to try to find them on our own. Things seem to be getting out of hand, and it's bothering me. I'm mad as hell at that woman for trying to take our land. Yet I'm fearful of what might happen to me if I confront her. I also have a weird sense of hope that my parents could be safe somewhere out there." Tears welled in her eyes. "Brett, I'm so confused."

They stood together on the balcony as the day broke, feeling the gentle warm wind that sprang up. He stayed by her side and waited in silence for her to continue. He was a good listener.

She shook her head, and her long brown hair fell around her face. "I'm sorry. There is something about you that gives me comfort." She stepped closer to him and leaned against his warm body.

He embraced her, careful not to hold her too tightly. She tilted her head up at him. "I don't know how I survived this long without you."

He held her gaze. "Are you alright now?"

"Yes, thank you."

"Then we should go and see what the police have found out."

***

After breakfast they entered the Government Building and approached the information desk. Seeing Diane's familiar face eased their anxiety. "Good morning, Diane."

Her blue eyes sparkled. "Mr. Kelsall and Miss Jones! I'm sorry but Mr. Nichols isn't in to work yet. I don't understand the delay, but I'm sure he'll be along soon."

"Actually, we're not here to see Mr. Nichols. Instead, we would like to speak with the Chief of Police. Which way do we go to find his office?"

Diane hesitated. "Sorry, my mistake. Would you like me to escort you there?"

"No, just point us in the right direction."

"Take the hallway to your right and follow it to the end. There is a sign above the door. Just walk in and someone there will assist you."

"Thanks "

They found the spacious room and inhaled the distinctive smell of fresh brewed coffee that filled the air. Kayleigh marched up to the front desk and spoke to a woman dressed in a blue police uniform. "Excuse me, my name is Kayleigh Jones, and I recently filed a missing person's report on my parents, Mr. and Mrs. Ted Jones. I would like to know what kind of progress has been made, if any, into their disappearance."

The woman in blue clicked on her computer and scanned it. "What are both of their names?"

Kayleigh sighed. "Ted and Carole Jones. They have been missing for over three weeks."

The woman frowned. "Bear with me." She continued to search. "I've found your original alert, but not much has been added. Seems very little information is known about their disappearance."

"Really? It's been three weeks! That's odd. May I please speak to the Police Chief?"

"I'm sorry, he's not here now. Is there any way we can contact you?"

"Yes, we are staying at the Peace and Plenty. You can leave a message with the front desk." She fought back her tears and looked at Brett. "Let's go."

***

"Kayleigh, come on, we need to get out of here; let's pack a lunch and take a plane ride; you'll feel better on the beach."

"Sounds good."

They settled into the front seats of the plane, and Brett said, "We'll fly along the coast until we see that tall beacon, then circle over the salt pond and land by the beach."

He flew the plane low enough to clearly see the objects below and easily found the salt pond.

Kayleigh eyes scanned the terrain below them. "Brett, something is wrong down there."

"What is it? What's wrong?"

"There are two men pointing their guns at another man."

"What the...?" Brett took a good hard look. "Hold on! I'm going to buzz them." He swept his plane lower.

The men below were startled and took aim at the plane. Bullets struck the plane's fuselage. In a bold maneuver, Brett turned the plane on its side and attempted to gain altitude. As it started to climb, the plane's left engine shut down and then burst into flames. "Kayleigh, brace yourself. I'm going to ditch her."

The plane landed on the water with a thud, sending water washing over the cockpit as they skimmed across the waves. "Damn! We're headed for the reefs. We need to abandon her. Follow me."

He turned toward the rear of the plane and opened the hatch that led to the walkway above. "Come on!"

"Brett, I can't move! My foot is caught under the seat!"

He looked back at her and noticed the look of terror on her face as she struggled to release herself. Her panic was obvious as she tried harder to pull her foot out. In another minute, she managed to rotate her leg, and her foot broke free from the obstacle holding it under the seat.

"Kayleigh!" Brett cried, "come on, we have to get out of here."

He took her hand and helped her through the hatch. "We must jump just in case she blows. Stay away from the engine but be careful not to get tangled in the reef. Just jump as far away from the plane as possible. Can you do that?"

"I'll have to."

He launched himself into the water then turned to look up at her. "Come on, Kayleigh, jump—now!"

She took a leap and plunged into the water. "Help me!"

He grabbed her just as a spark from the engine fire landed in her hair. "Hold your breath, we're going under the water."

He took her hand and pulled her with him beneath the surface, then helped her swim away from the aircraft. When he judged that they were far enough away, he pulled Kayleigh to the surface where he patted her head to make sure the spark had died.

"Come on," he said, after steadied his breathing, "we have to make it to shore."

"Brett," Kaleigh's voice was breathless with fear. "My foot hurts. I don't know if I can swim that far."

"Don't worry, I'll help you." Together they made it to the shore where Brett kept out a sharp look for the men with guns.

CHAPTER FOURTEEN

Ted was awakened by a disturbance in the marina's office. When he heard gunfire, he knew it was time to move. Carole was sleeping by his side. He placed his hands on her shoulders and shook her. "Carole, wake up, we got to get out of here now!"

Carole opened her eyes. "What's wrong?"

"Throw something over your nightgown, then grab our money, personal documents and don't forget the deed." Ted peered out the front window; it was dark, and he couldn't make out any activity.

Carole was fully awake now and shuffled through the bureau drawer. "I got everything."

"Let's go, follow me and be quiet, we're going to the skiff at the end of the dock."

"Aren't you going to lock the door?"

"No!" They scurried along the dock until they reached the small boat. "Slide inside and lie down." He lowered himself down beside her and covered her with his body.

The commotion at the office had ceased. They heard men's voices and footsteps on the dock. "There ain't nothing here worth taking, not like the other marinas; they ain't got shit here. What about that houseboat?"

"Nah," said a second voice. "Don't bother, it's old. I'm sure it's not worth our effort; besides, it looks like one of those fancy ones they rent in George Town. Let's get out of here while that guy's still out of commission"

Ted and Carole waited in the darkness. After what seemed like forever, the sound of a boat engine echoed across the water. They felt waves rock the skiff as the boat passed by. When the roar of the engine diminished to a hum in the distance, they relaxed. "Carole, you'll be okay now. I'm going to the office to see what happened."

Ted helped her off the skiff and walked her back to the houseboat, then ran up the dock to the marina office which housed a small store that was stocked with beer, soda, bottled water and a limited supply of food items. "Anybody here? Hey, Ed, are you alright?"

He heard something move in the far end of the office and approached with caution. The floor was marbled with drops of fresh blood. Ed was slumped over on the floor behind the counter. His face was ashen.

"Hey, man," Ted exclaimed. "Where are you hit?"

"Just my arm. When I reached for my pistol, they shot me, then stole my gun."

"Let me see." Ted looked at the wound. "We got to stop the bleeding. You got anything around here I can use?"

"There are some rags by the sink."

Ted packed the wound with a terrycloth face cloth and wrapped it with a torn piece of a dishtowel. "That should help, but you need to get some medical help. Where's your VHF?"

"It's over by the front window."

Ted picked up the receiver which was on channel 16 and called for help. "May Day, May Day, May Day, there's been a robbery and shooting at Cave Cay Marina. Man injured. Need medical assistance." He repeated the distress call, and then there was a response. "The Royal Bahamian Police are on the way," Ted told Ed.

Ed grimaced. "I may need to go to Nassau; that means you'll be on your own here."

Ted nodded. "We'll be okay, we're not going anywhere anytime soon."

***

"Lenny, where'd that guy go?

"What guy?"

"The one we were supposed to whack?"

"Not the one in the plane?"

"No, not him, you idiot! Didn't you have a hold on that guy?"

"Hell, no! I was shooting that wise guy out of the sky. He was a ballsy one. Bet he's sorry he messed with us. I heard the plane crash. Don't worry, he ain't gonna screw with us no more."

"Yeah, but what about the guy who was saying his prayers?"

"I think they both might have been praying."

"Cut the crap, Lenny, where is he?"

"Hell, if I know, Vinny, you should have been holding on to him."

"This ain't getting us nowhere. Big Gina's gonna be pissed, and she's real ugly when her orders get fouled up."

"We'll tell her about the guy in the plane."

"Yeah, and then what? Our orders were simple—kill the guy and throw him in the pond. We better canvas the area cause if we can't find him, we're in deep shit."

***

Brett helped Kayleigh to shore and examined her foot. Her ankle was bleeding from a wound she sustained by trying to pull her leg free during their frantic attempt to escape through the back hatch. Her skin was scraped and turning purple, plus her foot was puffing up like a balloon."

"I know it must hurt, but it looks superficial, and I can't feel anything that might indicate it's broken. I have a first aid kit on the plane. Try soaking your foot in the water while I go get it."

"I'm sorry, Brett, I should have been more careful."

"Kayleigh, stop. Nothing's going to change that now."

He looked at his beloved plane with disbelief. "Kayleigh, I need to get back there and put that fire out!"

The sound of boats approaching startled him. He saw two fishing boats circle the plane with men holding fire extinguishers in their hands. They were dowsing the fire. Within moments the flames were gone.

"Are you alright?" Brett asked Kaleigh. "I need to get out there before they help themselves to my equipment."

"Go ahead, I'll be alright."

He dove into the water and swam back to the plane. "Thanks, guys. Your quick thinking saved her. What can I do for you?"

"Nothing, man, you got yourself in a heap of trouble."

"That's for sure. She's fully insured, but I can't imagine getting her fixed around here."

"Hold on, dude, bet Master Harbor Marine and Repair can help. They do all kinds of boat repairs. Mac, their main mechanic, is damn good at it, too. They got a place in George Town."

Brett looked at his plane with weary eyes. "How will I ever get her back there? I can't fly her with only one engine."

"We can tow you, but you gotta pay for the gas."

"Sure, I can do that. Is there any place to get gas in Williamstown?"

"No sir."

"Then we'll siphon some gas from my plane. I'm sure there's enough to do the job, but I need to check the sponsons. I don't know what kind of damage the reefs caused."

"Jump aboard; let's see." The boat circled around the plane, and to Brett's surprise, the sponsons had little damage. Just some scratches and scrapes, but there were no gouges that would cause leaks in them. "Not bad, some cosmetic work, and she'll be fine."

"Hey," Brett added, "one more thing, would you be able to give my cousin a lift?" He pointed to the shore where Kayleigh waited. "She hurt her foot, and I doubt if she will be able to get herself back into my plane. I need to get my first aid kit and wrap the wound."

"Got ya covered. Get your stuff; I'll give you a lift."

Kayleigh sat at the water's edge soaking her foot. The bleeding had subsided some, and she sat patiently while Brett dried and wrapped her ankle with an ace bandage. "See if you can stand."

"Hold me, my leg is wobbly."

"Do you think you can make it to the boat?"

"I'll try."

She struggled to walk. Brett didn't want her to fall, so he picked her up and carried her to the waiting fishing boat. "All set?" he asked after he put her down on a seat.

"That I am. Thanks."

The men in the boats attached lines to the sponsons. Brett perched himself outside the cockpit between the engines. He glared at the black soot that covered the left engine cowling, then at the bullet holes that riveted it. His scarlet face reflected his intense anger. It was hard for him to fathom the destruction inflicted on his special plane. "When I find those guys, I will show them no mercy!"

The arrival of the fishermen saved the day. From his location he watched as they cautiously guided his plane along the top of the waves. The extremely unconventional scheme worked well, and the plane limped gingerly up the coastline.

CHAPTER FIFTEEN

The two boats with the seaplane in tow arrived alongside Master Harbor and Repair. They caught a mooring buoy and secured the seaplane to it. Brett slithered off the plane's fuselage into the boat with Kayleigh aboard, and the fisherman escorted them to the marina.

They helped Kayleigh out of the boat onto the dock, and she stood by Brett's side. "Thanks, guys, you're the best. Fill your tanks with gas. I'll cover the costs."

Brett looked at Kayleigh's injured foot. "We need to get you to the clinic as soon as I'm done here. Just a few more minutes until I decide what to do about the repairs. There's a bench over there. I'll help you over to it, and you can sit until arrangements can be made for the work."

Brett spoke to the owner about repairs needed on the fuselage and the sponsons, and they agreed on how to proceed. Getting a new engine posed a difficult situation; while the plane was fully insured, getting the engine to Exuma might take up to six months or more. The whole situation was very disheartening.

He returned to where Kayleigh waited. "Why don't you stay here while I run back to the hotel and get your parent's rental car."

"That sounds good. I don't think I could walk to the clinic from here. I'll say put and watch the boat traffic."

Brett hiked back to the Peace and Plenty. With each step he fought to calm his emotions and hold back the anger welling up inside him. He entered the hotel and approached the front desk. "Hi, Kayleigh had a small mishap and hurt her foot, so I'd like the keys to her parent's rental to give her a lift back here."

The clerk, whose name was Roberta, wasn't sure whether she should give him the keys and hesitated.

"Look, I'll bring it right back." She reached for the keys and reluctantly gave them to him.

He returned to the marina and helped Kayleigh into the compact car. Once settled in, Kayleigh wrinkled her nose. "This car smells funny, like it's been fumigated with something."

"Yea, I noticed that, too, but at least you don't have to walk."

They arrived at the clinic which had all indications that they were about to close. When they entered, they heard someone say, "Sorry, but our office hours are over."

Brett bellowed. "No, they are not! This woman needs attention, and I'm not leaving until someone looks at her leg wound."

At that moment, the doctor appeared. Seeing the defiant expression on Brett's face, he asked, "What's going on here?"

"You a doctor?"

"Yes sir."

"Well, I don't care what your schedule is, you need to help us. My cousin hurt her foot, and I need you to look at it to make sure it's not broken."

The doctor rolled his eyes. "You're another one of those pushy Americans; bring her into the exam room."

The nurse positioned Kayleigh on the exam table while the doctor removed the ace bandage. "You got yourself a nasty wound, but there are no breaks. Looks like you may have damaged some tendons. I'll dress it and apply a boot. Change the dressing daily. It'll take about a month for it to heal. Try to keep your foot elevated. Do you have any allergies?"

"No."

"Good, I'll prescribe a weeks' worth of antibiotics. Any questions?"

"No, sir, thank you."

Brett helped Kayleigh to the car parked outside the clinic. When he opened the door, he noticed something brown and fuzzy on the floor below her seat that he hadn't seen before. "Wait a minute, what's that stuff on the floor?" He leaned closer for a better look. "Looks like a pile of dead scorpions; no wonder the car smells strange."

"They're deadly, aren't they? How could so many find their way into the car?"

"Well, there is a good-sized hole in the floorboard. Maybe it was parked over a nest? Or maybe someone planted them in the car. Who knows, lots of strange things are happening on this island."

"Oh Brett!" she exclaimed, "my parents could have been stung by them and died. How terrible! What is going on here? Every corner we turn seems to be worse than the one before; it's almost like we are cursed."

***

They returned to the hotel and Kayleigh settled herself on top of her bed. "This is better."

"You seem comfortable; why don't you take a nap while I go to the police and file a complaint?"

Brett returned to the Government Building. All offices were closed for the day except the police department, and he went directly there. The woman who Kayleigh had dealt with was at her desk. Her identification badge read Mrs. Albury. She looked up as he entered.

"Hi, I was recently here with my cousin."

She smiled at him. "Yes, I remember you. Do you have any good news about the missing people?"

"No, I wish I did, but now I have another problem."

The woman's smile vanished. "What is it?"

"Someone shot down my plane over the salt pond on Little Exuma, and I want to file a complaint for the damage they caused."

"Seems that you're having a great deal of bad luck. As you know, there is no police presence on that island. The population there doesn't support our department."

Brett bit his tongue. "I'm aware of that, but I would like to file a complaint anyway."

He explained the situation he'd come upon while flying over the salt pond. "It looked as if those men were going to execute the man they were holding. If he isn't dead, I'm sure you'll be hearing from him soon. Seems this place is a haven for underhanded people."

Mrs. Albury listened with increased interest and went through the tedious task of filling out the paperwork necessary to enter a complaint.

Brett left with an empty feeling that he hadn't accomplished a thing. As he walked down the stairs outside the building, he questioned himself. Was coming here a tragic mistake?

CHAPTER SIXTEEN

The sight of the seaplane startled Vinny. "What the …?

Brett barrel rolled his plane and came closer to the ground. Lenny yelled, "I'll take care of him," and he aimed his automatic high-powered rifle, pulled the trigger, and pelted the plane with an array of bullets.

Mr. Nichols took advantage of the distraction and fled. He ran up the road to the Hermitage plantation, then raced around the building. He looked back; not seeing anyone following him, he continued into the heart of Williamstown and kept running until he arrived at Santana's Beachside Snack Shack. A good number of customers sat around the open bar. He stopped and leaned on the wooden building. He was panting hard, his heart racing.

"Mister, you better sit down over here." A pleasant plump black woman invited him in. The shack overlooked a white sandy beach, and the azure water was a welcome sight.

"What could be the matter; you look like you just seen a ghost."

Mr. Nichols managed to limp over to a stool. His body trembled. The woman handed him a glass of ice water. "Sir, rest here for a while. Whatever you're running from must be very evil."

He remained breathless and agitated and every few seconds he looked around to see if he had been followed. He took sips of the water and eventually his deep wheezes abated as he regained control of his breathing.

He looked at the woman. "Did you see that seaplane? I think I heard it crash."

"Yes, sir, man, that big bird hit the water hard. Big black clouds filled the sky. Could be he sunk."

"I hope not; he just saved my life."

The woman could clearly see his face was still flushed. Her smile flashed, showing dimples in her cheeks. "You just stay put, relax a bit. I'll be right back."

His thoughts were racing, and his eyes continued to dart at the road.

The woman returned with a dark tinted drink. "Here, sir, this will help."

He lifted the drink to his mouth and inhaled the sweet scent of rum. "Thank you; I guess I needed this, but what I really need is to find a way to get back to George Town. I'm late for work."

"Work? Yes, of course, you are all dressed up. How'd you get here?"

"Some guys assaulted me when I left my house to go to work and were about to shoot me when the seaplane distracted them."

"What did you do to get them mad at you?"

"Seems some angry woman sent them to kill me because I wouldn't let her steal another person's land."

"Good grief! There are nasty people everywhere. Don't you worry, my husband is out back. He'll be glad to give you a lift to your job."

***

Brett didn't know how to break the news to Kayleigh, but he knew he must return home. He had a business to run, and the only way he could get a new engine for his plane was to do it himself. There was no easy way to tell her.

By the time he returned to the hotel, his mind was made up. He found her sitting on the balcony outside the suite with her foot propped up on a pillow. "Hi, there!"

She turned toward him and smiled. "How'd you make out?"

A wry grin covered his face. "What do you think? They'll investigate it, but it's really out of their jurisdiction."

"Brett, how awful."

"No, not really. I should have expected it." He touched her foot, "How are you doing?"

"Seems a little better."

He took a deep breath. "Kayleigh, I need to go back to California."

Dismay shot through her. "Brett, not now, you can't leave me here like this!"

His smile vanished. "I don't have a choice. I have a business to think about, and I'm not about to wait six months to get a new engine for my plane. Believe me, it's not an easy decision. If you want, you can come with me."

Tears streamed down her cheeks. "You know I can't leave here without knowing what happened to my parents. There are so many questions and no answers."

He bent down and embraced her, as a wave of emotion overwhelmed him. "I'm sorry."

Her hands worked their way through his long, tangled hair, and she kissed him deeply.

He slid his hands lower until he touched the small of her back. He looked into her lovely chocolate-colored eyes, then returned her deep kiss. "I'll be back as soon as I can." His voice shook with emotion.

There was no way of denying that their feelings for each other had blossomed. He picked her up and carried her to his bed. "Tell me now if you want me to stop."

"Don't stop," she whispered.

Brett carefully placed her on the bed and removed the boot from her foot before slowly unbuttoning her blouse. He looked at her and smiled, all his anxiety gone. "I love to look at you because you are so beautiful you take my breath away."

She was overwhelmed with emotion. Her eyes glistened, and she was unable to utter a word.

He continued to undress her. With a teasing grin he dropped his clothes on the floor and they melted into each other's arms. Their mouths were flooded with passionate kisses as they released their pent-up desires. Gentle kisses became more urgent as desire swept over them. The gentleness turned into lustful love making as they explored one another's bodies. Eventually exhaustion overcame them with sweat covering their bare limbs. Spent, they finally lay silent in each other's arms.

Kayleigh's hands caressed his solid chest, then she rested her head gently on his shoulder and stroked his hair. "Brett, please don't leave me here all alone."

He kissed her tenderly. "Kayleigh, you know I must go. Don't make it any harder than it is. I promise I won't be gone long. Now let's just enjoy what we've discovered about one another. My mind and my heart are overwhelmed with happiness."

"What lies behind us and what lies before us are tiny matters compared to what lies within us"
Ralph Waldo Emerson

CHAPTER SEVENTEEN

Kayleigh sat on the balcony watching the sea birds and boats as they passed by the hotel. Her eyes drifted to the island beyond where Brett had landed his seaplane. She decided that she needed to go there and talk with the people on the blue and white sailboat before she missed the opportunity. The image she'd seen was so vivid and real—she knew it was meant to be a sign.

With that in mind she made her way to the lobby and stood in front of Roberta who was behind the desk. When she got her attention, Kayleigh smiled. "Hi, I'd like to book a boat ride over to Stocking Island."

Roberta exchanged a grin. "Miss Jones, how is your foot?"

"Believe it or not, it's doing remarkably well."

"That's good to hear. You know that there are no hard walkways on the island, so be careful walking on the sand; it might be a little tricky to move about with that boot."

"Yes, ma'am, I'll be careful."

"Good. Now let me tell you that you're in luck. The shuttle boat just returned to our dock, and they are reloading now for their next group of guests. They make a trip every two hours daily, so stay for a while if you wish and enjoy yourself."

"Thank you, see you later."

Kayleigh climbed aboard the 20-foot open boat and with the help from the boat's first mate, she settled herself on a seat. It was a short wait while people filled the boat. When the boat was loaded, the captain guided the craft away from the dock and headed across the harbor. The one-mile crossing went quickly, and the boat pulled up on a gorgeous white sandy beach to let the passengers off.

At first Kayleigh stumbled; walking in the soft sand with the boot on her foot was more difficult than she imagined, but she was determined. She looked down the beach beyond the volleyball court and was relieved to see the blue and white sailboat still at anchor. She slowly walked along the beach and passed by a bunch of people involved in a riotous volleyball game.

She took her time and eventually made it to the sailboat. There was a woman sitting in the cockpit who was intently writing on a notepad. Kayleigh stood silent, trying to decide what to say; soon the woman looked up. Her eyes darted toward the volleyball court but quickly returned to Kayleigh. She looked her over, starting at her feet, then up her body, and stopped at her face. "Hello, may I help you with something?"

Kayleigh was relieved by the woman's friendly manner but felt it would be awkward to ask about the image at this time. "No, I'm just curious on what you are writing; you seemed so intent."

The woman's soft brown eyes seemed inviting as she spoke. "I am a freelance writer from Devon, England, and I'm involved in a research project for my company."

"Yes, I picked up on your British accent, it's quite nice. Would you mind sharing your story with me?" Kate smiled at the stranger.

"Why, of course I will. Let me get closer to you, you'll never be able to get up here, nor will you be able to stand that long." She descended the swim ladder and walked over to where Kayleigh stood. "Come sit down on these chairs. My husband, Lance, is involved in a volleyball game with his mates, and he won't be back for a while."

Kayleigh sighed, took in a breath, and released it. "How did you get here? Not on that boat, I hope."

"No, of course not. We flew to Nassau where Lance found this sailboat, and we were able to put it aboard the mail boat which transported us to George Town."

"How exciting; so, what are you writing about?"

"I have an interest in the history of the Colonists and their families, the ones who first settled here in the 1700s."

Kayleigh played it coy. "I've heard of them. They were rich men who owned plantations in the Carolinas."

"Right, there were two prominent families, the Rolles and the Kelsalls. Neither did well growing cotton so their slaves were released. Mr. Rolle gave many of his slaves parcels of the vast amount of undeveloped property he owned, and they formed their own towns like Rolleville and Rolle Town. The Kelsalls wanted to keep most of their property for their family."

Kayleigh was waiting for the right opportunity to bring up the image of the sailboat she saw. "That seems selfish, don't you think?"

"The Kelsalls held a family seat in Devonshire, England, as the Lords of the Manor of Kelsall, and were prominent members of the government, and that trait followed them here."

"That's cool."

"In my research I discovered there was a haunted house called Henock in Devon which is rumored to have unexplained occurrences befall visitors on the property. I found that intriguing as it's like what is known to happen at the Kelsall's Hermitage House here on Little Exuma. Both properties housed slaves and have several tombs on the land."

Kayleigh curiosity was piqued; where was this story heading and why was she telling her all this stuff? "Have you visited the Hermitage House?"

"I've been by it but have never been inside, and it felt a little creepy to me."

Finally, Kayleigh had her chance to broach her question. "Well, I've been there, and yes, it's very creepy. In fact, I was inside the house when I saw an image of your sailboat. Why do you think that would happen to me?"

Kate's eyes went wide with astonishment, and she practically shouted. "Who are you?"

Kayleigh held her emotions tight. "My name is Kayleigh Jones, and I'm not bewitched, so please calm down. I need help finding my parents. They came here to check out some property they inherited, and something happened to them. When I saw the image of your sailboat, I took it as a sign. Do you have any idea why I saw your boat?"

Kate's bright shiny smile was replaced by an agitated glare. "No, of course not! How would I know?"

Kayleigh didn't want to push her luck, but she suspected Kate knew more than she was letting on. "Worst of all, there is someone involved in trying to steal the land. This whole thing has been a terrible nightmare. My cousin's plane was shot out of the sky, and I hurt my foot when we crashed. Now he's gone, and I'm all alone." Kayleigh was overwhelmed with fear and loneliness. Her eyes filled with tears and sobs shattered her body.

Kate wanted to hug her and tell her that her parents were safe, but she knew Lance would never allow such a thing. She was torn watching the poor girl suffer. "Please calm down. Let's go for a walk." Gazing at her foot, she reconsidered. "I'm sorry, I guess that's not an option. Can you make it to the Chat and Chill? I'll buy you something to drink. I know a nice cold Corona Beer would suit my fancy. I don't want to leave you here alone in such a state of mind."

Kayleigh nodded, tears still streaming down her cheeks. "Why don't you get your beer, and I'll meet you there—I can't walk fast."

"Don't be a silly, lass, just wait while I get some cash."

They walked at a slow pace toward the restaurant. As they passed the volleyball court, Kate smiled at Lance, but he was so involved in the game that he didn't pay much attention to her or the woman by her side.

The Chat and Chill was busy but not crowded. They found a table, and Kayleigh sat down; she was exhausted and was glad to be out of the sun. Kate looked at the tears that still leaked from Kayleigh's eyes. "I'm going to get myself a beer, what can I get for you?"

Kayleigh dabbed away her tears. "I don't know, no alcohol. I feel too down for that."

"How about a lemonade?"

"Sure, I can do that."

Kate made her way to the bar and ordered the drinks. "Please put a splash of vodka in the lemonade; my friend's foot is bothering her."

Kayleigh watched Kate at the bar; she was certain that she was hiding something from her, but what? She glanced around at the people in the bar; they were smiling and laughing, acting carefree and seemed to be thoroughly enjoying themselves while basking in a picturesque tropical paradise. And she wished that she were any place but here. The chaos that surrounded her was almost overwhelming.

Kate returned with the drinks. In her heart she knew she must share her secret with Kayleigh but was having a tough time deciding on how to present the news. She took a sip of her drink. "Oh, that's good and cold; the sun was getting to me."

Kayleigh began to relax and was interested in Kate's chattering which was taking her mind off her current dilemma.

Kate took a deep breath, then bent over and looked into Kayleigh's reddened eyes. "Kayleigh, I am sorry. I do have a secret I must share—your parents are safe and well. I can't reveal more than that, but at least this information should give you peace of mind."

The news was shocking. How did Kate know about her parents? "Where are they? I need to see them. Tell me more."

"Please don't beg me for more information. All our lives would be in danger if I revealed more. Just take care of yourself and keep this awareness to yourself."

CHAPTER EIGHTEEN

Big Gina Marino stomped up the stairs leading into the Government Building and swung open the impressive doors. Diane saw the large woman enter, and she cowered at the sight. In a shallow voice, she meekly asked, "How may I help you today, Miss Marino?"

Gina's artificial smile couldn't hide the hardness in her face. "I'm here to see that poor excuse of a man, Nichols."

"But...but . . ." Diane stuttered. "You don't have an appointment, and Mr. Nichols isn't seeing anyone today. His office is closed to the public."

"Come on, girly, I know he's in there, and don't bother escorting me, I know where his freaking office is located."

The intimidating woman boldly marched by Diane and down the hall until she was outside his office where she threw open the door.

Mr. Nichols looked up at the sound of the disturbance. Gina saw the look of astonishment on his face, and she brazenly took steps closer, then stood hovering over his desk.

"Hi, there, just because you managed to save your mangy hide doesn't mean you're off the hook. Now let's talk."

Her presence was both frightful and distressing. Nichols remained frozen in his seat, watching, and waiting.

"Well, what's the matter, Nichols? The Kelsall clan seems to have either left the area, or they're no longer interested in pursuing the bogus plan to claim ownership to what belongs to me."

He knew there was no escape from this woman's power over his life or death and the welfare of his family. He was a desperate man. "I take it that you must have secured the needed paperwork to proceed with your ownership we discussed during your last visit."

"Hey, cut the BS. like I told you before, I don't need any paperwork. Your job is to make it happen."

"And how can I do that?"

Gina reached into her voluminous handbag and pulled out an envelope. "You can certify this as authentic." She handed him the envelope which he opened and pulled out a document. "This is a deed to the property," he said but frowned. "Where did you get this?" He took a closer look at the paper. "This paper looks authentic. Where did you get this?" he asked with dismay.

Gina's eyes narrowed. "You don't need to know any details. All I need is for you to certify it as authentic, and at the same time, destroy any other deeds."

His heart sank as he realized she was laying a trap for him. If he certified her claim as true and also destroyed the Kelsall's deeds, there would be no evidence to prove that she had not legally inherited the property.

On the other hand, the Kelsalls would surely contest the validity of Marino's deed. The fact that he was complicit in a fraud would be revealed, and he'd not only lose his job but probably go to prison. Or be killed by one of Gina's goons.

If he refused to certify her deed, he and his family would be in immediate danger. He was well caught between a rock and a hard place. "So, if I certify this as a genuine deed, you'll leave me and my family alone?"

"Yes, as long as you do things my way." Her eyes hardened, and he held back a shiver of fear. She was not a woman to cross.

"So, what will it be?" Gina demanded. "This or your family?"

Nichols sighed. "Have it your way. I'll authenticate this and destroy any other deeds. But I can't keep the Kelsalls from contesting ownership."

"Don't you worry, I'll handle the Kelsalls." An evil light danced in her eyes.

Nichols swallowed hard. "I'll need some assurance that you will leave my family out of this arrangement."

"I can assure you all you want, but if you turn on me, all bets are off. So just do what must be done."

She reached for a framed photograph on his desk and studied the picture of his wife and two teenage girls. "Beautiful family," Gina said. "It would be a shame if something happened to them."

She returned the frame to the desk and stepped away. "I'll be in touch," she promised and walked out of the office.

Nichols remained seated, his hands shaking as he listened to the clicking sound of her expensive leather heels on the tile floor fade down the hallway. He was as good as dead, but he had time to get his wife and daughters as far away from the Bahamas as possible.

***

Kayleigh spent most of her day on the balcony gazing at the soothing water and thinking of her encounter with Kate. She knew she should be relieved that her parents were safe, but that wasn't enough. She was angry; why wouldn't she tell her more? *Why can't I see them? When will Brett be back? I miss him so. I don't like being here alone.* Her cell phone rang, surprising her so that she nearly dropped it in her excitement. "Hello."

"Hi, Kayleigh, it's Lou. I'm here at the Exuma airport."

With disbelief she listened to his voice. "Lou, you're here in Exuma? How come?"

"Babe, I missed you and came to see how you are managing. I thought we might make amends."

Kayleigh's first thought was how dare he call her! Then she hesitated and sighed. "Tell me what your plans are."

"It's just a quick visit, can't stay long, just an overnight, but I'd like to get together. What do you say?"

Her thoughts overwhelmed her. On one hand she wanted to tell him to jump in the nearest cove. On the other hand, she was lonely and confused. There was nothing keeping her from seeing what he has to say for himself. "Lou, that's so nice of you. Can you come to George Town? I'm staying at a place called the Peace and Plenty. We could have dinner."

"That'll be fine. I'll rent a car for a day. See you soon."

She had a couple of hours before he would arrive, so she took her time. She changed into a colorful dress and took extra care with her makeup and hair. Then she went to the lobby and tried to relax in an overstuffed wicker rocking chair. Her phone rang and she saw that it was Lou.

"I'm parking my car," he said.

"I'm waiting in the lobby. Come on in."

Lou walked into the lobby, removed his black aviator sunglasses, and strode toward her. She admired the casual but upscale way he dressed.

She stood to greet him, accepting a casual kiss on the cheek. "Lou, you look great, this is a grand surprise."

His eyes gave her a once over. "What's with that boot on your foot?"

She smiled back at him, but she didn't relay the cause of her injury. "Just a freak accident." Wanting to avoid an inquisition, she added, "I get to remove it next week."

"What about your folks? Have you been able to locate them?"

"No, I haven't a clue to as to where they are—there are only thousands of islands in the Bahamas, but I'm not about to give up looking for them."

A silence settled between them. With nothing left to say he asked, "Where's a good place to eat?"

"I've heard the Two Turtles Inn is good, plus there is a band playing there tonight. I'm sure you can tell, George Town is nothing like South Beach, but if you don't mind, it's just a short walk from here."

"Don't you think I should drive you?"

"No, I'll be fine." In the few minutes they'd been together, she was reminded of his manipulative manner. Well, she wasn't going to fall for his gesture of tenderness. "Ready? Let's go."

He took her hand, and they walked along the sidewalk that skirted the Harbor. He surveyed the array of boating activity on the water surrounding them. "It seems like a busy boating community, but not much action. Don't you miss Miami? You could fly back with me and spent a romantic weekend together."

Just yesterday she was feeling she'd like to be anywhere other than here, but now she hid those thoughts. "Lou, Miami is the farthest thing from my mind, and I'm not coming back to work for some time, not until I find my parents."

He stopped and held her shoulders. "Kayleigh, I miss you. I didn't come all this way just to have dinner."

She looked at him, wondering why everything was always about him and his needs? "Lou, what we had was nice, but it's over. You just can't give me what I need."

"Do you really mean that? Am I that bad?"

"Please, Lou. This is nice surprise, and thank you for coming to see me, but I've made up my mind so let's not spoil the evening."

The Two Turtles Inn was across the street from the park and the straw market. A crowd was gathering, and it was abuzz with activity. They found a table in the corner and ordered a drink and looked over the menu. The band was playing a lively song which sparked the revelers to crowd on the dance floor. "Sorry I can't dance with this boot on, but at least we can enjoy our meal and listen to the music."

"Yeah, that's no problem." His eyes followed several women dancing to an erotic song.

When he dragged his gaze back to hers, they made small talk and ate their meal. "This conch chowder is really good," Kaleigh noted.

"Yes, my meal is good, too. This grouper is fresh. Must have been caught today." Yet he picked at the food on his plate.

The night seemed to drag on. Kayleigh noticed that his enthusiasm had diminished. Finally, she asked, "Should we head back now?"

He nodded. "Yeah, why don't we."

They left the spirited crowd and crossed the street to the sidewalk when Lou felt something swish by his head. "What was that? Kayleigh, did you hear it?"

"I'm sorry, Lou, hear what?" Another bullet buzzed by her.

"If I didn't know better, I'd say someone's shooting at us."

Kayleigh froze. "But I didn't hear any gunshots, did you?"

"Come on, let's mingle with the people at the straw market." He grabbed her hand and pulled her along until they were lost within the racks of sandals, straw hats, and tee shirts. Kayleigh was frightened, and she could feel her heart pound but wasn't about to tell him of all the mishaps that she had encountered since arriving in Exuma. She simply wondered if she would be able to survive until Brett returned.

Lou wiped the sweat off his lips. "Why would anyone want to harm us? Are you sure you want to stay here? This is no place for you. Kayleigh, please come back to Miami with me."

"It's tempting, Lou, but as I told you, I can't leave until I know what happened to my parents. Let's go now, the sun's starting to set, and the street is packed with people. I think we'll be safe enough to return to the hotel."

The events of the evening had taken a toll on Kayleigh's emotions. The sky was dark by the time they reached the hotel, and the moon's light softly illuminated the darkness, lending a hint of romance to the moment. Lou leaned his body against hers. "Kayleigh, I'd like to spend the night with you."

She was about to protest but didn't resist his advances. He pushed the hair away from her face and kissed her.

She backed away. "No, Lou, I can't. Please find yourself someone new. If you want to stay, you're welcome to sleep on the couch, but you can't join me in my bed."

He dropped his arms and stepped away from her. "I'm disappointed in you, Kayleigh, I thought I meant more to you."

She locked her eyes on his. "You did at one time, but I've told you. It's over. Don't make it so difficult. You captured my heart, and I really did love you, but I know now that you can't give me what I need. It's always about you. You always put yourself first. Lou, you just don't get it; I'm important, too, and right now I don't see any hope for us in the future. Let's remain friends, can we do that?"

"Well, if that's how you feel, I'll be on my way." He pulled car keys from his pocket. "Just let me know when you plan to return to work. And be careful. Something dangerous is happening here."

"Bye, Lou," she said as he hurried away. "Thanks for the visit." She closed her eyes to hide the tears and quickly made her way into the hotel lobby.

CHAPTER NINETEEN

Carole couldn't get over the events that transpired during the night at the marina. But when the marina manager returned from Nassau, she insisted Ted move the houseboat to another island.

"Carole, I'm telling you, I don't feel comfortable running in the waters around here."

"Don't be silly, Ted, you've had boats all your life. It can't be that different."

Ted stood rigid, and he was tense. "Carole, you're not listening to me. The houseboat doesn't belong to me, although that's not my main concern; it's the navigational hazards that I'm uncomfortable with."

Carole pleaded. "Ted, this place is too isolated. It's just a matter of time before someone or something else happens here."

He didn't like it, but she had a point and reluctantly he agreed. "Okay, Carole, I'll see what I can locate."

Ted understood her concern, because he too was worried about their safety, and he intently studied the charts. Later in the day, he brought a chart to Carole.

With kindness in his voice he said, "I think I found a place for us. Come here, and I'll show you on the chart." He pointed to the area. "It's called Staniel Cay, and it's about 25 to 30 miles north. There are two marinas with slips, or if you'd rather, there are moorings available. It also has a general store and two restaurants. By the looks of it, we won't be that isolated. I'll do my best to get us there, although I can see some tricky passages. You'll have to help me navigate; can you agree to do that?"

Carole smiled and wrapped her arms around him. "I'll do whatever I can to help." She pursed her lips while her hands cupped his face and kissed him tenderly.

***

Kayleigh had a restless night. The visit from Lou, plus the fear of being shot at had upset her. She was overwhelmed with extreme anxiety that she couldn't shake. Maybe she should have let Lou stay. No, what good would that do? She knew he wasn't good for her, that she deserved better. She had never liked being manipulated by him. And besides, what would Brett think of her?

She just lay in bed, seemingly paralyzed, unable to make a move to get up. By late afternoon she realized she had wasted the whole day in bed. She got up, dressed herself, and went to the restaurant where she ordered a lobster salad and a glass of wine.

She slowly sipped her drink, gazing at Stocking Island directly across Elizabeth Harbor. Tomorrow, she decided, she was going back there to find Kate. She needed to know why Kate wouldn't tell her more about her parents' whereabouts and what had made them hide away without letting her know what was going on. Nothing made sense.

***

The next morning arrived among Kayleigh's nighttime twists and turns. She dressed quickly and left her boot behind; it was just too clumsy for walking in the sand. Ditching it a few days early shouldn't impede the healing process. She slipped her feet into her comfortable flip flops and headed to the dock where the shuttle boat was located. It was mid-morning, and the shuttle was about to depart with only a few passengers aboard.

She took a seat in the bow of the boat. The boat was mostly empty due to the lack of people, but the captain left on the scheduled time. A warm wind shifted through her hair, and it soothed her, but her anticipation grew stronger the closer the shuttle came to the island.

She kicked off her sandals and slid over the boat's side onto the fine soft sand. "That's much better." She looked down the shoreline and was relieved to see that the blue and white sailboat was still anchored there. She took her time ambling along the shoreline. When she reached the sailboat, Lance and Kate were in the surf enjoying a midmorning swim. She had no idea how long they would frolic there, so she sat in one of the sand chairs on the shore and watched as they romped playfully in the water.

After a while Lance drifted toward the boat and climbed aboard to disappear down the hatch. Kate walked to the shore and looked at the woman sitting in her chair. A quizzical look covered her face, and she was about to chase her away when she realized the interloper was Kayleigh. She walked closer. "Hi, Kayleigh, what brings you back here?"

"I came to see you, because I've been unable to sleep since you told me about my parents, and I'm here to find out more!"

Kate's body grew tense, and she glanced over her shoulder looking for a sign of Lance, but he was nowhere in sight. "Kayleigh, I don't have anything to add. Please accept what I told you and be happy that they are safe. Now please leave before there is a scene."

Kayleigh was astonished. "What do you mean by that? What kind of scene are you expecting? No, I will not leave. I demand to know more, and I won't leave until you tell me the whole story."

Kate raised her eyebrows, and her bright brown eyes glared at the girl sitting in her chair. "Please, Kayleigh, don't speak so loud, you will get me in a heap of trouble." She looked at Kayleigh's feet. "I see you are not wearing your boot today. Let's go for a walk, and I'll explain a few things."

"All right. What's the big deal; you act like you're committing a crime?"

"Lance is going to play a game of volleyball, so let's stay away from the court."

She walked over to Kayleigh and extended her hand. "Here, let me help you up." When Kayleigh got her bearings, they headed further down the beach.

"Kayleigh, I'm deeply sorry about your situation. That is why I told you about your parents, but because of a current obligation, I can't reveal anything else. But I've been thinking about the Hermitage House. Why don't we go there together?"

Kayleigh's anger seemed to abate while she thought of Kate's suggestion. "Why do you want me to return there?"

Kate tried to remain patient and practical. "For one thing, you saw an image of our sailboat, which you took to be a sign, and apparently it was one. Just maybe you'll see another image that will lead you to your parents."

Kayleigh stared at Kate for a long moment. "This is ridiculous. You could just as easily tell me where they are. This whole situation is the dumbest thing I've ever encountered. Going back there won't solve anything. Besides, that place really creeps me out." With that she turned to go.

"Kayleigh, please wait. I would like to help you, and if we went together, I could do more research on the paper I'm writing."

Kayleigh paused to think about Kate's suggestion. Could going back really reveal any clues? "Do you have any idea how we would get there? It's a long dinghy ride."

"Can't we rent a taxi? I'll pay for it."

She questioned the notion. "You will?" Kayleigh gave the idea more thought. "Tell you what, my parents' car is in the hotel's parking lot. We could take that, then we wouldn't be in a hurry to get back. And you could drive because you are used to driving a car on the left side of the road."

"It's a deal," Kate said. "Let me put some dry clothes on. Today's a good day—Lance will be busy all day."

The two women walked back to the sailboat with purpose in their stride.

CHAPTER TWENTY

Lou was disappointed with the outcome of his planned visit; he sulked as he strode to his rental car, opened the door, and slid behind the wheel. He gave one last glance at Kayleigh who was opening the door of the hotel.

He felt guilty for leaving her behind. This was no place for a woman to be by herself. Had someone really shot at them earlier in the day or had he imagined the sound of bullets whizzing by his head? He drove out of the parking lot onto the Queen's Highway and headed toward the airport. There were no flights scheduled after dark, so he would have to find lodging for the night.

Had he imagined the sound of bullets? After all, he hadn't heard any shots ring out. Someone would have had to use a silencer on a handgun, and that was really a farfetched idea. Things like that didn't happen to ordinary people who were simply walking through a straw market.

The idea of being shot at bubbled through his mind, making him agitated which caused him to have a foggy focus on the road ahead. There were no streetlights along the road, and he was the only car on the road. He tried not to think about the idea of being shot at but being on the dark remote road made him uneasy. Suddenly a pair of headlights loomed in his rearview mirror. A truck sped up and hung on his bumper. He picked up his speed, but the vehicle behind him did the same. Was someone following him? He slowed down and hoped the truck would go around him. In the next moment, the vehicle behind him bashed into his rear bumper. "What the hell?"

He picked up speed, but the next bump was more forceful. A shot of fury mixed with ice cold fear shot through Lou. He checked the rearview mirror again only to be blinded by powerful headlights. He stepped hard on the gas pedal, and the car sprang forward with greater speed, but the rental car was no match for the truck that was now alongside him.

The truck driver swerved into the side of Lou's car in an effort to force his car off the road. The darkness, the accelerated speed, and the poorly maintained road were against Lou. He lost control of the car which plowed through the thick overgrowth of brush at 60 miles an hour and continued until it crashed into a large tree where it stopped abruptly.

The car's front window was shattered, and Lou's body hung on top of the steering wheel. There were no seat belts or air bags in the rental car to save him.

Vinny and Lenny got out of their truck and scrambled through the brush. When they reached the car, they were unable to determine if Lou was dead or alive.

"Vinny, you better finish the job. No way of knowing if he's gone, and I ain't gonna check."

Vinny took his pistol and placed it behind Lou's ear and pulled the trigger. "There, that's done. This guy's seaplane will just rot away now, and no one will be the wiser. Now let's cover the car tracks." They scattered dead branches over the area, leaving the car and the corpse hidden from sight.

***

Ted and Carole left Cave Cay at daybreak. The early morning mist had dissipated, and warming rays of bright sunlight shone through the cabin of the houseboat. Carole brought Ted a hot cup of coffee. Smiling she said, "I thought you might like a pickup."

"Thanks, sweetie, the seas are calm, but the forecast predicts them to pick up later. Let's hope they don't whip up until we reach Staniel Cay."

Carole placed her hands on his shoulders. "Is there anything you would like for me to do?"

"No, but please watch the charts and see if there are any navigational questions you might have. Thanks, honey, with any luck we should be there by early afternoon."

Carole let out a big sigh. "Ted, I can't wait."

As the day progressed, a warm wind sprang up. By noon they were off Great Guana Cay. "Ted, be careful around here; you need to stay between the shore and a large sandbar to the west that runs the entire length of the next island, named Bitter Guana Cay. When you reach the end of the island, turn 90 degrees west, then head straight. There is a red light off Staniel Cay. Make another 90 degree turn east to the marked channel entrance."

Ted absorbed her input. "Okay, thanks."

When Ted made his 90-degree adjustment he was surprised that the wind was whipping up. The waves began crashing over the bow of the boat which rocked furiously.

"Carole!" Ted bellowed, "secure things down! This is going to be a rough ride. I need you to help me find that red light so we can turn back east."

Spray from the waves covered the window in front of the helm, limiting Ted's visibility. He found himself grabbing on to the wheel with all his might. He felt moisture running down his back.

Carole hovered over Ted's shoulder, searching for the light. Then out of the mist they saw the red beam. The boat's forward momentum had slowed because of the pounding waves, and it seemed like forever to reach the light that appeared so close.

"Carole, I'm going to have to go beyond the light before I change directions again."

Carole's fear was evident. "Why? Why can't you just turn when we get to the light? We need to get out of these waves."

"Carole, please calm down! It's bad enough that I have to manage a boat I don't know how to handle in an area I've never been to before."

Tension was high as Ted made his calculated turn, but the wind caught the broad side of the boat, pushing it back toward the light. "Damn it!" He pushed the throttles forward, and the boat headed north, away from the light. Once they were above Staniel Cay he was in open water. The waves were relentless, but he managed to swing the boat in an easterly direction. The waves were behind them now, pushing them toward the island.

"I have it now," Ted said with relief. "All I have to do is avoid the sand bar and head for Happy People's Marina."

Carole smiled. "That's an appropriate name. Let's hope it makes us happy."

The channel was well marked. Ted followed the recommendations and headed for a hill in the background. He slowed the boat down when they entered Staniel Cay Creek, and the wind died down.

"We made it!" Carole cried out.

Ted relaxed just a bit. "It's not over yet, but at least we're here in one piece,"

Rays of sunlight filled the interior of the boat which helped to brighten their moods. Carole's eyes were warm with love as she embraced Ted, kissing him softly on his cheek, and she whispered, "Thank you."

CHAPTER TWENTY-ONE

The Cessna 172 Sea Plane descended through the clouds just above Leo Kelsall's home, circled around Big Bear Lake, then splashed down on the water and came to rest on a small sandy beach. Brett slipped out of his plane and looked toward his grandfather's cabin. To his surprise he saw him briskly walking in his direction with a backpack strapped to his shoulders.

"Hi, Sonny, I'm ready to go, no need to waste time."

Brett gave his grandfather a questionable glance. He stared at him for long minute without speaking as he tried to get his thoughts together. "You sure you want to do this? When was the last time you flew on a jet plane? Let's just talk about this for a while."

"Don't worry about me, sonny. I'll be fine, now let's go."

Brett's mind was vibrating with curiosity. "Gramps, you're not going to need those boots and long pants when we arrive in Exuma. Do you have any shorts and sandals?"

"Are you crazy? I ain't got no need for them Jesus shoes; I only wear my boots. Nothing more comfortable than them."

Brett shook his head in disbelief. "But Gramps, you must understand it's gonna be hot there. How about a bathing suit?"

His grandfather smiled. "Yep, got one of them packed right back here. I jump in the lake now and then. It's cool and refreshing in the summer."

"I imagine it is. Do you have a pair of old blue jeans we could cut to make into shorts?"

"Why would I want to ruin a pair of perfectly good pants?"

Brett noted a glint of humor in his grandfather's eyes and considered the options, then decided to let it go. "Have it your way, there are shops in George Town if you change your mind."

"That's better; I knew you'd come to your senses." Then he reached his hand deep into his hip pocket and retrieved something. When he opened his fist, Brett saw two hunks of gold. "Here you go, these are for you. One is to pay for your engine, and the other is for my share of the trip."

The gold nuggets glittered in the sunlight. "Gramps, I can't take them. The engine is covered by my insurance claim, and we can discuss the trip cost later."

"Don't be silly, son, now take the damn stones!"

Brett didn't want to have to discuss the transaction any longer, so he reached for the gold and placed them in his shirt pocket. "Thanks."

"That's better. I can't wait to meet that impostor and give the bitch a piece of my mind. I'll teach her not to screw with me. She'll think twice before she ever tries to steal my land away from me. She's in a heap of trouble."

Brett rolled his eyes and felt the realization in his gut that maybe this wasn't such a good idea. Reluctantly, he turned around and headed back to his plane and listened to the sounds of footsteps following close behind.

***

Kate took a minute to change into dry clothes then pulled the dinghy close to the sailboat. She lowered herself into it, started the motor and drove it up on the shore where Kayleigh stood. "Hop aboard. We'll use this, it will give us more control of our time."

They pushed the small boat back into the water and headed across Elizabeth Harbor. Small frothy waves broke over the bow as the dinghy scooted through them. The seagulls flying above seemed to be guiding them on the right course. They arrived at the Peace and Plenty and beached the dinghy on the sandy beach.

Kate looked around, searching for the parking lot. "Where's the car?"

"The parking lot is on the other side of the building, but first I have to get the keys. They are kept at the front desk."

Kate frowned. "Why?"

Kayleigh sighed. "Because the rental is in my father's name, and the staff is being picky on who drives it and where they go."

"Well, that's bloody rude. Just tell them you're taking it for a drive. I'll meet you in the parking lot."

Kayleigh mumbled something under her breath and followed the path to the lobby. When she entered the room, she was greeted by Roberta who was behind the front desk.

"Hi, Kayleigh, how are you doing?"

"I'm well, thank you, but I need a favor. I have to go to the clinic for a check-up. Would it be possible to take my father's rental car?"

Roberta noticed Kayleigh wasn't wearing the boot on her foot. "Looks like you've recovered."

"Yes, but I don't want to overdo it until the doctor releases me."

"Here you go, please be careful," Roberta said as she handed Kayleigh the keys.

"Thanks, I'm not sure how long I'll be. It depends on how many people are ahead of me." She dashed back to the parking lot with the keys. "All set. You drive."

Kate grabbed the keys and climbed into the car. "What's that smell?"

"Some sort of insecticide, I think. There were a bunch of dead bugs in here. They must have come through that hole in the floorboard. Let's go!"

Kate drove the rental car south on the Queens Highway. When they reached the outskirts of George Town she asked, "How much longer?"

"It's not far now, once we go over the bridge at Ferry, we'll be close. Besides, this is just a big waste of time. All you have to do is tell me where my folks are. This subterfuge is nothing but a bunch of BS."

"Bollocks! You know I can't do that."

"No, I don't know that," Kayleigh practically snapped. "I don't get any of this. Why?"

"I told you. I can't tell you."

The car bumped over the old rickety bridge, and the beauty of the stunning tropical setting surrounded them. "Look how gorgeous that beach is." Kate effectively changed the subject.

"Yes, it's a magnificent paradise, isn't it?" Kayleigh said, thinking to herself, *and it belongs to me.*

A few minutes later, the Hermitage House appeared on the knoll above the road.

"We're here," Kate said with satisfaction.

Kayleigh wrinkled her nose. "This place grosses me out. I hope this won't take long."

Kate parked the car, and the two made their way up the hill to find their way inside the old building. Kayleigh's hands were sweating as she dreaded each step she took. "Kate, nothing's happening. I think we should leave."

Kate was deep in thought as she studied the walls of the building. Everything about the place fascinated her. "This place is awesome. I'm not ready to go yet. Where were you standing when you saw the image of our sailboat?"

"I don't remember." Suddenly Kayleigh started feeling her heart thump. Her breaths came in rapid succession. "I got to get out of here now!"

Kate was aghast when she saw the aura that surrounded Kayleigh and froze in place.

Kayleigh shrieked, "Oh, no, Lou! It's Lou, and he's dead! How can that be?" Tears filled her eyes. "Kate, I need to get out of here now! And I'm never coming back! This place is too freaking creepy!"

When they were outside the building, Kayleigh's fear turned into rage. She glared at Kate as fury boiled out of her. "Kate, you don't know or care about me! All you want to do is protect yourself from Lance's wrath and use me as a guinea pig for your stupid article! Take me home. I never want to see you again!"

"That's not completely true!" Kate protested. "I do want to help you find your parents, but I can't betray a confidence. I'm sorry." Kate opened her arms. "Here, let me give you a hug."

Kayleigh backed away. "Get away from me! Let's go!"

They walked down the hill, got into the car, and headed north. No one spoke a word as they made their way back. Suddenly Kate yelled, "We're snookered; some blokes are coming at us fast, and I think he's going to ram us!"

Kayleigh glanced at Kate and noticed the pupils of her eyes had grown as big as saucers as she looked in the rear-view mirror. A truck approached rapidly from behind.

Kayleigh turned to look at the oncoming truck and screamed. "Holy shit! They're trying to kill us!"

Instantly Kate pushed the gas pedal hard, and to her surprise the car took off like a rocket, but the truck gained on them. Desperately she tried to outrun them but felt a jolt when the truck struck the car's rear bumper. They hit it again with more force, tearing the bumper off the car.

Kate looked at the rear-view mirror again into the eyes of the man driving the truck. "Oh, my God, it's those gangsters that threatened Lance and me on the beach!"

"What guys?"

The old bridge was in sight; in a flash they were crossing the bridge, but Kate's success was interrupted when the truck hit them harder and pushed the car though the railing.

"Oh, no!" Kayleigh screamed as the car plunged off the bridge. "We're going to drown!" she screamed as her body thrashed about.

"Just hold on tight!" Kate screeched.

The car was in a nosedive off the bridge and splashed into the water on its side. Kayleigh's twisted body was thrown against the door. Kate managed to open her door and yelled, "Kayleigh, get out now!"

"I can't open my door! The water is coming in fast through the hole in the floorboard. Help me!"

Kate saw the rising water. "Give me your hand and push hard with your feet. Quickly, before we're underwater."

Kayleigh reached up and caught Kate's arm, then pushed herself upward with all her might.

They held each other tight. "Good," Kate huffed. "Now we have to jump out!" The car was already half submerged.

Together they splashed into the water while the rental car slid along the sandy bottom and was swept fast into deep water before going beneath the bridge and into even deeper water.

The two women were drawn beneath the turbulent water for a long moment before popping up. They gulped for air as they grasped one another. Kayleigh started to sob, but Kate silenced her with a quick admonition. "Hush, I hear the truck up on the bridge!" A squeal of tires filled the air above them.

Kate pulled Kayleigh to one of the bridge's supports where they were hidden from anyone above. "Shhh!

"There goes the car!" a triumphant voice called out from above.

"There was no time for them to get out," a second voice yelled.

"Then let's get out of here before traffic comes along!"

They heard two doors slamming and then tires squealing as the truck took off. In moments all they could hear was the sound of the engine receding. Soon it was quiet beneath the bridge, the only sound the girls' heavy breathing.

"Oh, my God," Kayleigh managed to choke out.

"Thanks be to God," Kate agreed. "They think we're dead." Then she noticed that Kayleigh's body was trembling. "Come on, let's get out of here." She looked up and down the coast. "We'll swim to that cluster of palms," she said, pointing downstream. "If they come back, they won't be able to spot us there."

The two swam side by side. By the time they reached shore, their bodies were rigid and full of adrenalin. Kate looked at Kayleigh, whose face was ashen, and she noticed her body was still trembling.

Kayleigh's thoughts were on an emotional roller coaster ride. She was frightened, mad and sad all at the same time, and relieved to be alive. For long silent moments the two rested on the warm sand. Finally, Kayleigh placed her hand over her heart, feeling the rapid beats while some reality seeped back into her brain. "I'm screwed big time! The car was part of the ongoing investigation of my parents' disappearance. I should never had taken it." Her voice waivered with apprehension.

Kate sighed, "Hey, don't think you're alone. Lance will be livid when he finds out I was with you."

"Don't tell him!"

"Kayleigh, just look at me. I'm a mess, he'll be suspicious of my taking the dinghy without telling him of my plans."

Kayleigh was consumed by her own problems and not supportive of Kate. "I'm sure you'll figure it out, but what are we going to do now? And why the hell do those guys want us dead?"

Kate stood up. "It must have something to do with that car. Which just might be a clue as to why your parents are on the run."

Mouth open with shock, Kayleigh stared at Kate as she tried to take in the comment about her parents.

"We need to get out of here," Kate added. "Let's walk back toward Williamstown. There is a bar on the beach not far from here. Carmen works for Santana, the owner, and is a sweet woman. I'm sure she'll help us get back to the hotel."

They walked a short way when Kayleigh complained, "My foot really hurts. I think I reinjured it. Kate, can we rest for a minute?"

They sat for a while, until Kate got restless. "This is getting us nowhere, let's go."

Kayleigh hobbled along in the soft sand as Kate scanned the beach for any signs of the waterfront bar. They continued onward with Kayleigh lagging behind. Kate ignored her as she searched the beach until finally, she spotted the bar ahead of them. The sandy beach and bright sunlight seemed to engulf it. A crowd of people were inside eating and drinking and laughing.

Kayleigh relinquished her hatred toward Kate, and the two hugged one another with relief. "I don't know about you," Kate finally said, "but I'm getting myself a beer. I need something to settle my nerves."

Kayleigh looked surprised at Kate's announcement. "A beer? I don't think I could get one down. I'm still too upset."

"Come on, girl, that's behind us. We need to focus on what to do next. Now get a grip!"

Kayleigh gave her a glare, then thought about it and changed her mind. "Hey, why not? Besides, I need to vent and talk to you about what just happened to us. So, yes, I'll have one, too."

*"You gain strength, courage, and confidence by every experience
in which you really stop to look fear in the face... You must do the
thing you cannot do."*
Eleanor Roosevelt

CHAPTER TWENTY TWO

G ina Marino was a female mastermind who was a successful,
savage drug lord involved in trafficking, racketeering,
extortion, and assault with murder. She met her acquaintance
Luigi Gallo in Las Vegas, Nevada, where the tantalizing allure of
skimming cash from the casino's winnings brought them together.

Unfortunately for them, gaming regulations now intensely
scrutinizes and penalizes any questionable activity in the Sin City as
the current environment promotes a family entertainment venue.

With that in mind, they investigated the up stick by organized
crime bosses in the Bahamas, known as Bahama's Amusement Ltd.
Their research led them to the Exuma Island chain, a magnet for the
rich and famous who live in mansions on their private islands. Gina
and Luigi settled for an ideal spot for their new casino on Little Exuma
because of its remoteness and its beautiful beaches. The only glitch
was the Kelsall family who had laid claim to the land back in the
1700s.

Gina's street shoulders, Vinny and Lenny, were attempting to
explain their recent intimidation tactics and the murder of one of the
alleged members of the Kelsall family. "Boss, we offed the guy with
the seaplane, so that's one down. The older woman has disappeared,
and we don't see her coming back after spending a day inside a tomb."

"Yeah, but the bitch escaped and saved her husband, plus they
never returned to the states. So where are they? There's no excuse for
that kind of sloppiness. Luigi doesn't like losers." She took a deep
breath. "Now tell me about the younger woman, the one who had the
nerve to get her DNA done and tell that pussy Nichols about it, saying
that I'm not Leo Kelsall's daughter but an imposter. Her revelation
caused me headaches because my credibility was damaged. Then I
remembered that counterfeiter who made me a fake passport. He's
just as good making a deed that will pass muster. Nichols is scared
shitless that we'll put a hit out on his wife and kids, so I think I settled

90

that problem. He's probably made the other deeds disappear, too, and replaced them with mine.

"Well, we don't have to worry about that guy with the seaplane. He's out of the picture; and don't worry about the girl who was with him, we just ran her car off the bridge at Ferry. We're pretty sure she was swept out to sea inside the car, along with the British woman we kicked off the beach a while back. Can't figure out how those two found each other, but we're pretty sure they're at the bottom of the sea.

"Pretty sure isn't good enough! Find out and terminate all of them, and don't mess it up this time! You guys are on borrowed time. Capeesh?"

***

Kate was exhausted mentally and physically—and what she had planned as a goodwill gesture had turned into a horrible nightmare. Those men were out to kill them, but the lady Carmen at Santana's turned out to be a saint. She gave them free drinks and arranged for transportation back to the hotel.

She and Kayleigh stood on the beach where she'd left the dinghy and regretted that she had coerced Kayleigh to go back to the Hermitage House. To top it off she knew Lance would be upset with her behavior. Most likely he'll be livid when he finds out that the men who ran them down saw her face and now knew that she was somehow involved with the Kelsall clan. Thank God that they probably are convinced that she and Kayleigh are now at the bottom of the sea.

She looked at Kayleigh who was beside her. "Kayleigh, dear, please be careful. I know I put you through a traumatic experience which was totally uncalled for, and I'm sorry for that, but I must go now."

Kayleigh remained silent, but Kate could see the frightened look that covered her face. She pulled the dinghy into the water and climbed in. "Don't forget to notify the police about those men."

Kayleigh nodded and swallowed hard before she spoke. "I'll do it in the morning. I just can't deal with any more drama today. I'm too stressed. Besides, I need to take a shower and get the saltwater off me. Maybe the warm water will calm my nerves."

***

91

Kayleigh paced around her room thinking about the pandemonium that surrounded her. She was at a loss on how to explain the car's disappearance to Roberta, the clerk at the front desk who would be expecting her to return the car keys. Her mind flipped to Kate, and she wondered if she had made it back to the sailboat without alerting Lance of anything suspicious.

Thank goodness Kate knew Carmen was a friend of Santana, the owner of the sand bar. When they had arrived at the bar, Kate explained their situation to Carmen who asked how they had gotten involved with such vile men.

"Just last week," Carmen explained, "some men tried to kidnap a gentleman who works at the Government Building in George Town. When the man showed up here, the poor soul was petrified. He said they were about to assassinate him."

"Yes, Carmen, we didn't know they would be after us, too, and part of the problem is there are no police in Little Exuma," Kate had explained.

"Yes, I know that is a problem, and I shall bring that to the mayor's attention. We can't have these hoodlums roaming around our city. Meanwhile, you can alert the police in George Town. Now stay put while I see if I can find someone to give you two a lift back there."

***

Kayleigh felt as though she had been beaten up. Her body ached all over from thrashing around in the car as it fell off the bridge. She looked around her bedroom in the midst of her helplessness, sitting alone on the side of her bed. What should she do first, she wondered when her cell phone's ring startled her. She was so overwhelmed with emotion she could barely speak. "Hello," she whispered.

"Kayleigh, this is Brett...Kayleigh, are you there?"

She spoke louder. "Brett, where are you? Things couldn't be worse here! Please hurry back. I'm not sure I can survive another day."

Brett paused, uncertain of what he should say next. "I'm sorry for not calling sooner, but it took a hell of lot of maneuvering to get all my bases covered. I just arrived in Miami, and soon I'll be on my way to Nassau with Gramps. My plan is to catch the mailboat and load my engine on it. If all goes well, we should be in George Town within a day or two. It all depends on how long it will take to get my engine from the airport cargo depot to the port where the boat is docked."

She paced about the suite and gazed out at the water as she reflected on his words. "Brett, you can't bring your grandfather here! They will kill him!"

"Kayleigh, what's gotten into you? You sound distraught."

"Oh, Brett! Things have gotten bad here. They killed Lou, and just yesterday they tried to kill Kate and me!"

"Lou? Kate? What are you talking about?"

"Brett, I can't explain it all to you now. I'm too upset. Please hurry, but don't bring your grandfather here!"

Such anguish seemed excessive to Brett. "Kayleigh, calm down, what's going on?" In an instant the line went dead. "What the hell?" He called her back, the phone rang, but she failed to answer. Then he heard the voice mail prompt. "Kayleigh, hang in there, I'm on my way!"

Kayleigh was stunned by her actions, and so fraught with the threat of danger she could scarcely function.

"What' wrong with me?" She closed her eyes and grabbed her head with both hands; when she tried to open her eyes, her lids wouldn't move. She stood there like a frozen statue. Finally, her panic subsided, and she opened her eyes, ran to her bedroom, then buried her head in the pillow and remained there for most of the morning, consumed by intense loneliness. By noon she felt better and realized she must face the reality of her situation.

She rinsed her face with cold water; looking at her reflection in the mirror, she gasped, "I look terrible!" She fussed with her hair, then grabbed the boot lying beside her bed and put it on. The trauma of the car accident and her struggle to get out had reinjured her foot. Then she left her room.

With determination she approached the front desk. The same woman Roberta wrinkled her brow and watched Kayleigh walk toward her. "Good day, Kayleigh, how are you?"

"Actually, I'm not doing that well."

"That's too bad," Roberta said with a bit of sarcasm in her voice. Her extended hand waved in front of Kayleigh. "I'll take the keys back now."

Kayleigh drew a big sigh from deep within her lungs and looked straight into Roberta's eyes. "I'm sorry, but I can't give you the keys or tell you exactly where you might find the car, because it was run off the bridge at Ferry."

Like an angry school marm, Roberta questioned, "What were you doing in Ferry? You told me you needed to go to the clinic."

Kayleigh felt the burning sensation that covered her face and the tenseness in her body. "Yes, I'm sorry, I lied to you, but that doesn't change things; the car and the keys are gone, and I'm on my way to the police to report the accident. You see I was attacked by two men in a truck who may have something to do with my parents' disappearance."

Without a backward glance at Roberta, she left the hotel lobby, struggling to walk with the boot on her foot; she headed for the Government Building. She was just a few blocks into her walk when she heard heavy footsteps rapidly coming up behind her. She turned to see who it might be. To her surprise, a man with a hood in his hand was only a few paces away, and he seemed ready to cover her head with the hood.

Instantly Kayleigh raised her boot-covered foot and kicked him hard in the groin. Then she wailed, "Help! Help me! Someone please help me!"

Her shouts alerted a young couple leaving the realtor's office across the street, and they darted toward her.

The man with the hood jumped into the bed of a green pickup truck that was pacing him, and the driver took off.

Kayleigh's heart was pounding, but she was relieved that she was safe for now. "Thank you, I think that man was about to assault me."

The young man agreed. "It sure looked that way to us. Are you okay?"

"Not really, but I'm on my way to the police station. Did you get a look at the license number on the truck?"

"No. Sorry, we were focused on helping you."

"Would you mind verifying what you saw to the police? Circumstances have become extremely dangerous for me."

"Really?" There was a note of uncertainty in the man's voice, and the woman was tugging at his hand, pulling him away. "I would really like to help you, miss, but I can't involve myself or my girlfriend in any kind of danger; we are only here for a short visit. Good luck to you." With that, the couple hurried across the street.

Kayleigh stood silent on the sidewalk while broken sunshine peeked through the drifting clouds. "Well, that was a bunch of shit luck."

She swallowed hard, wondering about what could lie ahead and frightened that worse was yet to come.

CHAPTER TWENTY-THREE

Kate started the boat's motor, then pointed the small watercraft toward the island across the harbor and waved goodbye. The gentle waves on the sea helped ease some of her agitation, but when she approached Stocking Island, she felt herself tense up again. She guided the dinghy past the deserted volleyball beach, then slipped behind the sailboat and secured it before climbing the swim ladder. Her heart fluttered with trepidation.

Lance was in the cockpit waiting for her. "Kate, what happened to you? You're a sight!"

She knew she must fess up; it was the only proper thing to do. She looked him in the eyes, took a deep breath, and paused.

"Well, Kate, are you going to tell me what's going on?"

"Lance, I am so sorry, but I befriended Kayleigh Jones. You remember her mom and dad who we helped rent the houseboat you drove to Cave Cay?"

"You what?"

"Lance, please don't be so cheeky, and just listen to what I have to say. Kayleigh was in the Hermitage plantation house with her cousin Brett when she saw an image of our sailboat. Do you remember Carol telling us about the image of the tomb when she was inside that house? Well, this Brett has a seaplane, and when they flew over the island, they saw our boat, and naturally Kayleigh was curious about the connection, so she paid me a visit while you were playing volleyball with your mates."

Lance interrupted her. "You told her about her parents, didn't you?"

"Oh, Lance, please let me finish. This is not easy."

He dropped his eyes for a second. "Go on."

"To answer your question, I only told her I knew they were safe. Nothing more. She left, but she came back and demanded that I tell her more. She was so distraught I suggested that we revisit the Hermitage House hoping that she might see an image of where they were."

"Kate, this is tosh!"

"This is not getting us anywhere, and I need to clean up. I'll finish this later." Then she slipped away into the cabin, while Lance brooded.

Later when the two of them had time to think about things, they sat on the beach. The stars above and a bright beam of moon light illuminated their faces which helped improve Lance's temperament. Kate continued to explain the day's saga to Lance who listened with keen interest. He moved closer and placed his arm over her shoulder. "I'm sorry for not understanding the danger you were in and happy that you kept your wits about you to survive the onslaught of those two henchmen."

He paused. "But I'm disappointed in you for breaking my trust. I know it was not your intent to put us both in danger, and you are sorry for the damage your behavior has caused, but none the less, it's now up to me to fix this mess."

***

Brett and Leo stood in the cargo hold at Lynden Pindling International Airport alongside the crate that held the new engine. Brett discovered the protocol to move the crate to the mailboat dock at Potter's Cay. "Gramps, I've rented a truck to take the engine to the dock myself, so you wait here while make arrangements."

The next morning, they dropped the crate at the dock in the midst of many multi-gallon containers of food, water, lumber, furniture, hardware, and much more. All of which was being lifted on to the mailboat by a 70-foot crane lashed to a steel boom crutch.

"That should do it." Brett eyed his grandfather who was still dressed in his mountain man clothes. "We better get our tickets and check out our room."

The ticket agent sat in a small wooden building behind a half open double door. "That will be $40.00 each for the trip, a meal, and a bed. You can board anytime. We're due to depart around 2 this afternoon. Arrival in Georgetown is about 4:30 in the morning Just be mindful to not to get in the way of the men loading the cargo."

They found their way aboard. "Let's check out our room. I think we will have to share it with a couple other passengers or staff."

They walked around until they found their room, tucked behind the wheelhouse. Brett opened the door, and they squinted as they entered the darkened interior. There was one window and an overhead light and three sets of bunk beds. "Kind of dingy but clean enough for one night. Gramps, what bed do you want?"

"I'll take the lower bunk by the door."

"Then I'll take the one by the window. Let's leave our backpacks on the beds and go outside to watch the activity. It's gonna be a long night."

They stood on the deck and rested their arms on the rail overlooking the water. Below them the crane continued to hoist the cargo onto the main deck. "Look, Sonny, they just lifted an old Chevy onto the foredeck. That car's got to be a classic."

"More like an old clunker that burns a lot of gas, but it's probably sentimental to the owner."

They continued to watch the activity when the ship's Captain passed by on his inspection rounds and stopped to talk. "Good day, I'm Captain Gray, welcome aboard. Our accommodations are minimal, but we offer an evening meal, a clean bed and coffee in the morning. I'll get you to George Town safely. I've been doing this for some time now, and I know the route well. Do you have any questions for me?"

"Yes, I do," Brett replied. "I have a crate somewhere on board. When do you think it will be available for me to transport it to the marina?"

The captain smiled at Brett. "Don't expect it to be off loaded for three or four hours after our arrival. You see, we are obligated to accommodate our local customers first. The grocery store has priority because the residents anxiously await our arrival so they can resupply their provisions. Your crate will be placed on the dock by mid-day. I recommend you just relax and enjoy the journey. Don't forget to do some star gazing tonight. The view is spectacular."

Brett sighed. "Thanks," and the captain walked away. "Gramps, let's sit over there on that bench in the shade."

He considered calling Kayleigh but didn't know what to say. He didn't understand why she'd hung up on him, but he couldn't stop thinking about how distressed she seemed about the danger she was in. What's happening there? Why was she so adamant on not wanting Gramps to visit and clarify the fraudulent landgrabber's hoax. But there was nothing he could do until their arrival, so, he let it pass. They'd be there in the morning.

CHAPTER TWENTY-FOUR

Kayleigh was angry with the couple for walking away and not wanting to get involved with her predicament, but she understood their hesitation—they were on vacation in a foreign country and frightened at the attempted abduction in broad daylight.

She stood still on the sidewalk, trying to control her frazzled nerves. When will Brett be here? He should not have left her alone with those men on the loose. Finally, she took a step on her wobbly legs and limped on toward the Government Building. She stopped often to look behind her, paranoia and fear consuming her as she moved onward. She sighed. "Only one more block, and I'll be there."

She felt a wave of relief as she opened the large front door and entered the building. Diane, the receptionist, was sitting at her desk. Her blue eyes sparkled, and she flashed a bright smile toward Kayleigh. "Miss Jones, what brings you in today?" She hesitated for a moment after noticing Kayleigh's demeanor. "Are you alright? You look frightened."

Kayleigh tried to maintain her composure but lost her conviction, and a flood of tears streamed down her cheeks. "Diane, I've been having a terrible time, and I need protection from those hoodlums who are trying to kill me!"

"Someone wants to kill you?" Diane tried to comfort her by placing an arm across Kayleigh's shoulders. "Come with me and sit down so you can explain your troubles to me."

"Please no! Just take me to someone in the police department who will listen to me. This is a serious matter. I need help!"

Diane focused her attention on the front door, thinking danger may be just outside. "Come with me, I'll take you to our chief detective." She escorted Kayleigh slowly down the long hallway that led to the Police Department.

Kayleigh stopped to rub her hands over her face in an attempt to wipe her tears away. "They just won't give up. It seems they will do anything to get that property. When I awoke this morning, I wondered if this would be my last day. Brett is on his way back, but he won't be here for a day or two."

They entered the police station which by now was familiar to Kayleigh. The policewoman who had taken the information on her missing parents was sitting behind her desk working on the computer in front of her. Diane approached her. "Excuse me, Mrs. Albury, this is Kayleigh Jones."

"Yes, we have met, have you any news about your missing parents?"

"That's a story for another day. I have more pressing issues today."

Diane interrupted. "Mrs. Albury, is Detective Stevens in? Miss Jones needs to have some time with him."

Raising her eyebrows, Mrs. Albury scanned Kayleigh's appearance. "Yes, of course. I'll notify him that you are on your way."

Diane knew her way through the maze of desks in the room to the detective's office and knocked on the door, then entered the room. "Good afternoon, sir, I'd like to introduce Miss Jones; she was accosted this morning and wishes to discuss the terrifying events that have led up to that incident."

The detective was a tall man with cocoa colored skin, dark eyes, and a muscular build. "Thank you, Diane. Miss, please have a seat. Would you like some water or a coffee?"

"No sir."

He scanned the boot on her leg as she seated herself. "Please tell me what's going on that's made you so upset."

Kayleigh spent the next hour explaining the harrowing events that she had encountered since she had arrived in George Town in search of her missing parents. Before she finished, she mentioned, "There is another perplexing occurrence I need to share with you. My friend Lou who lives in Miami came to visit me for a day last week, but it seems he never returned home. I believe there is a missing person's alert in place for information leading to his disappearance."

Kayleigh never disclosed the images she had seen while inside the Hermitage House. She felt that might discredit her, and she didn't want to appear as a kook because she needed his help. "Please add his name along with my parents to your missing person's file."

The detective contemplated all the details that she had shared with him. "Miss Jones, I will increase the surveillance of the Peace and Plenty Hotel while you remain there, and I will speak with the Mayor of Williamstown about the recent events you have described."

"Sir, there is one more important item I must mention. My cousin Brett will be arriving on the mailboat that's due soon, and he is bringing his grandfather who insisted he come to straighten out the property dispute with that woman gangster, but I am afraid she will try to kill him to claim ownership over the land."

"Miss Jones, we will make a concerted effort to prevent our island from being taken over by any crime family or underworld crime network here on Exuma." He stood. "Please feel free to contact me at any time. I will arrange for a patrolman to escort you back to the hotel. You can wait up front with Mrs. Albury while I give the officer instructions."

She reached for his hand. "Thank you." She scanned his pleasant face but was nonethelss skeptical of his ability to deal with the savage world of underworld crime bosses.

***

Leo and Brett stayed on deck after they finished their meal and did some stargazing. Brett kept thinking of Kayleigh and was still baffled about all the calamity she was going through since he'd left her. The two men stayed on deck for a while but finally grew tired. It had been a long couple of days. "Gramps, what do you say let's go to bed."

"Sure, Sonny, I'm nodding off myself."

They returned to their cabin and settled into their bunks. Two crew members who reeked of body odor were asleep in the other bunks.

Leo awoke in the middle of the night. Between the stale smell and snoring of the other men plus the continuous rumbling of the big diesel engines, he was unable to get back to sleep. Besides that, the never-ending swells of the sea that pitched the ship side to side were getting to him and he felt nauseous. He got up, dressed, and stumbled around in a groggy manner, then made his way over to Brett's bunk.

He pushed on his grandson's arm. "Sonny, I got to get out of here and get some fresh air before I puke."

Dim lights from the bridge cast a hazy light through the window by Brett's bunk so he could see Leo's shadow hovering over him. "Huh?" He sat up. "What's going on, Gramps?"

"I don't feel all that well. Thought I'd go outside for some fresh air."

Brett looked at the time. "It's 3:30, and we're scheduled to get to George Town by 4:30. Hold on, I'll go with you."

They wandered around the deck and found a place to sit. They could see a few dark humps of land in the distance. Moving closer, a few lights began appearing on the land. The water calmed as the ship slowly moved through the darkness.

"Gramps, I think this is the harbor, but I can't make out the channel yet."

"Guess they don't have any markers because it looks like we are headed for that dock that's all lit up."

Soon the clanging of equipment echoed in the night and shouts from men could be heard as the huge lines were unfurled and secured to the cleats on the dock. "How's your stomach feel? I'm going to get myself a cup of coffee."

"I'll pass."

They sat in the galley for some time as the crew members moved about the room. Then they returned to their cabin and rested until faint rays of sunshine filtered through the window.

"Gramps, you ready? Let's take our stuff and get off the ship. I want to check with the guys at the marina and arrange for them to haul my engine over there. No sense to you coming along. I won't be long. Find yourself a cool spot over by that tree and wait for me. When I'm done, we'll go to the hotel."

The wharf was cluttered with people anxious to find their goods. The crane was back in action unloading food and water to the trucks waiting to bring supplies to the grocery store. It was a busy and confusing scene. Leo worked his way around the antsy people who were pushing others out of their way trying to identify where their cargo was stored. Finally, he found a grassy spot under the tree and waited for Brett.

He looked around in awe. Everything was so different from the mountains. The water was a shade of turquoise that he had never seen, and the air was warm, maybe too warm. People were everywhere, but they were a happy and friendly lot. There was so much action he failed to see the two men who were watching him.

The crane stopped in midair and unexpectantly dropped a heavy load on the dock which made a racket, and for an instant people stopped what they were doing. In that moment Leo jumped in surprise when he heard the crash.

Vinny and Lenny moved closer to get a better shot. "You missed him! Damn, can't you do anything right?"

"Shut up! You saw him move at the last minute."

"It wasn't him; it was you. Now let me get him."

Leo felt a stinging sensation on his arm. Upon inspection, he saw that the sleeve of his shirt had a growing spot of red.

"What's going on? I've been shot!" He grabbed his arm to put pressure on the wound and looked through the crowd. Then her heard two distinct gun shots ring through the air. Screams arose from within the crowd, and they moved apart to expose Vinny and Lenny's bodies on the ground. People started to panic when they saw the bullet holes in their foreheads.

Brett heard the commotion and came running off the wharf in search of Leo. He breathed a sigh of relief when he saw him standing under the tree. The area was so cluttered with people he had to push some out of his way. He was alarmed when he reached Leo whose shirt was covered with bright red blood. "Gramps, what happened?"

"I'm not sure. Just felt this sting in my arm, then I heard the gun shots, but nothing else other than those guys on the ground over there. Don't think I had anything to do with it. Just got in the wrong place at the wrong time."

"Let me look at your arm."

Leo removed his shirt. "It's just a graze. I'll survive."

"Yeah," Brett said after examining the wound, "a large band aid is all you'll need."

Then Brett recalled Kayleigh's warning. *Don't bring your grandfather here, they'll kill him.* "I'm all set, let's get out of here."

CHAPTER TWENTY-FOUR

Kayleigh heard her cell phone ring and answered it. "Hi, Kayleigh, it's Brett, I'm here."

"Thank God! When will I get to see you? Hold on, what's all that noise? It sounds like police sirens."

"Oh, that!" He tried to be nonchalant. "Some guys just got shot, and the police are surrounding the area. We are at the wharf right now. I arranged for the marina staff to get my engine when it's offloaded. Then all hell broke out. Do think you could pick us up with your parents' car? I don't think Gramps can walk to the hotel."

"What's going on; I don't understand."

"Kayleigh, I want to get away from here before we are stuck for the duration of the investigation. Can't you please come and pick us up?"

She hesitated. "Brett, I'm sorry, I can't do that right now. You'll have to walk. Just take your time and rest when he gets tired."

"But he's old, and it's too hot for him to lug his backpack all that way."

Kayleigh sighed; she must fess up. "Brett, the car is gone, and I can't leave here right now. Please, just find away."

"It's not that easy. We're caught in the middle of a big crowd, and I'll never find a taxi."

The whale of sirens echoed in the air and within moments the police surrounded the area. "Kayleigh, I got to go. We'll be there when we can. If we wait much longer, we could be stuck here all day."

"What the hell is going on?"

He stopped the conversation. "I got to go!"

***

"Come on, Gramps, grab your stuff; let's get going, looks like we're going to have to walk to the hotel, and I don't want to get involved in this mess."

They circled around the tree and headed across the open field. Across the street was a gas station and next to it was a strip store plaza with a pharmacy. "Gramps, you wait outside while I get some kind of patch for that wound."

Brett returned with a large-sized band-aid. "Remove your shirt and let me apply this patch to your arm. Now, put a clean shirt on so we don't give the cops any reason to stop us."

They weaved their way through a line of people crowding into the grocery store who were blocking their way. "It'll take us about an hour to get to the hotel from here. It's close to a three-mile jaunt. Kayleigh has no way to come for us, and it looks like the street is blocked off by the police."

"That's a long time to walk in these boots, and it's mighty hot around these parts, too hot to be lugging this bag."

Brett was beside himself; this situation was not part of his plan. "Gramps, there is no other way. How's your stomach feel? Are you still nauseous?"

Leo wiped the drops of sweat that covered his brow and the back of his neck. "My stomach is growling, and I could use a glass of water."

Brett stared off at the rays of sunlight overhead, thinking of how he'd tried to warn Leo about his choice of clothes. "Tell you what we'll do, walk on a little farther and look for a place to stop for a cold drink and a bite to eat. You'll be able to rest and cool off."

They walked on for a while when Leo stopped. "Sonny, I need to stop here and catch my breath."

Brett could see that Leo was short of breath, and he was getting much too hot. He needed to do something now before Leo passed out. He looked around and saw a man standing on the porch of a grey concreate building. He was smoking something that looked like it could be a joint. "Stay here, I'll be right back." He approached the man on the porch who appeared disheveled; his hair was matted, and he was dressed in a soiled and tattered tee shirt which exposed the many tattoos on his arms. "Say, I'm looking for a place where I can get a cold drink and some food."

"This place is a bar, and they sell drinks and snacks. For a nicer place you'll have to go farther north about another mile or so."

"Thanks."

Brett ran back to his grandfather who looked exhausted. "Let's go here. This place is a bar, and they serve snacks. At least you'll be able to get something to drink and rest for a while."

He hiked up the two backpacks, and they walked up the stairs of the building. He opened the door, and they entered a dark room which was covered in a thick fog of smoke, loads of it, and inhaled a mixture of cigarette, cigar, pot, combined with a burnt smoke stench from a greasy grill. Ten bar stools lined one wall of the bar. There were a few tables around the room and a pool table at the far end.

"Gramps, you go sit at a table while I get us something cool to drink."

Brett rested his arm on the bar and waited for the bartender to take his order. "What's your name, I'll run you a tab."

"The name's Brett Kelsall."

"Really? You are a Kelsall; well, I'll be dammed."

Leo collapsed onto a chair and waited until Brett returned with two draft beers and a glass of ice water. "I ordered hot dogs and chips. Take a drink of the water."

Brett looked around the room, noticing a heavy-set man sitting nearby; he seemed clean-cut with dark hair and eyes and was dressed in a black t-shirt and shorts. He held a cigar up to his mouth; a full martini glass sat on the table. Brett thought the guy looked out of place and wondered what he was doing in a bar like this.

"Gramps, drink up, the dogs will be here shortly. I'm going to go outside and call Kayleigh, maybe she can get us a taxi."

***

The bartender placed the two hot dogs, chips, and beers on the table. "The kid said you were Kelsalls; they have quite a history in our town."

"Yep, we are here to check on our property. Brett went out to make a call and should be right back. Thanks." Leo drank the water, then looked at the hot dogs and sipped on his beer, but he was hungry and got tired of waiting for Brett to return. He couldn't wait another minute and ate the hot dog and chips, pushed his plate aside, but he felt as though he was still hungry, so he ate the other one and drank the second beer. He glanced at the door, still no sign of Brett. What the hell! "Hey, bartender, how about another beer?"

After finishing the third beer, he glanced around the room looking for the rest room. Seeing the sign, he got up from the table and found his way to the back hallway. He was about to leave when the big guy who had been sitting at the other table burst into the

106

bathroom. Leo was surprised by the abrupt entry. "Sorry, I'll get out of your way."

The man dressed in black remarked, "Not as sorry as you're gonna be, old man!" He grabbed Leo and jabbed a gun beneath his jaw.

"Hey, what's going on?"

"Shut up, you're coming with me."

"Hell, no, I'm not. Let go of me, you're nothing but a big bag of blubber!"

"I told you to shut your trap!"

***

Her phone rang, and Kayleigh answered right away. "Hi."

The sound of her voice made Brett smile. "Kayleigh, Gramps is having a rough time walking. Do you think you could get us a cab? We are at this place called The Cellar, which is a real dive."

"I've never heard of it."

"I can see why; believe me, you aren't missing anything." He paused. "I can't wait to see you. I dream about you a lot."

"Brett, I missed you so and needed you here. It's been terrifying for me facing all this alone." She continued to explain all the recent events she'd been through. They talked at length when Brett stopped her abruptly. "Kayleigh, I need to check on Gramps; he's really having a hard time. Call me back when you get us a ride, thanks."

Brett returned to the table in the smoke-filled room, but Leo was gone. He scanned the room. Gramps wasn't anywhere in sight, and what about that other guy sitting at the next table? He wasn't there either. He returned to the bar. "Excuse me, but did you see where my grandfather went; he's no longer sitting at that table."

"He just finished the dogs and fries; maybe he's in the john, you know some old guys have to use it quite often."

"Good idea, I'll check that."

Just as Luigi shoved Leo out into the hallway, he heard Brett's voice. He opened the door to a storage closet, pushed Leo in and joined him, holding his hand over the old man's mouth. "One word out of you, and you're a dead man!"

Brett searched the men's room, but Leo wasn't there. If he had gone out the front door, he would have seen him. He left the men's room and looked around. He noticed that a door at the far end of the hallway was ajar. He opened it and found steps leading from the back door to a parking lot where an old beat-up pickup truck was parked. He noticed the front bumper was ripped in half and the front of the hood had multiple dents, plus one of the headlights was smashed. The vehicle looked like it was on its last legs.

He went back to the bar. "He's not there. Are you sure you didn't see anything unusual? He wouldn't leave without me."

The bartender replied, "Look buddy, I'm a bartender not a babysitter!"

Brett wanted to pound him with his fist but used restraint. "Point taken. How do I get in touch with the police?"

The bartender gave Brett the phone number to the police station. When Brett turned his head, the bartender placed two one-hundred-dollar bills Luigi had given him into his pants pocket.

Brett entered the number on his cell phone, and someone answered on the second ring, "Hi, I'm Brett Kelsall. My grandfather and I arrived on the mailboat this morning. We stopped at a place called The Cellar to rest, but while I was on the phone, he disappeared. I need help to find him."

"No, he's not demented! What do you mean you can't help me? Why not? Come on, that's just wrong! Okay, I guess investigating two killings would be a priority. I'll come by and fill out a missing person's report."

Brett paid his tab. "I guess every cop in town is at the wharf; a couple of guys got shot. Listen, I need to meet someone. Here's my number; if my grandfather shows up, give me a call. Thanks."

Then he called Kayleigh. "Hi, it's me. You're not going to believe this, but Gramps is missing. I'll explain when I see you. Gotta go."

He left the building with both backpacks, but he had a bad feeling, so he walked around to the back. The pickup truck was gone, which shocked him. He'd have bet a month's salary that it was too far gone to drive. Not to mention he could have sworn that no one was in the truck.

His heart sank as he wondered if the guy with the cigar had kidnapped Gramps and used the truck to get away.

CHAPTER TWENTY-FIVE

Luigi subdued Leo with a choke hold and found some old rags to gag him. When the old man regained consciousness, he dragged him out the back door. His cell phone buzzed. "What the hell?" He released Leo, who fell to the ground. Luigi placed his foot on Leo's chest and put the phone to his ear. "Yeah, what's up?"

"Hi, I just heard about the commotion at the wharf. My two men just got shot; did you do it?"

"Hell, no! Gina, you must know those guys of yours were nothing but two freaking screw ups."

"How did the cops track them down; that makes no sense?"

"I'll call in some of my men to replace them; besides, I just found old man Kelsall. Those dopes couldn't do a simple caper on their own. Don't want to waste the old man just yet."

"Good luck, they are a stubborn lot. My men's truck should be nearby. You can find it in the parking lot behind that downtown bar, and the keys should be in the ignition. Meet me at the red brick house on the beach just past Smithies convenience store. You'll see my car in the driveway."

***

Brett left the Cellar lugging the two back packs and trudged his way toward the hotel. His mind was entangled in his own thoughts. He blamed his absentmindedness for Leo's disappearance—he'd been consumed with a longing to hold Kayleigh in his arms again. He stopped in front of the police station and hesitated. He didn't relish spending his time filling out the needed paperwork, but he really thought that someone other than himself needed to search for Leo.

He walked up the steps of the Government Building and entered. Diane was sitting at her desk and greeted him with enthusiasm. "Mr. Kelsall, you're back! I know Miss Kayleigh must be very happy."

Brett peered into Diane's sparkling blue eyes. "I don't think she'll be happy with what I have to tell her, but Diane, right now I need to talk with the police."

"I'm sorry, but most of the officers are involved in the goings on downtown, but feel free to speak with Mrs. Albury. You know the way. I'll let her know that you are on your way."

Brett walked into the Police Station and stood in front of Mrs. Albury's desk. She tried to but couldn't ignore his presence and finally looked up. "Hello, Mr. Kelsall, what can I do for you?"

"I'm here to tell you that my grandfather Leo Kelsall has been abducted."

She sighed. "You Kelsall's are taking up a lot of our department's time."

Brett scowled at her. "Yeah, we are, but it's not our fault. If you ask me, the George Town police need to work harder to eliminate the current threat of the gangster element that is penetrating the area."

Brett turned to walk away.

"Wait a minute, Detective Stevens has been hard at work doing just that, but right now he has a pressing investigation downtown. The murders seemed to mimic a typical gangland slaying."

"Well, add this to my report, my grandfather was hit by what seems to be a ricochet bullet, and now he's missing. Maybe it wasn't a ricochet after all, and now he's not available to give the police details."

"Mr. Kelsall, please take a seat and give me a brief description of the incident. Don't be dismayed, there's a lot of action going on behind the scenes."

Brett felt better after Mrs. Albury took his information. Finished with providing details, he left the station which was only a couple of blocks to the Peace and Plenty. He walked into the lobby and found his way to the room. Kaleigh opened the door, and Brett dropped the backpacks to embraced her, not wanting to let her go.

Her brown eyes glistened as she took a good look at him, noticing his unruly hair and the scraggy beard that covered his handsome face but she melted into his arms.

"Kayleigh, I missed you so much and am so sorry about leaving you here alone."

She pursed her lips and rubbed her hands across the muscles of his chest. "Brett, forget that. You are here now, and together we will make some sense out of this nightmare." She closed her eyes and ran her fingers through his hair while they kissed.

Brett broke away. "Let's save some of this for later."

She laughed. "You're right. Now tell me what happened to your grandfather. I'm not going to tell you I told you so, but you should have listened to my advice."

He dropped his eyes. "I know you were right, and I shouldn't have left him alone. I'm pretty sure that he was kidnapped by a rough looking character at the bar. And I'll bet that Gina Marino is behind it. He said he wanted to give her a piece of his mind, so maybe now he has a chance to do just that."

"That's a scary thought," Kayleigh said, "but we are dealing with gangsters who will stop at nothing to get their way. I had a good talk with Detective Stevens, and I believe he will do whatever has to be done to prevent the mob from over running Exuma.".

"Good luck with that thought, Kayleigh. I just left the police station, and they have an attitude about us. In fact, they wish we would just go away. But we must find your parents and Gramps. We can't give up."

"And we won't. I'm going to find out what happened to my parents no matter what. Even if I face more turmoil myself."

Brett placed his arms around her shoulders and hugged her. Then his lips moved softly over hers. She responded with abandon. When she came up for a breath, she smiled at him. "I think I can deal with anything as long as you're here with me."

CHAPTER TWENTY-SIX

Pink sunlight shone through the open hatch on the sailboat and caressed Kate's body. She awoke to the warmth of the rays, then rolled over to kiss Lance, but his spot on the bed was empty. That jolted her up. She went on deck only to see the dinghy was gone. She was pissed—the least he could have done was tell her where he was off to.

She returned to the cabin, brewed a pot of tea, and brooded. Where could he have gone so early in the day? The morning wore on and still no sign of Lance. She was back on deck sipping on her tea and ruminating; where was he? She hoped he's safe. Broken sunshine passed over the boat when she heard the hum of a small motor approaching the boat. Relief surged through her.

Lance moved the dinghy closer to the boat, and she grabbed the bow line and secured it to a cleat on the sailboat. Kate's nerves were wound up tight, and she wanted to scold him but couldn't. He came aboard, and she greeted him with a kiss. "Lance, I was so worried, it's not like you to leave without telling me, and why so early?"

She noticed an expression of concern that covered his face. "I'm sorry, Kate, I didn't think I would be gone this long, but George Town is in a total state of bedlam. All hell broke out just after the mailboat started to unload its cargo. Two men got shot at the wharf. I'm not sure what happened. I heard two gunshots. People were screaming. It was a major mess. The police arrived and isolated the area. Then they started their investigation and tried to calm the crowd."

Kate was curious. "Do the police know who shot the guys?"

Lance avoided her eyes and tried to hide his cocky grin. "I don't think so, but I'm sure I would know it if they did."

Kate noted the sly look on his face and refrained from asking anymore questions.

"I went there to get firsthand information about the upcoming National Family Island Regatta. I was hoping we could enter our sailboat in the competition but found out that wouldn't work."

"Why not? Are we not good enough? That would be a fun challenge. It sounds so cool!"

"Kate, just relax; I kept asking questions. I found out that the boats must be built in the Bahamas, and the crew members need to be born and raised in the Bahamas."

Kate was irritated. "That's tosh!"

"I know but those are the rules. I did find out that they have a volleyball tournament that me mates and I can participate in."

Kate smiled. "The regatta idea sounds like fun. It should generate a lot of enjoyment and excitement."

They embraced, and Lance pressed his lips on hers. She felt his warm body react to hers. "That's better."

***

Ted and Carole sat at the outside bar adjacent to the Happy Peoples Marina and sipped on cold drinks. They were quiet, nothing much to discuss, so they enjoyed watching the gulls while the sea breeze rustled the palm trees.

Carole pointed. "Ted, I'm going to look at the announcements that are posted on the bulletin board over there. Just curious of what I might find out."

Carole read the notices, mainly related to boat issues, but she saw a poster that caught her eye. The poster read: *Missing People: A senior couple vacationing in George Town have gone missing. Approximate ages around 65. The man is slim about 6 feet tall with gray hair. The woman about 5-foot 5-inches with salt and pepper hair. She weighs around 140 pounds. If sighted, please notify the George Town police.*

A sudden rush of chest pressure overwhelmed Carole. "Oh, no! We'll have to leave here. What if it's a trap by the gangsters?" She rushed back to Ted.

She kept her voice low. "We need to leave this place now! We can't delay. They are after us!"

Ted noticed Carole's face was pale, and her body was tense. "Carol, calm down, what's going on?"

"Go look for yourself. It's a missing person flyer! About us! If someone turns us in, we are doomed. We can't trust anyone. I just want to go home!"

Ted walked to the bulletin board and read the flyer. He returned with a shocked expression on his face. He took Carole's shaking hand in his. "We aren't going to take the boat any further. The only way we'll leave is on the mailboat. It stops here every other week. We'll book a ride to Nassau, then get a plane ride home. I've had enough of this island life to last a lifetime. Let them follow us to the states, then the FBI can get involved."

The fright in Carole's eyes faded. "Oh, my God, what a good decision. I can't wait to leave. Let's go back to the boat and make plans. We don't need to be exposing ourselves to anyone."

"Carole, wait a minute." He removed the flyer from his pocket. "Here, put this in your bag. Now let's go."

***

Brett showered, shaved, and put on clean clothes then joined Kayleigh on the balcony where the pale turquoise water gleamed in the sunlight. She seemed lost in her thoughts as she gazed across the harbor. She looked at Brett and her broad smile crinkled the lines in her face. "Oh, Brett, you smell so good."

He wrapped her in an embrace and kissed her. "You taste delicious."

Standing back, he admired her smile and the gold flecks that glittered within her deep brown eyes. "I'm truly sorry for leaving you alone to deal with all that stress and those assaults on your life. It must have been an extremely perilous time for you, but I admire your spirit and stamina; you're such a trooper."

"Brett, I'm beyond that now, and yes, at the time it was unimaginable. It overwhelmed me so that I wanted to be anywhere but here. When I went to bed, I didn't know if I'd make it to live another day."

He hugged her tightly. "I guess I'm batting zero. I let you down and did the same to my grandfather. But I'll make up for it, I promise. Together we must devise a plan to rid ourselves of these pieces of shit and come to some type of understanding of what we expect to gain by doing all this or just focus on finding your parents and gramps, then leave all this behind us."

"Brett, that goal seems impossible to me, but let's explore the possibilities. I think the reality of all this is that we are screwed. The people we ae dealing have no morals; they are wicked and will stop at nothing until they get the property and build their casino. They already think they bumped me and Kate off. If they find out we're alive, they'll come after us with a vengeance. Stopping them is a bigger job than we can manage. The government needs to step in and stop it, and I don't see that happening."

"Kayleigh, please don't give up on me." He gently touched her face. "There has to be a way."

CHAPTER TWENTY-SEVEN

Luigi drove the wreck of a pickup truck through George Town with Leo's blanket-covered body bouncing around in the bed of the truck. He was bound, and his mouth gagged with a dirty rag Luigi found in the storage closet of the Cellar.

Luigi pulled into the circular driveway in front of a red brick beachfront home. He got out of the truck and walked around the corner of the house to the ocean side of the home. Soft waves hugged the sand, lapping it with soothing sounds. Luigi saw Gina sunbathing on a beach towel draped over a weathered chaise lounge.

"Hi, gorgeous, you look good enough to eat."

She got up from the lounge and embraced him. "We'll save that for later. Do you have the old man?"

"Yeah, he's in the back of the truck. He is pretty frail and didn't give me much of a struggle."

Luigi heard the voices of two men down by the shore. He looked at them working on Gina's boat. "I see Russo and Sebbie got here."

She nodded. "They arrived a little while ago and filled me in on their plans to waste the young Kelsalls."

"They're good soldiers."

She grinned. "Enough of that, I want to see the old coot." Her naked body was firm, and her skin glistened with a covering of suntan oil. She led Luigi back to the driveway, then peered into the bed of the pickup, jerked the blanket off him and smiled. "Well, well, if it ain't my old man."

Leo scowled at the sight of her. She reached into the truck, bending over him with her naked breasts in full view and removed the gag from his mouth. "Hi, Daddy," she said, the words dripping with sarcasm.

Leo erupted with rage. "Bitch! You ain't no kin of mine! You're just a whore like your damn mother!"

"Pops, your face is scarlet, don't have a heart attack before we come to an understanding. And how dare you speak so unkindly of

116

my mother; she is such a fine woman who I understand you enjoyed screwing."

"Shit! She was nothing but a gold digger who played nice until I discovered her devious motivations. It was then she revealed her vicious nature. A forked tongued sinister monster, and it looks like you ain't no different. You're out to steal property that ain't rightly yours, and I ain't gonna let that happen."

"We'll see about that. Torture may be the only alternative. If you don't survive, that'll be your tough luck, old man." She stalled. "You've got to know by now that we've captured your niece Carole and her husband, and they are suffering severe beatings because they won't cooperate. You'll have their fate on your conscience because you are the only one responsible for their dire situation. You should have never given them that deed. That belongs to me." She deliberately withheld the information about the fake deed she'd given to Nichols. She was determined to get a genuine deed as a backup.

"You're an evil woman with no heart."

"One more thing, Pop, the two younger ass holes are cagy ones. Carole's daughter went over the bridge and out to sea, but we have no way of proving she's dead. And your grandson Brett is a tough one, but we'll find a way to get to him, too. Then all of you damn Kelsalls will be history." She looked at Luigi. "Put this old codger in solitary for a week, then we'll talk again. He might be more cooperative when he's starving."

She turned away and sauntered back to her place in the sun.

Luigi looked at Leo. "She's a hell cat, and I can't wait to enjoy her charms."

Leo rolled his eyes. "Take these shackles off me, lover boy."

Luigi grabbed Leo and dragged him off the truck, then hauled him into an empty room where he removed the restraints. "It's kind of dark in here, but you'll get used to it. If I had my way, I'd eliminate you now, and the hell with the damn drama." He slammed the door, and Leo heard the clink as the lock slid into place.

***

Brett and Kayleigh sat in the outside lounge eating their evening meal. The horizon behind them was fading into a dusky blue, and the sea breeze settled down, allowing the scent of saltwater to linger in the air. Kayleigh was silent and distant, trying to figure out why he hadn't followed her advice on leaving his grandfather at home.

"This fresh grouper tastes great. I was famished." He took a sip of his beer and questioned her about the events that had occurred during his absence.

"Kayleigh, you told me about two people, a woman named Kate who you were with when your parent's rental car was run off the bridge at Ferry, and then there was some guy."

"What would you like to know? I already told you about them."

He looked at her intently. "How did you and Kate get in that situation?"

Kayleigh felt a twinge in her gut and developed a lump in her throat as she relived the events in her mind and hesitated before answering. "Brett!" she said with an air of exasperation. "I told you I confronted her by her sailboat, and she told me my parents were safe but wouldn't explain where they were. Then she suggested we return to the Hermitage House, and maybe I would see another image which would give me a clue to where they were. I didn't want to go, but it made sense to me at the time."

Brett listened and searched her troubled eyes. "So, you went, and you saw another image."

"Yes, it was not of my parents but of Lou."

"Lou, your pilot friend?"

"Yes, and he was dead. Oh, Brett, it was shocking. It was my fault, too."

"Your fault? How's that?"

"Because he came to visit me and wanted to stay the night, but I told him no. So, he left. If he hadn't gone, he would still be alive today."

Kayleigh grabbed her chest, and her body began to tremble uncontrollably.

Brett swallowed hard and moved over to embrace her as tears fell down her cheeks. "Kayleigh, I'm so sorry, I didn't mean to make you relive the horror."

He brushed her dark hair from her face and attempted to console her, but she backed away, then she began pounding her fists on his chest. "I am so mad at you for leaving me here all alone! You didn't have to go before we found my parents. That damn plane means more to you than I do. If Lou was alive, I wouldn't be here right now, and your grandfather would be safe."

Brett hesitated, then he surrounded her with his body. The physical effect of his embrace was enough to halt her outburst, and she look lovingly into his eyes. "I'm sorry," she whispered.

They stayed wrapped in one another's arms, allowing the silence to bring them peace.

CHAPTER TWENTY-EIGHT

Sailboats were starting to accumulate in Elizabeth Harbor, and sailors looked for a perfect spot to anchor their craft while they registered for the Regatta competition. Brett and Kayleigh left the hotel together. Kayleigh was on her way to the clinic for her checkup while Brett was headed to the marina to see the progress of the engine installment on his sea plane. He walked along the harbor and marveled at the workmanship involved to build the vessels anchored there.

He had lost patience with the slowness and unpredictability of the time frame for the completion of his project and wanted to know when his plane would be ready to fly. When he arrived at the marina, he found the chief mechanic working on a sailboat and was confused.

"Hi, Mac."

The mechanic looked up then quickly looked away.

Brett stood there. "I thought you'd be working on my seaplane; what's up?"

He nodded. "Sorry, Brett, I hate to disappoint you, but the Regatta will be my priority as it has been for years in the past, and it will last for the next two or three weeks. These sailors pay me well to take care of their vessels. They work very hard all year long to have the best boat, and they are here to prove that they deserve the reward of being the best sailors in the Bahamas. The competition is very fierce."

"That's not what I wanted to hear, but I appreciate your honesty."

"One more thing, Brett, after I install your engine, you will need a certified aircraft mechanic to approve my work and make sure it passes a special inspection. I'm not sure if there are any here on Exuma. You may need to hire one from Nassau, but during the Regatta the mailboat will be busy bringing supplies and people here and will be making extra runs, eliminating their stops on the other out islands."

Brett frowned and finally allowed his agitation to show. "Okay! What other good news do you have for me?" he said snidely.

Mac shrugged his shoulders. "Not much, just be prepared for a lot of excitement and activity over the next few weeks."

Brett wanted to protest but bit back his words. There was no way he could change things, so he simply flashed an artificial smile. "Thanks for the info; looks like I'll be in for a unique experience."

He muttered to himself as he walked away, brooding all the way back to the hotel to express his displeasure with the delay of the engine repair to Kayleigh.

***

Later in the day he and Kayleigh sat next to each other on the water taxi which was on its way to Stocking Island. Kayleigh gingerly put her foot up on the edge of the of the boat's hull and wiggled her toes. "It feels great to wear sandals again, but I still must be careful. I don't want to wear that clumsy boot again. Although it did come in handy when that guy attempted to kidnap me."

Brett smiled at her and still felt guilty about leaving her on her own while he got the engine for his plane. He looked deeply into her wide brown eyes and placed a kiss on her check. The taxi danced on top of the water, scooting around the many sailboats anchored in the harbor.

"I'm looking forward to meeting your friend and finding out the reason she won't tell you where your parents are hiding."

She placed her hand on his thigh. "Don't get your hopes up; if her husband is around, she'll never talk to us. She told me that he doesn't want her to have any association with us because of all the problems I've caused her."

"He has a point, Kayleigh, you know you are a troublemaker." He winked at her, and she picked up the hint of humor in his voice.

They landed on a white sandy beach in front of the Chat and Chill restaurant. "This is such a beautiful spot, Brett. I envy Kate."

"Don't be silly, we have an incredible piece of property, and we shall enjoy it's splendor someday."

She smiled. "You're right; now let's get on with our mission."

Brett took her hand. "Be careful, no more accidents." He steadied her as she jumped out of the boat, her feet sinking into the warm soft sand. "Their boat's still there; that's a good sign."

"You know, I've never met the guy, but the way he's acting makes me suspicious that he's hiding something."

Kayleigh squeezed Brett's hand. "Well, let's see if we can solve the mystery."

They walked along the beach and passed the deserted volleyball court sporting a sign restricting private parties and bonfires. "Brett, this seems strange; usually this place is packed."

They watched the sailboat floating gently in the light breeze, but it too seemed unoccupied.

Brett sighed. "Guess nothing's going right today," and he turned to walk away.

Before she followed, Kayleigh caught a glimpse of Kate's head pop out of the hatch. "Wait, Brett, stop! She's on the boat!"

Kayleigh ran toward the boat yelling, "Kate, Kate!"

Kate looked at her then popped back into the cabin. Kayleigh ran over and stood beside the boat. "Kate, I know you're in there; please, I need to talk with you."

Kate emerged from the cabin. "Kayleigh, you need to stop this nonsense; you're acting like you're off your trolly. Go away. Having you around is too dangerous for us. You nearly got us killed, and Lance was furious. As soon as the Regatta is over, we are leaving."

"Kate, you can't do that! You must tell me where my parents are."

Brett spoke up. "When my plane is fixed, I'll take them back to the states."

Kate darted a look at Brett. "Let me know when it's ready to fly. Until then, leave me alone. You two must get a grip. The people who are after you will stop at nothing until they achieve their goal, and anyone who gets in their way will die. Now get stuffed!"

CHAPTER TWENTY-NINE

The room was dark, damp and barren. Leo kicked the mattress on the floor and inspected the small bathroom that had a toilet, a sink, and a small window above his head which allowed a trickle of sunlight to filter into the room. He sat on the mattress and spent his time planning his escape.

He was hungry and tired and soon fell asleep on the mattress. He didn't know how long he had slept when he was startled by the sound of someone opening the door. He quickly sprang into action.

The door opened, and Luigi stood rigid and seemed confused because Leo was not in sight. "Hey, old man, where are you?"

There was no answer. Now curious, Luigi stepped into the room. The door slammed him on his back, knocking him off balance. Leo hung by his hands on the back of the door and with his rugged boots on, he kicked Luigi in the head. The impact knocked him on the floor. Leo jumped down and kicked him again.

"You no good freaking asshole!" Then with all his might he kicked him again, crushing Luigi's skull. Leo bent down and looked at the motionless body. "Sayonara, big guy."

Leo found the key in Luigi's pants and took the gun from the holster under the man's arm. He looked outside; seeing no one, he left the room and locked the door.

The sky was a dusky gray, and he slithered along the gloomy exterior of the building. There wasn't any human activity in the early morning. Not a sign of any other person around, nor any traffic on the road. When he had the chance, he darted across the Queen's Highway into the heavily wooded section of land that bordered the road. Surrounded by the trees, he felt more secure and stopped to rest.

***

Gina woke up when she heard noises coming from the kitchen. She slipped into her robe and investigated. The kitchen was large with all new shiny appliances. It opened into a wide living room surrounded by windows. Bright sunlight filled the room. The views of the ocean were breath taking.

She found Sebbie and Rosso rummaging through the pantry.

"Good morning." The sound of her voice startled them.

Sebbie turned toward her. "Oh, hi, thought we'd make you some breakfast."

She glared at him. "Sure you did. Make me some coffee, that's what I want." She searched the kitchen for Luigi; not seeing him she turned to the other two men. "Have you two seen Luigi?"

"No, we thought he was here with you."

"He spent the night with me, but now the louse is missing." She shook her head. "He must be outside; maybe he's checking on the boat? Russo, go check on him."

Russo uttered something under his breath, then left the two in the kitchen and walked out the door.

Gina moved into the living room. "Bring me the coffee when it's ready, Sebbie."

She relaxed on a soft leather sofa and sipped her coffee, watching the pelicans and seagulls fly by while she waited but grew restless and was relieved when Russo returned. "Can't find him anywhere out there. He just ain't around."

"How about the truck? Is it still in the driveway?"

"Yeah, it's there."

"Then go check on the old man; maybe Luigi's paying him a visit."

Russo sighed. "What else? Maybe he wants some time alone."

"Hey, shithead, don't be giving me no lip. I know you're Luigi's soldier, but I'm in charge of this operation, and I give the orders, so get used to it. Now get your sorry ass out of here and check on the old man!"

She took a queenly stance as he passed her.

"Don't I need a key?" he asked.

"If Luigi's in there, the door will be open.

"Sure. That's right."

Russo walked around the patio and down the stone walkway to the room where Leo was being held and tried to open the door. There was no response, so he banged his fists on the door. He knew if there was someone inside, they would respond to the ruckus. He turned to walk away when he heard a guttural scream which he didn't

124

understand. "Holy shit, that didn't sound right; there's someone in there. "Hey, let me in." Still there was no response.

He leaned against the rugged door and shouted. "Who's in there? Open the door!" Again, there was silence; he grabbed his gun from its holster, shot out the lock and pushed the door open. He saw Luigi sprawled on the floor. A pool of blood surrounded his head, and his eyes were open and dilated. He looked straight ahead but didn't respond to Russo who knelt and held Luigi's head with both hands.

"Boss, this is Russo, can you hear me?"

Luigi's eyes rolled back, and he let out a big sigh. Russo placed his sticky hands on his neck, trying to find a pulse, but there was none. God damn it, who could have done this? That old man was too frail, and no one knew he was in here. He stood up. How could this have this happened? Who had helped him?

He ran out of the room and back around the kitchen and burst into the kitchen. "Luigi's dead!"

Gina looked at him and his bloody hands. "What the hell are you talking about? What happened to you?"

"Looks like someone bashed in his head."

"What? How could that be?" Gina seemed shocked at the description. "Where is the old man?"

"He's not there."

"Well, where is he?"

"Don't you get it? He's not there! How the hell do I know where he is."

Gina sprinted out of the chair. "Don't tell me he did it. That's not possible. Someone had to help him."

Sebbie spoke up. "How did anyone know where he was? That's not possible, he didn't have a phone, and no one followed Luigi here."

Gina thought quickly. "No, and I don't think that the old man had anything but the clothes on his back. Come on, I'm going to examine Luigi. You might be wrong about no pulse. We still might be able to save him."

CHAPTER THIRTY

Leo collapsed by a sea grape tree and rested his back on the trunk. He was breathing heavily and felt exhausted. He hadn't eaten or had any water in the past few days.

He pondered his next move. He had to find someone to help, but who could he trust, even if he could find someone, a perfect stranger? No matter, the reality was that he couldn't just stay here hiding under a tree. He had to move along.

He pushed his body up, then stood still while attempting to get his bearings. He proceeded to work his way around the dense landscape that encircled him. Slipping and tripping between and over the many obstacles in the forest, he pushed himself until he became weary to the point of feeling faint. He wasn't accustomed to the humidity which drained him more, and he settled into a thicket along a small stream trickling with flowing water. He buried his head in the cool creek and quenched his thirst.

He wanted to stay put but forced himself onward. He walked until he discovered a car wreck which was buried within a tunnel of trees. The smell of something rancid overwhelmed him when he moved closer to examine the car. The front door was ajar. Curious, he looked inside.

To his surprise, he saw a decaying body slumped over the steering wheel. The sight and smell of the decomposed flesh instantly gave him the dry heaves. Backing away from the car, he finally composed himself and followed the rutted tire tracks back until he heard traffic passing close by. He checked the surroundings for signs of danger before daring to walk alongside the road.

Traffic was light, but he was hesitant to hail a car, unsure of any passing motorist's motives. When he saw a convenience store up ahead on the east side of the highway, he darted across the road. Outside the building were signs indicating a pharmacy and a grocery store located inside. He opened the door warily, looked around and approached the person behind the counter who backed away.

"Someone help me," he whispered, then realized how bedraggled he looked and sounded. His clothes were covered with grit and perspiration, his hair was an unruly mess, and his face was covered with bristly white stubbles of hair. "Please someone help me!" he said louder this time.

A man dressed in a white lab coat came out from behind the counter. "Mister, we don't cater to homeless beggars; please leave our store."

Leo protested. "I ain't homeless or a beggar. I'm Leo Kelsall, and I own property on this damn island."

"Do you have any identification?" The pharmacist stared at him warily.

"Yes, I do, but not on me."

"Without proper identification, Mr. Kelsall, what am I to believe? I could say I'm a doctor, but I'm not, and you know that. Now please leave."

Anger swept over Leo. "Look! I've been kidnapped and escaped the slimy weasel, and I need to find my grandson, Brett Kelsall, who is staying somewhere in George Town. You've got to help me. Stop asking your questions and get me some help. Please!"

The pharmacist was still skeptical of Leo's story. "Come over here and have a seat. Would you like some water? You must be sweltering; you're not dressed for the tropics. Where are you from?"

"California, damn it! What do you care? Pete sakes, man, can't you get me some help! Get my grandson; he invited me here to take care of some business dealings."

Leo sat in the chair, and as he did, the handle of the gun he'd taken from Luigi peeked out of his pocket.

The pharmacist reared away with alarm when he saw the weapon. "Look, mister, I don't want any trouble from you. Why don't you just leave?"

Leo caught the frightened look on the pharmacist's face, and when he backed away, Leo quickly slipped the gun into his boot, hoping no one would think to look for it there.

"What, leave? I can hardly walk. I'm starving—I haven't eaten in days! Where's your compassion? Can't you get me some help?"

By now a few people had gathered around. One person seemed concerned and gave Leo a candy bar. "Here, old man, eat this. I'll call the cops for you. They'll find your grandson for you. Where were you when you got separated?"

Leo stuffed the chocolate bar into his mouth. "We just got off the mailboat when all hell broke loose down by the docks."

"Yeah, that was a few days ago. You're right, there was quite a commotion downtown."

Shortly after Leo finished eating the candy, the front door swung open and two men in uniforms entered. The pharmacist greeted them. "Thanks for getting here so quickly. We have a vagrant here who seems confused. He told me he is here on business, but he has no identification or money, but he has a gun hanging out of his pocket."

Leo feigned surprise. "What are you talking about, Mister. I don't have no gun! Damn it, stop making up lies."

The men approached Leo. "Looks like you've seen better days. I think you should come with us so we can find out what's going on."

Leo locked his eyes on the man talking to him. "There's a criminal element on this island, and you guys need to get rid of it, pronto! Some gangster kidnapped me, but I outwitted the sumbitch. Then over there in those woods, I discovered some dead guy in a wrecked car. So, take me in; maybe you can find my grandson."

"First, you need to hand over the gun you got in your pocket."

"I'm sorry, I don't understand. Like I said I don't have no gun."

"Well, just in case, you need to know, it's against the law for people to possess a handgun in the Bahamas."

The two men towered over Leo, then they bent over him, one on each side and helped him stand.

Leo continued to act innocent. "You should be looking for the hoodlum who kidnapped me. He's the one who has a gun he shouldn't have."

The few people standing around moved out of the way. One person spoke up. "Don't worry, mister, you're in the hands of the Royal Bahama Defense Force. They are here to help monitor the crowd during the Regatta, and they'll take care of you."

Leo felt a slight glimmer of hope and smiled. "Thanks."

"I was taught that the way of progress was neither swift nor easy."
Marie Curie

CHAPTER THIRTY-ONE

Crowds of people started to gather along the shoreline. They came from every major island in the Bahamas to see the top-notch racing boats in all the categories from one to five. The competition was fierce, and it evaluated the skills and stamina of the participating sailors.

The Peace and Plenty Hotel was at maximum capacity, and the hotel guests were crowded tightly in the confines of the old building. The excitement of the regatta permeated Georgetown with unrelenting sounds of boisterous horseplay.

Brett and Kayleigh sat side by side on their balcony, gazing at the sunlit sea. While stroking Kayleigh's dark hair he asked, "What do you think we should do today?"

Kayleigh's enthusiasm suffered due the constant distress of her missing family members which exacerbated the tension between them. "Brett, how should I know? This place is making me crazy. I can't stand the stress. This whole escapade has been one big disaster. I should have never come here, and inviting you along hasn't made anything better."

"Aww, Kayleigh, that's mean."

She looked at his face, trying to figure out what he could be thinking when something inside told her that their relationship was going in the wrong direction.

"Brett, nothing you've done has made it any better."

He sighed. "Kayleigh, what can I do to make you understand that I want to help you?"

Her fixed look was harsh. "Brett, back off. Don't pamper me. I think our feelings for each other are out of line, and what appeared to be the right thing, now seems to be ending before it had a chance to begin."

He dropped his head in his hands. After a long moment, he straightened and stared across the Harbor. "Okay, I'm going to take a walk to the Government Building and check to see if they have any leads about Gramps' whereabouts."

She shook her head, her bottom lip trembling. "Don't waste your time The police are so busy with the regatta, you'll be lucky to find anyone who even cares about your grandfather. Besides, you are only reacting to your own guilt about his disappearance."

She rose and went back inside.

Brett watched her walk away; her emotional outburst had caught him off guard, but he was a good listener. He would consider her feelings. The constant uncertainty had taken its toll on them both. He took a breath and inhaled the light sea air, then set out to discover what was being done to find his grandfather.

***

Gina Marino was upset about Luigi's sudden death but knew that reporting it would cause more problems than she needed. Besides, Sebbie confessed that Luigi had planned on rubbing her out after they acquired the deed. Better to dispose of his body in the ocean, hoping the sea creatures would take care of her problem.

Leo Kelsall's assault had surprised her, and she realized that she wasn't dealing with a weak old man. In fact, she was pissed at him and knew she must act now, before he got to that Nichols guy and saw the fake deed she had made.

She ordered Sebbie and Russo to go into George Town. "You guys need to find the younger Kelsalls because they have become a royal pain in the ass, and it's time they are wiped out." The men got into the truck and left, leaving her to head out to visit the property appraiser at the Government Building.

George Town was abuzz with people, and hordes of them wandered all over, crowding the roads and slowing traffic, which annoyed her even more. Unable to hold back her irritation, she blew the horn of the car at them. "Get your sorry asses out of the street, you stupid sons of bitches!"

She finally pulled into the parking lot, took the briefcase she had placed on the seat next to her and proceeded up the stairs and into the building. To her surprise there was none of the usual busy activity. The reception desk was vacant, and the note posted on it instructed visitors that the offices were closed for the rest of the day. "How convenient."

She sauntered down the hall to the property appraiser's office and placed her satchel on the floor. To her delight, the closed door swung open easily. Mr. Nichols sat at his desk, busy working. He looked up to see the cause of the intrusion, and she noticed a look of astonishment covering his face.

Gina strolled in like an entitled guest. "Hi, there, do you remember me?"

His face turned scarlet, and he yelled, "Get out of my office. You're not welcome here."

"Nichols, that's not gonna happen until you validate my copy of the deed to my property. You've had ample time to complete it and to get rid of the other deeds. Now hand it over!"

"That land belongs to the rightful owners," he sputtered. "It's not your land. Now please leave and don't return."

"Not a chance," she said boldly. "You're dragging your feet. To expedite the completion of that necessary form, I'm giving you an incentive." He stood, and as he did, she reached in her pocket and produced a gun. Before Nichols could react, Gina pulled the trigger. The bullet pierced his left shoulder. "That should knock some sense into your pea brain."

The jolt from the bullet knocked Nichols off his feet and onto the floor next to his desk. She peeked over to see red blood soaking through his shirt. "You better get yourself some help. Looks like a nasty wound, and we wouldn't want you bleeding to death, would we? I'll be back when you're feeling better."

She exited the office and closed the door behind her. Then she bent down by the briefcase she had placed on the floor, opened it, and adjusted the timer on the homemade bomb inside. Satisfied, she left the building.

***

As Gina drove away, Brett entered the Government Building. He was surprised to see the usual busy place so quiet. He turned toward the police department, but as he did, he heard muffled cries for help. He followed the pleas and found them coming from behind the closed door of the property appraiser and rushed in.

Mr. Nichols had braced himself up and was leaning on the corner of his desk. Seeing Brett he begged, "Help me I've been shot!"

Brett rushed to him. "Come with me." Supporting Nichols, Brett helped him to the police department. Seeing them, Mrs. Albury immediately ran to their side. "Looks like he's been shot," Brett exclaimed. As the words left his mouth, a muted reverberation echoed from the hall, strong enough to knock the three to the floor.

The noise of the explosion was masked by all the sounds of the outside activities. Brett checked on Nichols and then helped Mrs. Albury up from the floor. They looked around the area but didn't see any noticeable damage. Brett turned his examination to Nichols' shoulder. "We have to stop the bleeding. Do you have a first-aid kit?"

"Yes, just a moment." She scurried off to the back of the police department which was vacant and returned with the kit. Breathless and agitated, her eyes were wide with concern. "What happened to Mr. Nichols? And what could have caused that blast?"

"I don't know how Nichols got shot, but the blast sounded like a bomb." Brett knelt next to Mr. Nichols whose face was ashen, and his shirt soaked with blood. Removing the shirt, Brett packed the wound with gauze and wrapped his shoulder with an ace bandage.

"Looks like the bullet went straight through, so you've got two wounds, an entrance site and an exit, which is sort of good news."

"Thanks, I needed to hear something positive," Nichols said in a weak voice. "That deranged woman continues to torture me because I refuse to certify a bogus deed to the Kelsall property."

"Yeah, she's a bold one who will stop at nothing to get her way. I'm afraid we are all in her line of fire," Brett said. "Unfortunately, the police have a busy week monitoring the crowds here for the regatta, but someone should be here soon. You two should be okay, no sense in all of us taking risks—I'm going to see what kind of damage that explosion caused. There could be more bombs hidden out there."

Brett walked cautiously down the hallway to the lobby, then turned toward Nichols' office. The floor was strewn with ceiling tiles, and there was a gaping hole in the wall outside his office. The door lay in pieces with fragments of wood and concrete partially covering what appeared to be the remnants of a homemade bomb. The window behind the desk was shattered into fine slivers of glass, letting in a sea breeze that ruffled the papers scattered around the room.

He jumped when he heard heavy footsteps approaching. "Mr. Kelsall, you need to leave this area, we'll take over. Our bomb squad is on the way."

The men escorted Brett back to the police department where Mrs. Albury was already being questioned. "As soon as we're finished here, we'll need for you to give us your account of any involvement in this intrusion."

***

Leo Kelsall was being held by the Royal Bahamian Defense Force and was currently being observed at the local clinic for the laceration on his arm, his severe dehydration, and the lack of a valid identity. He sat on a stretcher in the examination room looking at the nurse by his side.

"Can't you just find my grandson and release me? I'm better now, and I ain't gonna run away, because I got no place to go without him."

The stern-faced nurse ignored his request. "Sir, I'm not privileged to make that decision because the Defense Force has jurisdiction over that matter. Besides, you are in no condition to be discharged."

She was disturbed from the exam when the sound of the phone went unanswered. "Excuse me, sir, I must answer the phone." She left him sitting on the stretcher and rushed off.

A fretful look covered her face when she returned. "I'm sorry, sir, we are very short of staff right now, and that was an urgent call. I must move you to another room while I attend to this new patient's needs."

"Why do I have to move? That ain't fair, I was here first."

The nurse rolled her eyes. "I'll help you down; please move along. I'll take care of your needs as soon as possible, but the doctor needs this room now." Leo rubbed the bristles that covered his face and begrudgingly obliged. "Where do you want me to go?"

"Please! Just come with me; you need to sit in the waiting room."

Moments later chief detective Stevens entered the clinic with Brett and Nichols, who was weak and frightened. The doctor greeted them, and the nurse placed Nichols on the stretcher. "Are you a family member?" the nurse asked Brett.

"No, I was just giving the chief a helping hand."

"Then, sir, please have a seat in the waiting area." She pointed down the hall. "Just go around the corner. There's an older gent there waiting to be examined."

Brett looked at the other two men and shrugged his shoulders, then turned and walked away. When he entered the waiting area, he

133

saw a disheveled older man sitting by the window who was staring at him.

"My God, Sonny, it's about time you showed up!"

"Gramps, what the hell happened to you?"

Brett darted across the room, embraced his grandfather, and noticed the mischievous irreverent manner of the older man's smile. "I've been looking for you, but you must have been hiding out since you left me alone in that foggy smoke-filled joint. You shouldn't had done that to me."

Brett felt embarrassed. "I'm sorry; let's get out of here and clean you up."

"Nope, can't do that. I'm a ward of the Royal Bahamian cops. They need me to show identification and a passport, or I'll be sent to Nassau."

Brett was going to protest but stopped himself. Instead, he took his cell phone out of his pants pocket and called Kayleigh. As he looked at Leo, he worried that she would ignore his call. He was impatient and agitated and was about to end the call when she answered. "Brett, are you alright? I just heard about the explosion at the Government Building."

"Yeah, I'm fine. Made it out but there's a mess in there. I'm at the clinic with Mr. Nichols; he didn't do all that well. But listen, I found Gramps!"

"Oh, Brett, that's wonderful, how is he?"

Brett chuckled. "Seems to be a little ornery. Kayleigh, I need his passport and driver's license. They should be in his backpack which I left it in the closet in my room. Could you bring them to me? I'm in the waiting room at the hospital."

"I'm on my way."

CHAPTER THIRTY-TWO

Kate spread her beach towel on the ground by the shoreline of Elizabeth Harbor and sat down. A white cover up was draped over her bathing suit, and a large white hat covered her head; dark glasses hid her eyes which were focused on the line of dinghies with their colorful sails skimming along the water in front of her. The pages of the note pad lying by her side fluttered in the breeze.

The owner of the houseboat rentals had noticed her earlier when she walked by him as she searched for a suitable spot to watch the race, and he followed her. He was casually dressed with a baseball cap protecting his dark hair. A trimmed beard covered his dark but handsome face. He approached Kate and tapped her on her shoulder. His unannounced arrival caught her off guard, and she jumped

"Hello, Miss, I need to have a word with you."

A sign of uncertainty covered her face. "Yes, sir, how can I help you?"

His firm voice demanded her attention. "Seems that the houseboat you and your husband rented has never been returned, nor have you paid for the extended time you requested. I do hope my boat is still intact and remains here in the Exumas."

She stood and adjusted her sunglasses. "I'm sorry about the delay of the rental fee, but time seems to fly by. I can assure you that your houseboat is in a safe place." Kate looked over the crowd of people around them and wondered how he had found her.

"My husband is not here right now, but I'll remind him of the overdue payment. I'm sure he'll take care of it right away."

"I hope so, Miss, if I don't get the money by the day after tomorrow, I will have an arrest warrant issued on him for stealing my houseboat."

Kate was astonished by the accusation. "I can appreciate your concern, but that won't be necessary. You'll get your money soon."

The man tugged on his beard and grunted. "I'm not one to jest." Then he turned and made his way back through the crowd.

135

***

Kayleigh rushed to the clinic with the necessary papers in hand. The usual busy place seemed quiet. A nursing staff member passed by her, and a look of surprise covered her face. "Why, Miss Kayleigh, what brings you here today?"

"I was on my way to the regatta when my cousin Brett called and asked me to drop off some papers that he needed. He said he was with his grandfather, Mr. Kelsall. Do you know where I can find them?"

The nurse assistant's eyes widened with amazement. "You know that old man?"

"Yes, he's my great uncle, and he's been missing for a while."

"Follow me. It's a good thing you showed up because some men from the Bahamian Royal Defense Force have been trying to identify him. He has no identification on him and looks like a lost soul; they were planning to take him to Nassau. Although he did insist he was Leo Kelsall, which makes sense now."

Kayleigh trailed behind the girl as she led her into a large waiting room. She was feeling distraught after passing by the Government Building while the bomb squad personnel roped off the entrance, plus still on her mind were all the insults she had flung at Brett earlier. When she saw Brett's faint smile, she felt relieved and greeted him with her own wide grin. Holding up her hand full of papers, she said, "I've got all the credentials you wanted."

Leo sat beside Brett, and she bent over and hugged him. "So good to see you, Uncle Leo."

"Thanks, Kayleigh, it's great to see you, too!"

"Kayleigh, we must wait here until the men from Nassau return," Brett said. "They were called away to investigate the bombing at the Government Building. Besides, Detective Stevens is here, too. He's with Mr. Nichols who was shot by our nemesis Gina Marino. Even Gramps had an introduction to her, and he says she has a great body for a bitch."

Kayleigh frowned then glanced at Leo's glum expression and noticed how dirty and disheveled he was. His sweat-stained shirt clung to his body, and his face was covered with white stubs of hair. Standing beside him she inhaled his distinctive body odor. "Uncle Leo, we were so worried about you!"

With a sense of pride, he spoke, "Don't ya know by now, you can't keep this old coot down?"

She grinned and was careful not to blame Brett. "I guess you're right, but I'm sorry you had to go through such an ordeal. When we get all this identification business straightened out, we'll get you cleaned up and feed you a hot meal."

***

Gina slammed the door when she left the building and briskly walked to her car, climbed behind the wheel, and left the parking lot. The street was so crowded with people that her car crawled along the road until she reached the Cellar where she pulled behind the building and parked. She walked around the building, then up the stairs and entered through the front door. The cloud of cigarette smoke engulfed the room, reminding her of a mist hanging in the early morning air, but the smoke fumes permeated her nostrils and irritated her eyes. She rubbed them with her hand while glancing around the room.

Patrons filled the stools along the bar, and two men at the pool table were engaged in a game. Scanning the room, she spotted her target and approached the small table by the pool table where he sat. She stood in silence beside the man, watching him give her the once over with his eyes. He was a muscular man with a long scar on his left cheek. She couldn't read what was he was thinking from the glare of his dark eyes, but she felt a sense of evil lurking there.

"Gina Marino, I take it? Right?'

"Yes, and you are Vito, a friend of Luigi, who unfortunately has recently gone missing."

Yeah, that's right, bitch! He was a good man; we met in Miami when I had my construction business there. That was before I got involved with the crime syndicate here in the Bahamas; pull up a chair."

Gina sat down with her tough demeanor on full display. She lowered her voice so only Vito would hear. "Luigi and I were involved in illegal gambling like running numbers and horse betting in Vegas, but when we heard about the lucrative offshore gambling houses in the Bahamas that are generating billons, we decided to find a place to build the next gambling mecca."

"So, you gonna tell me what happened to Luigi?"

"That old man Kelsall got the best of him."

Vito slid his hand over his slicked back black hair. "I have a hard time believing that a robust young and very fit man like Luigi let some

80-some-year-old mountain man get the best of him and actually kill him."

"Well, believe it or not, that's what happened."

"Are you sure? It wasn't you who killed him after you discovered that he wanted to take over your operation? Lady, and I use that term lightly, no one on this island has any money. The rich and famous live on their private islands up and down the coast, and if they wish to go on a gambling junket, they can jet off to Monti Carlo or Dubai anytime they wish and spend their millions anywhere they wish. Plus, the Bahamian people aren't allowed to gamble." He leaned into her face. "Your scam is ridiculous! This is not the place for an operation like the one you have in mind. The locals will protect the Kelsall legacy. You screwed up when you failed to whack the old man in the mountains."

Gina looked around the room then leaned forward. "You know this caper has the making of a gold mine, just like Atlantis and Cable Beach on New Providence."

He scoffed at her. "You'll never make it on your own, and I ain't interested in any part of your so-called operation. So, get lost, babe. Besides, you are an embarrassment to the Bahamian family. You exposed yourself with your insignificant attempts to appear tough. And you have to know that the Chinese are the ones that buy the land and build the casinos. Once their projects are complete, that's when we make our move."

"You may scoff at me all you wish, but I am going to be the owner of 900 acres of Kelsall land. That old man did my mama wrong, and I will prove to the world that the land was passed down to me. All the obstacles will be eliminated as they should be. It's just a matter of time."

Gina believed in the mob traditions of honor, respect, and dignity; she was certain that this man was skeptical of her role because she was a woman, but that didn't faze her—she had lucrative assets secretly hidden in Bahamian banks. She glared at him, then rose, turned her back on him, then thew him a kiss over her shoulder, and walked away, disappearing through the cloud of foggy cigarette smoke obscuring the exit.

"Life creates paths to follow and roadblocks to overcome.
Blaze your own trail and follow your dreams."

Lee Lomas

CHAPTER THIRTY-THREE

etective Stevens waited while the doctor completed treating Nichols' bullet wound. He watched his friend's ashen face covered with a look of desperation and put his own feelings aside. Finally, the ordeal was over, and the doctor released him. "You're free to go. Make sure to follow my instructions. If you have any concerns, call me. I'll see you back here in 10 days. The detective will escort you home. I don't recommend you return to work until I see you again."

Nichols struggled to sit up, and the nurse standing by his side helped him into the wheelchair. He tried to smile. "Life has become complicated."

"Detective, take him down the hall to the lobby," the doctor added.

"Wait," Nichols said, "before we leave, I'd like to see Brett Kelsall who came in with us; do you know where he's waiting?"

"Yes, sir, he's with his grandfather in the waiting room."

A frown covered Nichols' brow. "His grandfather?"

"Yes, the elderly gentleman was found by our Royal Defense Force men who are in the area to help with crowd control. He was wandering around Smithies' convenience store. They brought the gent here to be examined; he was severely dehydrated, and he's in sad shape. Another thing, he doesn't have any identification with him, so they plan to take him back to Nassau."

"Our department has been searching for him," Stevens said. "I wish they had notified us, but I understand the delay; with the Regatta festivities this week we have been working with a limited staff. Where can I find them?"

The nurse pointed. "Just go this way—the waiting room is around the corner; I'll bring Mr. Nichols to the lobby where we will watch over him."

The detective briskly marched into the waiting room and approached the Kelsalls seated at the far end of the room. "Brett, thanks for your help earlier; you'll need to follow up with me tomorrow. I'm taking Nichols home; he's really shook up. Then I need to make sure our building is secure."

His eyes turned to Leo. "You must be Brett's grandfather."

"Yep, I am. And I'm waiting on the Nassau army to take me away."

"Why?"

Brett spoke. "That's because he didn't have any identification on him when they found him. How come they weren't aware of your search?"

"I just heard that, and I'm sorry; look, whatever you need I'll help you with it."

"Kayleigh just brought us his documents that were in his backpack at the hotel."

"Give them to me. I'll have the secretary copy them, and I'll take care of the details with the Defense Force. Mr. Kelsall, I'm sorry that your introduction to our beautiful island was less than ideal".

"Well, copper! In my opinion you need to do something to control that crazy woman who's trying to kill my family and, from what I hear, anyone else who gets in her way."

"Yes, we are well aware of that, and it's our upmost priority to keep you and your family as well as the members of our community safe."

The detective noticed Leo's jaw tighten.

"Sounds like mumbo jumbo double talk to me because my niece and her husband have been missing since the day they arrived. What about them? They could be dead for all we know. Just like the guy I found in his car!"

The detective didn't wish to escalate the situation and ignored the mention of the corpse found in the car. "I assure you that we are searching for them. You must know there are hundreds of islands in the Exuma chain. It takes time and men to search all of them. You are safe now and with two other members of your family who have the same concerns, plus you are here at one of the most treasured events. Boats from all over the Bahamas are here to race. Enjoy the occasion."

He paused, and there was a long silence. "Nice meeting you; you are free to go now. Don't forget to pick up your documents before you leave."

Leo nodded. "I need to get cleaned up; don't you agree? Tell the army they need to take that she-devil with them when they leave.

That'll get her off your hands before she causes more problems that you don't need."

***

Kate watched the man in the baseball cap walk away. Her mind was flooded with questions, and a sudden pressure developed in her chest. She bent down and picked up her towel and note pad, muttering to herself, "Bullocks!" The people around her turned to see what was wrong. She felt her cheeks flush. "Sorry, mates, pay me no mind, but that bloke upset me. I'll be leaving now."

She twisted and turned to make her way through the crowd who were pushing their way toward the shoreline with hopes of seeing the boats race. She couldn't turn her thoughts off. She knew that Lance would not want to leave the volleyball tournament, but he needed to know what was happening before someone showed up to arrest him for non-payment.

Finally, the crowd cleared, and she continued to walk past the grocery store to a vacant lot located just beyond it. The makeshift bleachers were placed on the sideline, and they were packed with people baking in the hot sunlight. Kate was in luck; Lance's team were currently resting in the shade of a large tree. She beckoned him to her side, and he sauntered over, holding a half full plastic bottle of water. His tan body was beaded with sweat. "Hi, love! I needed this break. The team from Cat Island were brutal, but we gave them a hell of a fight. It was a great game."

He swept his eyes over her and reached to move a strand of hair away from her face before giving her a tender kiss. "What about you? How's the race going?"

She smiled but her lips quivered. "Lots of excitement; there are some amazing sailors out there."

"Good, you can fill me in later," and he turned to go.

"Wait, don't run back just yet. I need to tell you about the bloke at the houseboat rental place. He scouted me out somehow and demanded we pay for the extended use of the houseboat by the day after tomorrow."

"I'll get on it, love. The final race is tomorrow; everyone will leave, and all this excitement will be over."

Kate sighed. "These Kelsalls are more trouble than I ever envisioned."

141

"Calm down, their lives are in constant danger; we need to do our part without being recognized. That would put us in danger, too. You do understand, don't you? Stay away from that Kelsall gal."

"Yes, I know."

He looked back at his teammates who were taking their place on the court. "Got to go. See you later, sunshine."

Kate watched as he joined the others. Undecided as to what to do next, she walked across the street to the strip store plaza and entered the Towne Café next door to the pharmacy. She found a seat under a fan and ordered herself a Corona with a lime and looked through her note pad.

CHAPTER THIRTY-FOUR

Gina was pissed. She got into her car and deliberated her situation. She knew she must ditch her car and evacuate the house she was renting. For sure, that old geezer will give the police information about the location. That's okay, she thought. She'll take the boat and find another freaking place, but she wasn't sure if she could trust the new men.

Impatiently she tapped her feet and glanced at her phone, wondering what was taking Vito so long. Minutes later Vito walked past, not noticing her sitting in her car. "Kiss my ass, you fool!" she shouted after him.

He turned around to see who was there, a shocked expression covering his face when he saw a Glock pistol aimed directly at him. Before he could respond, the sound of a bullet rang out. He placed his hand over his chest and collapsed.

Gina waited for a reaction, but no one came running out of the building or in from the street to investigate. She walked over to look at Vito. Standing over his body, she inhaled the coopery smell of blood as it oozed out from the large hole in his chest. A smile of satisfaction spread over her face. "So long, loser."

She got in her car, started it, backed up then drove it over Vito's lifeless body before leaving the parking lot.

***

Kayleigh followed the detective out to the lobby. She saw Mr. Nichols sitting in a wheelchair and went to his side, placing her hand over his. "I'm so sorry to hear about the attack on your life; don't worry, the detective will get The Royal Bahamian Police involved in our search for Gina. Then we all can sleep better."

A frightened look covered his face. "Kayleigh, I hope you're right. I don't think I can stand much more of her harassment. She threatened my wife and kids."

The detective returned to the lobby. "All set, Nick, let's go. Here's your papers, Kayleigh. Take special precautions, we are on high alert for the probability of another attempt to harm your family."

"I know; we'll be careful." She went back to the waiting room. "All set; let's go. Brett, why don't you take Uncle Leo back to the hotel, while I go shopping for more appropriate clothes.".

Leo wrinkled his brow. "Huh? Don't bother with that stuff. I don't need nothing new."

She smiled at him. "Seriously, you'll feel much more comfortable wearing cooler clothes. I know from experience; see you two later."

Kayleigh's first stop was the straw market. Tee shirts hung from the rafters and were arranged in piles on the multiple tables that consumed the building She browsed through the cluttered mess and held two shirts in her hands when a salesclerk slid up close to her. "Miss, let me help you while you look through our other selections."

Kayleigh wasn't in the mood. The place was overrun with people, and she felt uncomfortable, not knowing who might be lurking in the shadows. "I'll just take these two, thanks."

She was glad to get out of there and started to cross the busy street with its loud traffic noise as the drivers of the cars blasted their horns at the swarm of people loitering in the street. She was on her way to a sporting goods store that was located next to the Two Turtles. Halfway across the street she saw Kate moving up the stairs of the restaurant. "Hey, Kate!"

Kate turned at the sound of her name and saw Kayleigh approaching. "Surprise! Kate, wait up!" Kayleigh rushed forward and almost knocked a man over. "Oops, so sorry, sir, but I'm in a hurry!"

She rushed past him and focused on the woman who was turning away from her. "Kate, damn it, can't you be civil to me?" When she caught up to her, she shivered at the cold glare that covered Kate's face. "Aww, come on, you're being unreasonable."

Kate stopped abruptly and sighed with irritation. "What can I do for you, Kayleigh?"

Kayleigh moved closer and put her hand on Kate's arm. "Stop being a hard ass. Lance's not here. I just want to talk with you."

***

Gina braked her car in front of the Two Turtles. Police were directing congested traffic that accumulated in front of the Government Building. The glow of the yellow tape across the entrance had attracted onlookers and curiosity seekers who wondered what had happened there.

Gina growled. "This sucks." She needed to get out of here now, but she was caught in the traffic snarl. She'd just have to take her chances that the police wouldn't recognize her car. If she tried to push people out of the way, she'd only bring more attention to herself. So, she sat there and sulked.

She turned toward the Two Turtles and through the crowd caught a glimpse of Kayleigh hugging Kate. "My, my," she hissed. "They seem chummy. I wonder who that woman is with the Kelsall girl?" She picked up her cell phone and snapped a few pictures.

***

Kate gave in and tried to relax. "Let's go inside. I've had a trying day, and I intend to relieve my stress by having a few beers; care to join me? Lance is still playing volleyball. I think he's become addicted to it. He's in the tournament and loving the challenge."

It was cool and dark inside where a briny breeze floated through the open spaces. They found a table in the back and ordered drinks.

"I was actually thinking about you earlier," Kate said.

Kayleigh couldn't help but smirk. "Really, I find that hard to believe."

"Now you're being the cheeky one. Nothing special, but you came into my mind earlier."

The drinks came, and Kayleigh took a sip; she was trying to be calmer than she felt. "I hope they were good thoughts. My life is still full of drama. Brett returned with his grandfather in tow, and all hell broke loose. I don't need to bore you with the whole story, but he went missing for a few days. Anyway, he's back with us now." She sat back waiting for Kate's reaction.

"That means all your family is now in Exuma."

"Seems that way." She flashed a harsh glare at Kate. "If we only knew where my parents are we could leave all this behind. Have you had any contact with my mother lately?

Kate shook her head, avoiding further eye contact as she took a swig of beer. "No, but some recent pressure may make a difference soon."

Kayleigh took a deep breath. "That's a little double talk. Looks like this conversation is going nowhere, and I gotta go. I need to find my Uncle Leo some new clothes. He's still dressed like a mountain man." She twisted in her chair. "I'll pay for these drinks. If you're still around after the regatta is over, I'd like to know where you're hiding my folks. I don't appreciate all this secrecy."

Kate disregarded the jab, glancing her way with a sympathetic smile. "Be safe, Kayleigh."

"Thanks," she said wryly.

After paying for the drinks, she headed to the exit, passing a group of musicians who were setting up their equipment. "More noise," she muttered beneath her breath. On the other hand, music lifts peoples' spirits. She wished she was in the mood to party, but she had to finish her shopping.

Once outside it was only a short way to the sporting goods store which was well stocked with clothes and local crafts. She found what she had in mind and left the store satisfied.

On her way back to the hotel she couldn't help but wonder about Kate's statement of pressure that may cause her to reveal the location of her parents. Frustration at Kate surged through her as she hurried through the crowded street.

CHAPTER THIRTY-FIVE

The golden glow of sunlight illuminated the hotel room. Brett was sound asleep on the couch. Kayleigh was in her bed and started to stir, but her eyelids remained closed. She was startled when she heard a door slam and Leo roar, "I'm hungry!"

She looked through her eyelashes and moaned. "Sounds like I better get up." She slipped into her robe and joined the men.

"Good morning," she said as she opened the doors to the balcony. The sky was covered with a bright red glow which reflected on the boats anchored in the harbor. A warm wind blew into the room. "What a beautiful sunrise. How's everyone?"

Leo looked handsome dressed in his new clothes. A shave and shower had done wonders, and he seemed pleased with his appearance. "Good choices, Kayleigh."

She gave him the once over. The clothes fit him well. A polo shirt, dark blue shorts, and white New Balance sneakers. "Uncle Leo, why are you wearing those black socks. I bought you new white ones."

"Don't be silly, these are more comfortable."

"No! You can't wear them."

"Why not? Socks are socks; besides the white ones are too bulky."

She pouted. "Please, just try them for a day."

Brett handed his grandfather a tube of sun block. "Here, put this on your arms and legs; they look like they haven't seen sunlight in a long time."

Leo ignored the tube. "No time for this. You two are much too picky; when do we eat?"

Brett put his arm over Leo's shoulder. "Calm down. We eat all our meals in the restaurant downstairs. It won't take us more than a few minutes to get dressed."

Leo grumbled. "So, get to it. Time's a wasting."

Brett glanced at Kayleigh who nodded. "Okay, you can wait for us on the balcony."

Brett followed her into the adjacent room, admiring the way her dark hair swayed gently around her shoulders. When they were alone, he took her in his arms. "Let's kiss and make up."

She fell into his embrace and kissed him." When she came up for a breath, she said, "I promise to control my outbursts, and thank you for standing by me."

Brett kissed the tip of her nose. "You're welcome. Now, we better get ready, or we won't hear the end of it. You can't ignore a hungry man's stomach."

The restaurant staff was overwhelmed with customers and the wait time was long, but they were lucky to be seated on an outside table where they watched the boating activity, which helped Leo calm down. On the table was a pot of hot coffee and a basket full of Bahaman bread and some cinnamon buns, which sufficed until they were able to order their breakfast.

The boats were moving about, lining up in their designated categories. "They are getting information now for the first race."

Kayleigh added, "Yes, but there are five different classes for the sailboats," she said for Leo's benefit. "It's going to be a long day."

Sounds of the shouts from the crew rippled across the water, and their wait for the food to arrive went by fast. After breakfast they walked along the harbor, now crowded with spectators.

"Brett, I don't want to spend all day watching the races; besides, your grandfather's wobbly legs won't last all day."

Brett sighed. "The main race is due to start at 3 this afternoon. What shall we do until then?"

Leo had the solution. "Let's go see the property."

"Gramps, we can't do that," Brett protested. "We don't have a car.

"Why not, Sonny?"

Brett didn't want to go through the entire tale of how their car had been swept out to sea. "It's a long story, let's just say it's not available. That reminds me; I need to check with the boat mechanic at the marina. He should be able to work on my plane starting tomorrow. Let's take a walk."

Kayleigh interrupted their conversation. "The two of you have fun. I'm going back to the hotel. Brett, call me when the race is about to start."

Brett gave her a quick kiss and waved as she disappeared into the crowd.

Brett and Leo took their time walking to the marina on Kidd Cove where the seaplane was waiting for the replacement of the new engine, but the place was deserted. "Damn it, Gramps, I need to demand some action. They could assemble that engine in one day. My patience is over."

"Let's find a place to sit down for a while," Leo suggested.

They slipped through the growing crowd of people until they reached the park in the center of town and found a shady seat under a large banyan tree. Brett found them some cold drinks, and they did some crowd watching.

The day dragged on. It was extremely humid, and the wind died down to just a trickle, leaving the sailboats idling in the water.

Without warning the sky turned a dark purple, and the wind whipped across the park. The gusts had to be around 60 to 70 miles an hour. The squall captured everyone in the harbor off guard.

Frustrated sailors scrambled to control their sails. Raindrops turned into waves of water gushing over the regatta. Screams came from the sailors as well as the people on shore.

Boats slammed into each other; the sounds of sails being ripped apart by the wind was maddening, and the wreckage was a chaotic scene. Sailors were washed overboard and cries for help filled the air. Sailors' bloodied bodies were hurled every which way by the 8-foot seas.

The Royal Bahamas Police Force tried to control the panic, and Coast Guard boats were deployed to help the injured.

Brett's mind swirled with thoughts of survival. His heart beat fast as he looked for a safe place to take Leo. The cold rain pelted them with the strength of an unleased fire hose, and the fierce wind pushed at them with vengeance. Bodies of people lay on the ground, some of them unable to move.

"Gramps, we need to find shelter! Take my hand. I'll try to steady you. Try not fall."

Tents that had been erected to shade the people were scattered across the ground, covering people who had been inside when they collapsed. The roof of the straw market tumbled into the street. Clothes were drenched, and t-shirts blew away.

"Try to keep up with me, Gramps. Let's see if we can make it to the Two Turtles."

They made it to the street. "Watch your step. Let's go!" He felt Leo's grip slip out of his hand. Looking down, he saw Leo sitting in a puddle of water. "Come on, let me help you up." Brett wrapped his arms under Leo's armpits and lifted him up. "Are you okay?'

"Yep, think so. Nothing hurts, just took a bath."

Brett led Leo into the restaurant that was mobbed with other refugees from the storm. The wind and rain followed them through the doors, but in moments, they were safe.

CHAPTER THIRTY-SIX

A 28-foot Chris Craft with two 250-horsepower outboard motors was anchored in the water by the red brick house where Gina was staying. She finished packing her belongings in the boat's cuddy cabin. "Are you ready, men? Russo, you drive, and Sebbie, you ride shotgun. We're headed for Hog Cay which lies just south of Little Exuma."

"All set, boss."

"Russo, all eyes will be on the race, so skirt around the sailboats by hugging the shoreline of Stocking Island. Go at a leisurely pace; no time to draw attention to us."

"Yeah, I hear you. Hog Cay, is that where they have the wild pigs?"

"No! It's a private island and listed for sale at just under $75 million. No one lives on the island which has 7 beautiful beaches, a marina, and its own air strip. The main house is furnished, and it sits high on a knoll overlooking the sea."

"Sounds fancy, but we will be stranded there if the boat craps out."

"Right, so make sure it doesn't. Besides, we won't be there long, just long enough for things to settle down a bit in George Town. Seems we made a few enemies."

They traveled south for about a half an hour, moving slowly through the few ripples of the sea. "It's too damn hot! We're moving too slow. Can't even generate a breeze at this rate. Shit! I'm burning up!" Sebbie's face was flushed, and he was dripping with sweat.

"Settle down!" she scolded. She too was irritated; sweat droplets formed on her brow and began running in her eyes. "Damn it! This has turned into a bitch of a day! Where did you hide the bottled water?"

"It's in the cabin."

"Sebbie, go get us some."

He gave her a push. She glared at him, then moved aside, and he ducked into the room below, returning with a six-pack of cool water. He handed them out.

Gina grabbed hers and took a gulp. "That's better."

They could see the sail boats in the distance. "Not much action going on there. Those boats ain't going anywhere soon."

They were focused on the sailboats and failed to notice the change in the weather until the breeze picked up and a purple glow covered the boat. The wind and waves pushed the boat sideways which caused Russo to increase the power before they drifted west and interfered with the sailors. Soon drops of cold rain began pelting them. It became more forceful, attacking them with biting jabs of water.

Gina slipped into the cuddy cabin. Russo changed the course of the boat to run closer to Stocking Island, hoping that the island might block the buildup of waves. The scuppers were overflowing, and the bilge pumps were working overtime. They heard screams coming from the sailors in the harbor but could barely see the bedlam taking over Elizabeth Harbor as the visibility was about zero due to the gray curtain of rain blocking their sight.

***

Kate hesitated to leave her sailboat before 3 p.m., which was the time for the big race to start. She wanted to watch the finishing leg of the race. The air was still, not a good sign for a sailboat race. She jumped aboard her dinghy and began her trip across the water to George Town. She was concerned at the lack of a breeze. Without a wind, those boats weren't going anywhere. She was certain that the poor sailors must be disappointed. At this rate, they'd be sailing until midnight.

Seeing no need to rush, she took her time. By the time she reached the lee of the island she felt a cool breeze begin to push her dinghy, giving the 5 horsepower motor a little kick. The leisurely cruise became more intense. The waves surrounding her were building fast, and the wind was forcing her boat off course. Bucket loads of rain began pouring over her. She attempted to turn back when a huge wave washed over the dinghy. Gripped with panic, she screamed for help.

The sound of an approaching boat startled her. Through the gray backdrop she saw a larger white vessel approaching at a rapid speed. It was heading right at her.

She shrieked and blew a whistle. "Stop! Don't hit me!"

Russo heard the ear-piercing sound of the whistle but could barely see through the rain that pounded him. He saw something white but was unable to. recognize the dinghy being violently thrust around in the building waves. Again, he heard the whistle and slowed the Chis Craft down.

Gina came out of the cabin. "What's going on?"

"Look, there's a girl in a dinghy. She's going to be thrown overboard."

"So let her go; she's in our way. Run her down and put her out of her misery." Gina squinted through the rain and took a second quick glance. The girl looked vaguely familiar. "Hold on, Russo! That woman is a friend of the Kelsall girl. I saw them together. Save her, and I'll use her to get my land. This is perfect timing."

Kate waved. "Over here, please help me!" She clung to the dinghy while Russo slowed his boat to an idle and placed it between the waves and the dinghy. Sebbie reached out and grabbed Kate, lifting her aboard. She was dripping wet, her clothing clinging to her body.

"Oh, my God! Thank you. That was terrifying! I was on my way to the regatta. Are you going there?" She turned to look for her dinghy. "Wait…where'd my dinghy go?"

They all looked for it, but it was gone.

Gina and the men turned toward her in complete silence and stared at her. Kate sensed something was amiss. Panic rose within her, and a suffocating breath filled her lungs. "What's up with you people?" She backed away, grabbing for the side of the boat. "Oh, no! Put me back in my dinghy. I can't stay here!"

Gina grabbed her. "Don't worry, darling, we're not going to harm you. We just want you to stay as our guest for a bit." Standing behind Kate now, Gina shoved her. "Now get in the cabin and enjoy the ride."

Russo thrust the controls forward, and the boat shook as it crashed through the waves.

***

153

Kayleigh stood in front of the balcony doors which were closed and being pelted by the heavy rain of the raging storm. She was frozen in place, watching the spectacular sailboats being ruined by the unexpected turn of events. She watched in horror as people were hurled from their boats into the sea.

She got closer to get a better look at the results of the steadfast wind and rain. The waves were carrying people onto the shore as boats crashed into each other.

"Those people need help!" she cried out to the empty room. Without hesitation she ran from her room to the stairwell and swiftly scaled the stairs to the ground floor. She ran to a door leading outside and tried to push it open. Try as she might, the force of the wind was too great for her to budge it.

"Damn!" She turned and ran to the door that opened to the lobby which was packed with people seeking shelter. She threaded her way through the terror-stricken mob to the lobby door leading outside and barged through it. The weight of the heavy rain surprised her. She shivered at its chill but, undeterred, she ran toward the shore. She found a group of people who had formed a human rescue line, helping recover the injured who had washed up on the beach. Kayleigh heard sirens blast as two ambulances pulled into the hotel's parking lot.

She reached the sand and grabbed for a sailor's hand. "Come with me, I'll help you!" She remained at the edge of the harbor, helping rescue the injured until she became exhausted. By then the violence of mother nature's fury had abated, and a trickle of rain drops floated lightly on the sea breeze, leaving behind unconscionable damage in its wake.

***

Lance was concerned about Kate. She hadn't arrived to watch the final volleyball game of the tournament as she'd planned. He and a few of his teammates left the court together after the bleachers collapsed and assisted others to find safety in a nearby store.

As the skies cleared, the gathering began filtering out of the store. Lance paused outside the door. "I'll see you, mates, let's try to keep in touch. Hopefully we'll still play together on Stocking Island once the cleanup is complete. Let's do our best to help."

One of the players tapped him on his shoulder. "Doesn't look like your wife made it over. Would you like a lift back to your boat?"

Lance scanned the area, thinking that Kate could be somewhere around, then reasoned that if she couldn't find him, she'd assume that he got a lift back to their boat. "Sure," he said, "this place is a shambles."

"Just follow me, my skiff is at the wharf."

They made their way through the scattered debris and the people who milled about, gasping at the destruction.

"This way." Their shoes squished as they walked through the water saturated ground. As they approached the dock, Lance's friend started to look concerned. "I hope the skiff didn't get washed away."

It took a while before they found the friend's boat hidden beneath the dock they were walking along. A wide grin covered Lance's face. "Mate, you're a lucky man; that blow did you a favor and kept your craft safe. Hardly a drop of water in it."

"Right, chap. Jump in, and we'll be on our way to see how your boat did."

They weaved around the stranded boats and were cautious not to get tangled in their lines. Once out of the harbor it was an easy ride to Stocking Island. When it was in sight, they passed close by a half-submerged abandoned dinghy. "Hey, mate," Lance said. "Stop a moment; that dinghy looks familiar. I think it could be mine."

They pulled alongside, and Lance checked the identification numbers on the hull. Realizing it was his dinghy, his heartbeat kicked into overdrive. He stared across the water. He was at a loss for words as his mind swelled with uncertainty. "Where's Kate? My wife, she's not here!"

"Lance, calm down, " his friend said, placing a calming hand on Lance's arm. "Maybe the dinghy was loosened from your sailboat during the storm and drifted here. You're lucky to have found it. Let's bail her out and take her with us."

Working together, they quickly emptied most of the water out of the dinghy, then towed it behind the skiff. Lance placed his hands on his head as he looked in the direction of Stocking Island, trying to make sense out of what was happening. "There! Over there, that's my sailboat." The sailboat was washed up on the shore and tilted on its side.

"Looks like we gotta dig a trough to get her back in the water," his mate observed. "When she's free, I'll pull her off with my skiff."

They dug a trench behind the boat and tied a line around the cleats on the stern, then secured it to the skiff. Using the power of the skiff's motor, his friend was able to back the sailboat into the water where it floated freely.

There still was no sign of Kate. "Lance, I've gotta go; I'm sure your wife is safe. She's probably at the Chat and Chill waiting for you."

Lance had a hard time controlling the emotions that welled up in his chest but wasn't going to dump them on his friend. "Thanks for your help!" He waved as the skiff turned back toward Georgetown.

Lance tried to think positive. The Chat and Chill restaurant looked like it had survived the storm without damage. With any luck, Kate would be there waiting for him.

CHAPTER THIRTY-SEVEN

The storm passed. The sun sparkled in the sky once again, and the sea was crowned with the brightest of rainbows. Brett and Leo waited for the crowd to dissipate before venturing out of the Two Turtles. "I'm going to call Kayleigh." He punched her number, but there was no service.

Brett stood beside Leo. "Gramps, I can't reach her because the service is down. Are you ready to go back to the hotel?"

The old man nodded. "Might as well, Sonny, not much happening here, and they're going to have to get all these puddles out of here."

Brett noticed a grimace cross Leo's face as he tried to walk. "Gramps, are you alright?"

"Yeah, gotta a pinch in my back, but I'll walk it out. That trip into the water must have pulled something."

Brett was uncertain. "Are you sure you can make it back?"

Leo was a little indignant. "You betcha, stop acting like I'm a cripple. Besides, I'd like to get rid of these wet clothes."

Brett helped Leo out to the street and noticed the tension in Leo's pale face. "You doing all right, Gramps?"

"Look, Sonny, let's just get on with it!"

The gentle breeze carried a heavy smell of sea air. The Royal Bahama Police Force were patrolling the streets and helping to monitor the cleanup activity in and around Georgetown.

Leo grinned. "Looks like my copper friends have cloned their bodies. They're crawling around like a bunch of black spiders."

"Gramps, they need to have a high profile to prevent looting and to help those in danger."

"Yeah, I know, it's just there are so many of them."

"So, behave yourself, and you'll be fine."

They took their time walking at a slow pace and watched people helping to collect the tents in the park which they then examined for damage. The roof from the straw market had been moved off the road and now rested against the building. By the time they reached the hotel, both men had a shiny film of sweat covering their skin.

157

Kayleigh sat on the balcony watching the action below when she heard the door of the hotel room open. She turned to see the men enter and ran to them; she wrapped her arm around Brett and kissed him with an intensity that surprised him.

"I was so worried about you two," Kaleigh said.

Leo's face revealed a mischievous grin. "Hi, Kayleigh, do I get a kiss, too?"

She blew him a kiss and laughed. "Where did you go during the storm?"

Leo answered. "We held up at that turtle place."

"Thank goodness you're safe."

"It's a mess out there. Gramps was a trooper through it all, but he took a spill and hurt his back when we reached the street. The wind was literally trying to blow us over."

"I need to get out of these wet clothes," Leo said. "And you two need some time alone."

Kayleigh was just about to ask Leo if he needed help, but Brett touched her elbow. "Don't make a big deal out of it," he cautioned in a low voice. "He's a proud man. Just let him rest. If he needs anything we're here for him, and he knows it."

Her face softened, and she smiled at Brett. "You are graced with kindness." Her brown eyes were warm with admiration, and she stroked his hair then kissed him lovingly. "Let's go out on the balcony, and I'll tell you about my day."

***

Lance was overwhelmed with worry. No one at the Chat and Chill could help him trace Kate's movements prior to the storm. He was determined to find out more and took his dinghy across the harbor to Georgetown and tied it to the dock where the shuttle boat was kept. Then he proceeded to the police station which was located within the Government Building. The reception desk was empty, so he followed the signs to the police station.

Mrs. Albury was seated behind her computer. "May I assist you, sir?"

"I hope so. My wife Kate Robinson went missing during the storm yesterday, and I'd like to know if you have received any information about her."

158

Mrs. Albury typed her name into the computer. "Sir, it looks like all the missing sailors have been accounted for and there are no other new people listed on the police missing person log, but of course that could change."

"Bullocks! How can that be? People were being tossed off their boats like rats. The Harbor was full of floating bodies struggling to reach the shore."

"Sir, there are no unidentified people as you have indicated. I know you are upset, and I understand that it must be distressing to be unable to find your wife. I will place her name on the list and alert everyone in our department as well as the visiting Royal Bahama Defense Force to be extra vigilant in our search and rescue endeavors during these challenging times."

For a moment Lance was calm. "Thank you. One more thing, madam, I need a favor. My wife is friends with the Kelsall family members who are visiting here from America. I would like to find the girl whose name is Kayleigh. I know Kate has been involved in their endeavor to search for the missing people in their family. She may be able to help me."

"You say you know this girl?"

"Yes, but I don't know how to contact her."

Mrs. Albury sighed deeply. "I don't usually give out this information, but in your case if she's a friend of your wife and she may be able help you, that's a different matter. She and her cousin Brett are staying at the Peace and Plenty. Here's my card. Give it to the receptionist, and I'm sure she'll help you locate the Kelsalls."

Lance tried to smile. "Thank you for your time, and please, do your best to help me find my wife."

He left the building and walked up the slight incline to the Peace and Plenty. He headed straight to the reception desk. "Hi, I'm Lance Robinson, I just left Mrs. Albury at the police station. Here's her card, you can call her if you have any questions. She said that you would be able to help me find a girl named Kayleigh—she's a member of the Kelsall family."

The woman looked Lance and then at the card. "Is there some kind of trouble?"

"No trouble, just need to talk with her; she's a friend of my wife Kate."

"Just a moment. I'll notify her that you are here."

Lance stood back, glancing around the room, and waited.

Kayleigh received the call and was unsure of Lance's motive as he was never friendly and always made an issue when she would talk to Kate, but what the heck; she'd see what he wants. She approached him by the reception desk and felt a chill go through her body when she saw his angry glare. "Hi, Lance, what's up?"

He walked closer. "Have you seen Kate?"

She shivered. "No, not since before the storm. Why?"

"She's missing!" He tried to control his anger. "When I got back to the sailboat, she wasn't there. No one knows anything about her whereabouts, and I blame you and your family for her disappearance. You always snuck around, pumping her for information about your missing parents. You wouldn't accept that they are safe. You just wouldn't leave her alone."

Kayleigh felt her throat close. Brett and Leo were at the marina and couldn't help. "How dare you blame me, when you yourself don't have a clue about what happened to her." Not knowing what else to do, she turned to leave.

"Young lady, don't you leave. I'm not through yet!"

People in the lobby were watching them, and she knew she must defuse the tension before it escalated. "Lance, please calm down; let's get a seat on the patio and talk about this in a more civil manner."

She noticed some of the anger in his eyes start to fade away. "This way, follow me."

They found two comfortable chairs with a view of the harbor and the recovery effort workers cleaning up the remnants of the storm. "Lance, tell me about Kate's disappearance."

The change of environment helped lessen his agitation. He took a deep breath. "I was here in George Town playing in a volleyball tournament when the storm hit, and Kate never showed up like she planned, so a mate of mine gave me a lift back to Stocking Island. On the way there I found our abandoned dinghy drifting off the island. I checked with the blokes at the Chat and Chill, and no one can account for her whereabouts that day."

Kayleigh got it. "And you probably think she was abducted by the people who are out to get our property, but I don't know if that's true, do you?"

"No, but I need your help."

Kayleigh fidgeted in her chair. "How can I do that?"

"You can go back to the Hermitage House with your uncle and talk to the spirits. That's what you do, isn't it? That's how you found us!"

She cringed. "That place is freaky. I don't think I could ever go in there again."

"Kayleigh, please. I need your help."

She paused, thinking about his request. "If my Uncle Leo goes, too, I'd consider it, but on one condition. You know where my parents are staying. If I do this for you, you have to tell me where they are hiding. Mind you—you can't renege on your promise if we are unable to find out what happened to Kate."

Lance forced a small smile. "You've got a deal! I'll rent a taxi and take all three of us to Little Exuma. Let's go!'"

"Slow down, not so quick. Brett and Uncle Leo aren't here."

"Then let's go find them. We don't have time to waste."

"Never grow a wishbone where a backbone should be."
Ben Falcone

CHAPTER THIRTY-EIGHT

Russo continued to guide the boat on the course that would take them to Little Exuma. The storm's fury was lessening, and the rain drops became a fine mist before dissipating into a brilliant golden glow.

Navigation became much easier, and he carefully crossed into the Hog Cay cut, then slowed the boat to an idle to avoid the shallow areas. Passing them he docked the boat at an elaborate marina.

Gina and Kate emerged from the dark cuddy cabin, and their eyes adjusted to the magnificence of the island.

Sebbie also scanned the tropical paradise before him. "This place is for the rich and famous, boss, how did you manage a place like this?"

"I have a connection who knows the owner but don't get too comfortable; we won't be here long."

Kate pushed her matted hair aside while strands of it clung to her temples. She stared at the evil and malicious people on the boat.

She looked threateningly at Gina. "Why did you bring me here, and what are you going to do with me? I can't help you get that land. It doesn't belong to me."

Gina gave her a shove. "I have plans for you, and you are going to cooperate or else!"

Kate was terror stricken; her mind went blank. Her face wrinkled up while her eyes welled with tears.

Gina looked at her. "Buckle up, girly. I don't have time for your drama." She turned to Sebbie. "Take her to that small building over there and lock her in. Then meet us at the main house."

Sebbie roughed up Kate by twisting her arm up her back which was painful, and she thought he must get his kicks from twisting it. Kate whimpered in agony. It was a short walk up a hill overlooking the marina to a small building. The splendor of her surroundings was lost on her as the reality of the dire situation overtook her.

He opened the door and shoved Kate into the darkened room. She stumbled as he stepped back into the sunlight and slammed the door. Kate heard the clicking noise of the door being locked.

As her eyes adjusted to the dim lighting, she noted that the building was actually a small house. She walked around, noting that the place was nicely decorated with two bedrooms and a bath. It even had a washer and dryer. The closets held clean clothes that looked like uniforms along with some casual clothing and shoes. There was a small kitchen that was well stocked.

She sighed as her mood lifted. At least the place was not a dark dungeon. Not bad; she thought as she opened the refrigerator. She felt like a condemned prisoner who was going to get a steak dinner before her execution. She slammed the refrigerator door and tried to block the thought.

She wanted to get out of her wet clothes, wash her hair and rinse the salt water off. Continuing her exploration, she found a closet containing women's clothes. She grabbed a t-shirt and some slacks and headed to the bathroom. In the shower, the warm water soothed her anxiety.

***

Gina was amazed at the luxury of the main house. "I could get lost in this place." She opened the door leading to the pool and spa and smiled. Behind her she heard the men talking and the sound of ice clinking into glasses. She turned to see them raiding the liquor cabinet.

"Enjoy yourselves; that was turbulent journey." She joined them and made herself a cocktail. "Russo, did you notice if there are any zip ties in the boat?"

Russo poured more whiskey over his glass full of ice. "Huh? Zip ties, yeah, I saw some. Why?"

His curt attitude annoyed Gina. "Look, dude! I'm in charge here. There are a lot more like you to be had out there, so get those freaking ties now!"

He took a gulp of his drink and wiped his hand over his mouth before hurrying out of the room.

Sebbie stood still, watching, and waiting. She turned to him. "When Russo gets back, you two get the girl and bring her to me. Can't take a chance that she might get away like that old man did."

When Sebbie returned with the zip ties, the two men finished a few more drinks before heading to the smaller building where they'd left Kate.

"Sounds like our prisoner is taking a shower," Russo said, rubbing his hands together in anticipation. He stormed into the bathroom with Sebbi following close behind.

Russo pushed back the shower curtain.

Kate yelped in shock at the intrusion. "How dare you! Get out of here!"

She grabbed the curtain and wrapped it around her body. Water squirted the men in the face. Russo reached in the shower and turned the water off. "You're coming with us."

"Hell, no! I'm not going anywhere without clothes." Kate glared at them.

Russo jerked the shower curtain off her and pulled her out of the shower stall. He gawked at Kate. "Such a nice clean body shouldn't go to waste." He looked at Sebbie. "How bout we have a little fun before we take her to Gina? You hold her."

Russo moved closer to Kate and tried to grope her breasts.

Kate lifted her leg and attempted to kick him. "Get away from me, you animal!"

"Sebbie! Damn it, hold her legs."

"Russo, I can't do both. I'm not a contortionist. Here, she's all yours." He pushed her toward Russo.

Kate screamed. "Don't you dare touch me!"

Russo grabbed her by the waist, but she was slippery with soap and escaped his grip. She swung her arms and punched him.

"Bitch!" He tried to grab her again, but Kate was too quick for him—she made it to the open door where Sebbie tackled her.

She continued to violently thrash her arms, using her fingernails to attack Sebbie's face.

Finally, the two of them were able to subdue her. Sebbie wiped blood off his cheekbone. "Russo, let's go."

"Now?"

"Yeah! Come on, you can have your way some other time."

"But I was having fun, she was exciting me. I like it when they fight."

"Gina ain't gonna wait much longer, and if I was you, I wouldn't want to piss her off."

They dragged Kate outside and up the hill to the main house with Kate struggling and screaming the entire way. When Kate saw Gina, she yelled, "Keep these frigging creeps away from me!"

Gina ogled Kate's naked body still dripping with water. Her wet hair clung to her face, obscuring her features.

Gina shot an angry glance at the men and let out a frustrated breath of air. "What's going on here? You two are out of line! Sebbie, go get a towel." A cold glare covered her face. "Russo, you're pushing your luck."

Sebbie handed Kate the towel, which she yanked from him, then dried off. She tousled her hair and shook her head, allowing her tresses to fall into waves around her face. "That's better." She wrapped herself in the towel before turning to glare at Gina. "Your men are pigs! What the hell are your plans for me? I have nothing to do with that parcel of land you want. The people who own that land are complete strangers and have nothing to do with me."

"Really? I've seen you two together, and you seemed very chummy to me. I never saw strangers give each other hugs, have you?"

Kate stood still and got up her courage to ask again. "What's your plan for me?"

Gina sighed. "You, my dear, are my hostage, and I will use you to my advantage and get what I am seeking, or you will die. Now stand there while Russo puts these shackles around your ankles. He'll chain a few more together so you'll be able to walk around and fend for yourself. Don't try to escape or splice them off. If you do, we will have no choice but to put some on your wrists."

Kate closed her eyes and ran her fingers through her hair. "I guess you answered my question."

Russo finished tying her ankles and looked up at her. "I don't recommend trying to swim away; the current is strong, and you'll never make it to the next island without drowning."

Gina added, "That's it, dear, feel free to walk around and enjoy your stay in paradise."

Kate attempted to walk, but it seemed more like an awkward hobble. She left the house and slowly made her way back to the smaller house. All alone at last, her heartbeat was calm, and she snapped herself back to reality. "I can't run away, but somehow I will get away."

CHAPTER THIRTY-NINE

Asoft pink mist rose from the sea welcoming a new day. Brett and Kayleigh were up early enjoying the sunrise from the balcony. "Kayleigh, I'm going to talk with Mac today. I won't wait another day. He's going to put the engine in my plane like we agreed weeks ago. So, I'm going to the marina."

Kayleigh smiled at him. "Good luck, I hope your determination helps to accomplish your goal." She tried to conceal her doubts and gently planted a kiss on his check. "I know that you will give it your all."

He turned to leave the balcony when Kayleigh stopped him. "Wait, what about your grandfather? Shouldn't you stay until he gets up? He hurt his back yesterday. What if he can't walk?"

He shrugged his shoulders. "Nah, nothing can keep him down. Let him sleep. I'll be back soon."

After Brett left, quietness surrounded Kayleigh. She returned to the balcony where she relaxed on her chair overlooking the harbor. The sun's rays illuminated the untold destruction of the splendid sailboats that remained there. She searched her mind for some clarity of her own anguish and tried to comprehend the complexity of events that had evolved since she'd received a simple gift of a deed to land on Little Exuma, but she found no plausible explanation.

***

Ted made his way to the wharf on Staniel Cay where the mailboat was docked. The deck hands were busy securing the cargo, and Ted hailed one of them, "Excuse me, sir, where would I find your captain?"

The man paused for a moment and lifted his head, searching his surroundings. "He's the big guy with the white beard over there by the stern."

Ted looked toward the back of the ship. "I see him, thanks."

He approached the man and waited until he was able to get his attention. "Sir, I'd like to book passage to Nassau for myself and my wife."

The man paused, looked at Ted, still hesitated, then pulled on his beard as if he was considering the request. "Mister, I hate to disappoint you, but we are overbooked for the passage to Nassau until further notice. There was a devastating storm in George Town that resulted in multiple casualties. People are stranded there, and many of their boats have been destroyed. We are obligated to serve the people of the Bahamas by providing them with safe passage to Nassau. I hope you understand."

Ted felt his body tense while he tried to digest his disappointment and held eye contact with the captain. "I heard what you said, whether I understand, I'm not sure, but it is of the upmost importance that we book transportation on your ship."

"I can offer you passage once the crisis is past; until then it won't be possible. I'm sorry about your quandary. Have you considered hiring a private charter plane; they would get you there by the end of the day?"

"No, that's not possible."

"I'm sorry...if you are here when I return and I have room, you'll be welcome to join us; now please excuse me."

Ted stood there for a moment, rubbed his brow, and tried to think through how he was going to explain the news to Carole.

***

Brett found Mac working on a damaged sailboat. The smell of oil, diesel fuel, and machinery permeated the air. He was determined to make his desperation known. "Hi, Mac, I'm back, and I need you to stop and listen to me."

A surprised look covered Mac's face. "Brett, can't you see I'm busy?"

"Yes, but we made an agreement for you to install the new engine in my plane weeks ago. I've been patient with your excuses, but now I'm demanding some respect."

Mac reflected on Brett's words. "You know I've been busy with the regatta activities."

Brett tried to control his outrage. "Yeah, Mac, but the regatta is over, and my plane still needs an engine. It's time you started to work on it! You made your commitment to me long before the regatta began. It's over time for you to work on it."

"Yes, I know, but these are my people, and I need to help them. Many of them are stranded here."

Brett felt the heat rise in his face. "And I'm not stranded? Please explain the difference to me."

Mac paused, unable to respond.

"Mac, if I were able to fly my plane, I could help more than you realize. I could fly it to Nassau and pick up parts for you to fix the sailboats. I could transport the injured people to hospitals there for treatment that's not available here. I'll even give you a hand with the repairs. That should make your job easier."

Mac stood silent, looking at the water around the dock.

Brett waited, his gaze sweeping over the harbor and the crystal-clear turquoise water cluttered with disabled sailboats. The silence was maddening, and he was about to question Mac again when the older man spoke up.

"Brett, you're a fine man. I'll start working on your plane as soon as I complete the repairs on this boat, and I'll hold you to your word about volunteering to help the people of our islands."

Brett heaved a sigh of relief and fist bumped Mac. "Deal!"

CHAPTER-FORTY

L ance couldn't sleep. The sky was still dark when he opened his
eyes. His mind was swirling with questions. What had
happened to Kate? Where could she be? She could've
drowned, but her body hadn't shown up, and the police said there
were no deaths.

His gut feeling kept telling him her disappearance had to do with
the gang of underworld gangsters out to steal the Kelsall's land.

He closed his eyes again, but his sleep was fitful. When the soft
glow of a pink-orange sunrise crept into the sailboat, he got out of
bed.

Sipping on his tea, he planned his day, and his top priority was to
go back to the police station; he had to know if there was any new
information regarding Kate's whereabouts. He was not about to give
up hope.

He waited for the shuttle from George Town to show up at their
space outside the Chat and Chill. Once aboard he was on his way to
the Government Building. He entered and greeted Diane. "Hi, there,
I'm on my way to the police station," and rushed by, not waiting for
a reply.

When he entered, Mrs. Albury was sitting behind her desk
speaking with a police officer. He waited until she was free, then
approached her. "I'm Lance Robinson. I was here yesterday inquiring
about my missing wife.

She hesitated for a moment, and Lance picked up an uneasiness
in her behavior. The gesture seemed odd to him, and he eagerly
questioned, "Have you any new information for me?"

"Just a moment, sir, I'll be right back." She scurried off into the
maze of desks behind her.

Lance was confused. What could have caused such an abrupt
departure?

Within moments Mrs. Albury returned with Detective Stevens by her side. Lance's heart pounded in his chest, and he tried to hide his panic, thinking only the worst.

"Mr. Robinson, this our Chief Detective, Mr. Stevens."

Lance glanced at him. "Do you have any news about my wife?"

He shook his head. "No, sir, I'm sorry, I don't. The reason I'm here is that we have a warrant for your arrest. The warrant states that you are overdue on payment of a houseboat rental as well as possible theft of the boat."

Lance's jaw tightened, and he felt the hair at the nape of his neck rise. "This is tosh! I can't believe it! I did miss a rental payment, but there has been a storm, and my wife is missing. I just forgot about the payment."

"Yes, sir, I understand, but I have this warrant, and we must honor it."

"Bullocks! You people are off your trollies. My wife is missing! You should be looking for her, not harassing me about a late payment."

"Sir, the man who filed this warrant said he spoke to your wife and told her if he hadn't received the payment by yesterday, he would file the warrant with our department. Is that true?"

Lance was shocked, an angry scowl covering his face. "Yes, it's true! What are you going to do about it? Lock me up? I don't carry that kind of money on me."

"Please calm yourself. I have no choice." He turned to Mrs. Albury. "Contact the constable and have him place Mr. Robinson in jail."

***

Leo emerged from his room and wobbled into the sitting area. His eyes scanned the room in search of his roommates. Then he noticed Kayleigh sitting on the balcony. She snapped out of her trance when she heard movement behind her and turned around to see Leo standing there.

"Good morning, Uncle Leo, you surprised me. How are you feeling?"

He grimaced. "I've felt better. Maybe I'd feel better if I could get something to eat. You got anything here?"

Kayleigh moaned. "Gee, I don't know, maybe a few chips." Feeling annoyed she sighed. "I've told you before, we have to go to the restaurant for our meals."

Leo pouted. "Why didn't you get a place with a kitchen?"

"Uncle Leo! Be real, we weren't the first member of the Kelsall family to rent a room at this hotel."

"Oh, yeah, I'll have to speak to Carole about that."

Kayleigh finally lost her temper. "How dare you say that! For all we know, my mother could be dead." Tears streamed down her checks, and she sobbed.

Leo just stood there and watched with a helpless look on his face.

Kayleigh paused; she knew she was out of line and tried to calm down and control her emotions. Raising her hands to her face, she rubbed the tears away. "Uncle Leo, I'm sorry. Do you want to go downstairs to get breakfast?"

"Yep, sounds like a promising idea."

"What about your back? Will you be able to walk that far?"

"Just need to go slow."

"Okay, good. Wait here, I need to freshen up. I'll be just a minute."

Leo waited with barely concealed impatience, then jumped when he heard the outside door open. He was relieved when Brett walked in.

"Hi ,Gramps, looks like I spooked you."

"I'm waiting for Kayleigh; we were on our way out to get something to eat. Good to see you, Sonny, where have you been?"

"Went to see about my plane. I've got good news for a change. I'll tell you about when we're eating."

Kayleigh heard voices and peeked out of her room to see who Leo was talking with. Extending her head further, she saw Brett, and a wave of relief ran through her. "Hi, I'll be out in a minute."

Brett looked at Leo. "How are you doing today?"

Leo didn't reply.

"Gramps, you okay? How's your back feeling?"

He replied abruptly, "Been better—some food might help."

Kayleigh gingerly approached them, gave Brett a hug, and avoided speaking to Leo.

"Ready?" Brett asked, looking from Leo to Kayleigh.

She nodded, still uncertain of how her outburst had affected Leo.

Brett picked up on the tension in the room. "You both seem stressed. Is something wrong between you two, you're acting strange."

"Nothing's wrong other than my stomach is growling," Leo said, not wanting to make more of a fuss. "Not ready to run a mile though."

"Just take your time, no rush. I'll support you if you need assistance."

They took the elevator to the lobby. As they passed by the reception desk, Roberta stood up. "Miss Jones, I have a message for you."

Kayleigh hesitated. "Brett, don't wait for me, go find yourselves a table. I'll meet you there."

She was curious as to who would have left her a message and moved toward the reception desk. "Yes, what is the message?"

"Mrs. Albury from the police station asked that you call her when you find the time."

"That's it, nothing else?"

"No, ma'am, that's all."

She shrugged her shoulders. "Okay, thanks."

She found the men sipping coffee at a table.

"What was the message about?"

"It was from Mrs. Albury, but it was vague. It didn't sound urgent. I'll call her later." She smiled at Brett. "Your good news is more important. Tell us about it."

CHAPTER FORTY-ONE

K ate lay still, wondering why she wasn't feeling the soothing sway of the sailboat. Her thoughts warbled sluggishly in her mind. She gasped and her eyes opened wide when she remembered the horrible situation she was in. She glanced around the room, taking in the glimmer of sunshine peeking through the window.

She swung her feet off the bed and stood up. She was not fully awake and moved clumsily toward the bathroom. The confining grip of the ties around her ankles annoyed her.

Still naked, Kate opened the closet, found a gray women's uniform, and slipped it over her head, then wandered into the kitchen where she found an ample supply of food and made herself a spot of tea. She sat down in the breakfast nook to sip her tea and ate a croissant. She looked through the windows, studying the dazzling azure blue sea and the snow-white beach nearby.

Then she unfolded a map of the island she'd found mixed in with magazines that were piled high in the bookcase. "I've got to clear my mind and devise an escape plan," she whispered to herself. The map showed the island was strewn with multiple hiking trails plus as many as eight lovely, secluded beaches. She finally came up with a plan—she'd draw an SOS on one of the sandy beaches. Then anyone flying over the island would notify the Royal Bahamian Police, and they'll come to investigate. She giggled. Just like in the movies.

A renewed spat of energy filled her body. She'd need a crutch. The ties limited her balance. And she'd need lots of water and a hat to block the sun. She found a mop in the laundry room and removed the mop head. A wide-brimmed hat hanging on a hook was perfect for her escape. The refrigerator held numerous bottles of water. She filled the deep pockets of the uniform with the bottles, plunked the hat on her head, took her staff and set out to explore the island in search of a perfect beach.

***

From her place by the windows of the expansive living room Gina watched Kate hobble around and laughed at her stunted movements. "She'll wear herself out struggling to walk with those ties around her feet." They'd prevent her from trying to escape from the island, too.

She was waiting for Russo and Sebbie to return from the dock to check the boat before they headed back to George Town. The slamming of the door startled her, and she swung around, shouting, "For the love of Pete, Seb, were you born in a barn?"

He squinted. "Huh, what's the matter?"

A disgusted frown covered her face. "Never mind!"

She handed him a ransom note that she had formulated with instructions for the Kelsalls to pay a bounty for Kate's release. "Here, take this note and drop it at the front desk of the Peace and Plenty Hotel. Ask them to give it to any member of the Kelsall family staying there."

He grabbed the note from her. "That's simple."

"Not so fast. You're going to need a disguise. Wear your hoodie, mess up your face with grease or dirt, pull your hat down over your ears, and make sure to wear your sunglasses."

"Got it! No problem."

After he left, Gina gazed at the spectacular sparkling pool where she planned to spend her day sunbathing.

***

The three Kelsalls finished eating their meal and everyone seemed satisfied. Leo smacked his lips. "That was some good grub." They all stood to leave when Leo stumbled. Brett's quick action prevented him from falling. "I got you."

Leo grunted. "Damn legs don't want to work."

Brett held him in his strong arms. "Gramps, are you doing okay now?"

"Yeah Sonny, think I better lie down for a while."

"Do you want to get an X-Ray of your back?"

"Nope, don't need that. Just want to rest."

Kayleigh smiled and kept her eyes fixed on Brett. "Your news is fabulous. I'm so excited. When do you start?"

"Mac still must finish working on that sailboat, so he'll let me know when he's ready. Right now, I'll help Gramps back to the room."

"While you do that, I'll check with Mrs. Albury; can't imagine what she wants with me." She folded herself into Brett's arms and felt the warmth of his solid chest. "I'll see you two later."

Kayleigh passed by Roberta. "Thanks for the message. I'm on my way to see Mrs. Albury now."

She took her time strolling down the street, thinking of Brett, and a contented smile covered her face. The earlier hostile encounter with Leo had slipped her mind.

She entered the Government Building and was greeted by Diane. "Welcome, Miss Jones, how may I help you today?"

"I'm here to see Mrs. Albury."

"I'm sorry, she's not here at the moment."

"Humph, that's strange, she left a message for me to contact her.

Diane hesitated. "I know she was working on something involving Detective Stevens; let me give him a call. Please have a seat while you wait."

Kayleigh slid into the comfortable chair and scanned the room, trying to identify the source of the pounding noise, when she saw men wearing hard hats repairing a damaged wall.

"Diane, how is Mr. Nichols?"

She stalled for a moment. "I haven't heard any official word, but I have a suspicion that he won't be back. He's had enough of the Marino woman."

Kayleigh sighed. "Haven't we all?"

Time dragged on, and Kayleigh started to fidget in her chair. Just about the time she was about to complain, the detective appeared. "Miss Jones, nice to see you again."

She stood, unable to hide her displeasure. "I bet you are."

He ignored her curtness. "A new complication has emerged. Your friend Kate Robinson is missing."

Kayleigh nodded. "I know that."

He was surprised. "You do?"

"Yes, her husband Lance read me the riot act. He stated her disappearance was my fault."

"How can that be? The Royal Bahama Defense Force and my men have conducted several searches but have no leads, and for now we have not found a body."

"Another missing person. They're adding up, aren't they?"

"Miss Jones, please be patient. We are diligently working closely with our partners and continue to search for your parents as well as Mrs. Robinson and Gina Marino. Meanwhile still another gangster's body was discovered here in George Town. But that's not why I wished to speak with you"

"Oh, there's more?"

"Unfortunately, yes. Mr. Robinson is in jail for failure to pay his obligation for a houseboat rental. Were you aware of that arrangement?"

"No. Why tell me? I thought he had a sailboat. Why does he need a houseboat too—unless his current living quarters are becoming too confining?"

"I'm not sure, the problem is that he's incarcerated and has no way to withdraw the money he needs from the bank without paying his bail first, and he has asked to speak with you."

"Me? He doesn't even like me."

The detective rolled his eyes. "He's in a bind; would you consider his request?"

A calm came over her. "I guess it wouldn't hurt to talk to him."

CHAPTER FORTY-TWO

Detective Stevens led Kayleigh to the jail which was located behind the police station. It was a depressive, dark area, gray concrete walls with cells separated by bars. The typical incarceration facility. There were few occupants who were spread apart. He guided her to Lance's cell.

When Lance saw Kayleigh, he sighed with obvious relief. "I am so glad to see you!" She noticed a prickle of excitement cover his face. "Thanks for agreeing to see me."

Detective Stevens turned. "I'll leave you two alone. Miss Jones, when you are ready to leave, check with the guard at the end of the hall."

Kayleigh looked back. "I see him. Thank you."

Kayleigh was puzzled by Lance's change of attitude. "You must be desperate to ask for help from me."

"Kayleigh, I admit I was acting cheeky with you, but it was to protect Kate and your parents."

His statement aroused her curiosity. "My parents? How are you protecting my parents?"

Lance looked around, seeing only the guard watching a monitor. "Come closer, I don't want to alert anyone."

"Lance, you're acting weird."

"Please, just listen." In a hushed tone he continued. "When your parents first arrived here, the gangsters discovered they were part of the Kelsall clan whose claim to the property they so desperately wanted. This was an unexpected complication; their only alternative was to murder them before their presence was well known. That way they felt they could do whatever was necessary to navigate through the Government's old land registry system as soon as possible and rob your land to build their massive casino."

"Lance, this sounds surreal. How do you know this? And what has that to do with my parents?"

He shook his head. "Your parents' claim to the property is valid, so they are an obstacle to the gangsters' plans. There's more, but I

can't go into all the details right now. Please, please just trust me. I
need to pay the rent I owe on the houseboat, but I can't do that without
first paying my bail. Which isn't that much, but I don't have any
money on me, and with Kate missing, I have no one to ask for help."

"Wait a minute! I thought you owned that blue sailboat?"

"I do." Lance seemed desperate with his plea. "Do you
remember, Kate assured you that your parents are safe?"

"Oh, yes, I remember, and she refused to tell me where they were.
Which isn't right."

"Well, it was necessary due to the dire situation they were in. To
help them escape from the gangsters' notice, I rented a houseboat and
drove it to a secluded cay where they are safe, and the gangsters can't
trace them. They just seemingly disappeared."

Kayleigh put her hands on her head and stared at Lance. "This
story is beyond bizarre."

He begged her. "Please don't go! It's true. I can prove it, but I
need to get out of here before they launch a search for the houseboat
which would put your parents' safety in jeopardy."

She remained skeptical, but he seemed so genuine and truthful.
And if he was telling her the truth, she just might find her parents.
"Lance, I may be sorry for this decision, but I'll pay your bail, but you
must agree to repay me and tell me where my parents are staying."

Kayleigh looked at the guard, then back at Lance. "I'll be back."

He watched her disappear down the hall while he waited on the
edge of desperation.

***

Kate's shuffling gait took more energy than she anticipated. The
sun's glare was bright, so she lowered her hat, shading her eyes from
the brightness. She had been on the trail for almost an hour, and finally
she could see the bleached white sand beckoning her.

The beautiful small, secluded beach was hugged by a peaceful
cove. The bright sunlight made the translucent turquoise water glow
like a neon light, and she marveled at the sight. Feeling the cool water
bottle in her pocket, she removed it and gulped down over half of the
water in the bottle. Holding the mop handle for support, she lowered
herself down then splashed her feet in the cool water. "Oh, that feels
good."

Kate studied the sandy beach in search of a place to begin writing
her message. She noted the shoreline was strewn with empty mollusk

shells. The place was a sheller's paradise which was a bonus. She'd draw the message then outline it with the shells.

It was a struggle for her to stand again. Her weight made the mop handle sink deeper in the sand, and the ankle shackles restricted her movement. "Damn these things!" Finally, she stood upright. Using the handle, she outlined the SOS in the center of the beach then moved the shells and covered each initial with as many shells as she could find.

By the time her task was completed, she was exhausted, and the blazing glare of the sun was blinding her. She admired her work, and for a moment she felt her heart start pounding. A feeling of helplessness overwhelmed her, and it consumed her thoughts. If those thugs ever discovered this signal, she'd be doomed. She'd better get out of there before they came looking for her and catch her in the act.

She lamely struggled off the beach and was relieved when she reached the trail. The trees provided needed shade, but each step was torture. Sand was caught between the ties and her skin, and the constant rubbing tore her skin open. Feeling intense pain, she looked down at her ankles to discover they were covered in blood.

Kate was determined to go on despite the agony each footstep exerted on her torn ankles, but she refused to give up. She resolved to make it back to her captors without being discovered.

CHAPTER FORTY-THREE

Kayleigh and Leo waited outside the Peace and Plenty for Lance to pick them up in his rental car. He arrived on schedule and drove them to the Hermitage House in Little Exuma.

Before getting out of the car, Kayleigh turned to Leo. "Uncle Leo, I wish we didn't have to go in there; this place reminds me of a haunted castle, but I agreed because Lance promised he'd reveal my parent's location."

"What's the problem?"

"You'll find out for yourself. I can guarantee you will get to know what eerie really feels like."

"Kayleigh, stop the nonsense; I ain't afraid of any old, haunted house."

Lance wanted them to move along. "What's frightening about the place? It's nothing but an abandoned, run-down shack. Let's get this over and go inside."

Kayleigh glanced at Lance. "Please don't leave me alone in there."

He patted her on the shoulder. "Don't fret, I'll watch over you."

They walked up the hill and entered the building. Leo was curious and went on ahead of the others and wandered out of sight. Kayleigh and Lance stayed close to the door and idly waited for something to happen. Then Kayleigh felt a sudden rush of pressure in her chest. "Oh, no, this is horrible. I need to leave!"

Lance restrained her. "You can't go. We need to find Kate." He held her tight.

"Let go of me!" She sensed imminent danger. A feeling of claustrophobia overwhelmed her. "Lance, stop the walls, help me, the room is closing in on me."

Lance was alarmed and backed away with wonder he watched an aura of white light conceal Kayleigh's body. She seemed to disappear.

"Kayleigh, where are you?" He stood motionless, and soon she reappeared, panic-stricken as she tried to control her rapid breathing.

After exhaling a series of short breaths, she calmed down and retained her composure. "Lance, let's go outside."

As soon as they were out in the fresh air and sunshine he asked, "What did you see?"

"Now that you have put me through hell again, I want to know where you are hiding my parents."

Lance's face looked pasty white. "Kayleigh, I can't believe what just happened. Kate told me of seeing that white mist that surrounded you. It just blew my mind. Tell me what you saw?"

They became so embattled in their heated discussion and power play for information, they completely forgot about Leo.

***

Leo wandered throughout the dark, decaying structure, inhaling the musty fumes and stumbling on the debris that had accumulated throughout the years. He lost his footing and stumbled. Grabbing the wall, he steadied himself when he heard a man's voice cautioning him.

"Who said that?" He looked around in the darkness. Not seeing anyone, he felt his muscles tense. "Lance, is that you? Come here, so I can see you."

An elderly gentleman about his age walked up to him. "I'm not Lance."

"I can see that; who are you and why did you sneak up on me? What do you want anyway?"

"Leo, I thought I'd say hello and introduce myself."

"What the hell, how do you know my name?"

"I'm John Kelsall, and I know all my kinsfolk.".

"Huh? Are you batty? You expect me to believe that?"

"Your questions amuse me."

"Well, ha-ha. It ain't meant to be funny."

"Leo, let me explain. I am John Kelsall, and I built this house and lived here with my family. Before my time here expired, I willed my house and land to my children who were to make sure the Kelsall land remained within the family forever."

"Yep, that's old news. I've heard the spiel before." Leo tried his best to control a sudden rush of fear he felt when the temperature in the room chilled. "Okay, I get it. This is your house. Looks like you knew a bit about construction because this place is still standing.

181

Barely standing, but still intact. Good job, old chap. I'll run along, nice meeting you."

"Wait!" John commanded. "You need to listen to what I have to say."

Leo felt cold chills run down his back. Not knowing what John had in mind, he stopped and took a deep breath. "What do you want to tell me?"

John held a steady gaze into Leo's eyes. "Leo, as the elder statesman of the current Kelsall generation, you need to protect our land, but I'm not sure that you are capable of doing that."

"And why's that?" Leo couldn't keep the indignation out of his voice.

"Because you are a very selfish man. Your gold is more important to you than your family."

That keyed Leo up. "Mister, I gave my niece the deed to this property and my grandson hunks of gold."

"Yes, Leo, a deed to property that had no value to you as you never visited Exuma before. You are out for the revenge of Gina Marino who threatens to take away land you disregarded. The gold nuggets you gave Brett were only small tokens that you wouldn't miss. But you ignored the needs of your wife and son Scott to the extent that they left you all alone. As a result, you all had unfulfilled lives. You are fortunate to have such a caring grandson. He is someone to be admired because he overcame many difficult obstacles on his own. Plus, he strives to help others."

"Yeah, he's a nice kid."

John cleared his throat. "Leo, I'm not sure you are listening to me, but you must know that your time here on earth is running out. You are not a healthy man; maybe for the good of our family you could try to improve your legacy for the upcoming generations by surrounding yourself with those that you love, support and care about."

Leo was stunned by John's assessment of his life.

"There is an element of unknown and uncontrolled evil that surrounds you and your family. You need to be diligent and protect them from harm."

Leo felt overwhelmed by John's admonishment and felt his body shake. He closed his eyes and stood still in the dark awesome silence while wild thoughts whirled through his mind. When he opened his eyes again, he was alone. He walked toward the sunlit doorway and bounded out of the house.

Lance and Kayleigh were standing in the shade. When she saw Leo, she ran and embraced him. "Thank goodness you're alright. You were inside for such a long time. We were worried, but neither one of us wanted to go back inside."

He absorbed the warm tender hug. Confusion clouded his mind; the encounter with John Kelsall seemed so real, but how could it be? For an instant he pushed those thoughts aside. He smiled vaguely and looked beyond her at the sun kissed sea.

"This is a beautiful spot."

CHAPTER FORTY-FOUR

Her trek to the beach had exhausted Kate and her feet throbbed. She took a shower to wash the salt and sand off her, then found a man's tee shirt and put it on. After eating a snack, she went to bed.

When she awoke, her feet were in excruciating pain. She uncovered her legs and discovered her ankles were so swollen that the ties were hidden by the bulge of flesh overlapping them. She navigated slowly to the kitchen and packed a towel with ice, then stumbled to a recliner where she wrapped her feet in icepacks and elevated them.

Gina hadn't seen any activity from Kate during the morning and decided to check on her. Not expecting to see her laid up on the recliner, she grinned. "My, my, how did you get yourself in such a condition?"

Kate moaned and grimaced, her face revealing her agony. "I feel terrible. I overdid my exploration of the island. My feet are not meant to be so confined that I must take baby steps to walk. Can't you release me from this torment? I'm in no shape to be an escape risk."

Gina had no mercy. "You're a victim of your own stupidly, now deal with it. You did me a favor, now I have less to worry about. We'll see what the day has in store for us when the men return from George Town."

***

Kayleigh and Lance had yet to reach a compromise on who should reveal their information first, and Leo was irritated by their squabbling. He had no tolerance for such juvenile behavior and scolded them. "Can't you two get over it? One of you needs to tell the other the particulars you both agreed on before you went inside that building"

Kayleigh's eyes met Leo's. "Uncle Leo, don't you agree we need to know where he's hiding my mother, because he gave me his word.

Leo nodded. "That would be the manly thing to do, but it's apparent we're not dealing with a gentleman."

Lance objected. "That's vicious, old man, I need to know what happened to Kate before I reveal my secrets."

Leo bellowed. "Let's get out of here. Our visit here has put us all on edge. We need to relax a bit."

Surprised by his outburst, they looked at Leo. "I never thought to ask you, Uncle Leo, what happened to you inside? You were in there much longer than either one of us."

Leo shrugged and twitched. "Not much of anything. Just a bunch of rubbish strewn around that I had to plow through. Now let's go."

They returned to the rental car, and Lance drove them back toward George Town. As they passed over the bridge at Ferry, he turned to Kayleigh. "Is this the bridge where that pickup truck pushed you and Kate into the water?"

Kayleigh gasped. "You're right, that was a maddening day. Look at the rails; you can see the ones that have been replaced."

The road curved, and Santana's Beachside Shake was on their right. Leo barked from the back seat. "What's there? I sure could use a snack."

Kayleigh sighed. "Let's stop. Carmine is a sweetheart; I'd like to say hi."

Lance took a sharp turn, spinning the car's wheels in the sand, then it came to an abrupt stop. They got out and sat on a long bench that lined the bar and viewed the peaceful water and the sandy beach which was occupied with a few boats pushed up on the shore.

Carmine stopped to take their order, and she recognized Kayleigh. "Hello, my dear, so nice to see you again." She looked at the men, then asked, "I see you're out with men folk today, how is your girlfriend?"

Kayleigh flinched. "She's busy and couldn't make it today. This is my uncle and a friend. We stopped for a snack and a drink."

Carmine smiled. "They don't have a shady look about them. I hope those other men aren't bothering you anymore, although I've seen a couple more of that kind around here lately. Dear, you'd better watch out for them. They look like the troubling kind."

"Thanks, Carmine, I'll keep that in mind. We're ready to order."

Kayleigh was more relaxed; she took a deep breath, having decided to end the stalemate. "Lance, I've elected to tell you what kind of image I saw, but I fear it's not what you may have expected."

He took a sip of his drink, and with impatience, he practically barked at her. "Just tell me what you saw!"

She glanced at Leo then at Lance. "I saw an image that looked like a secluded beach with an SOS sign drawn in the sand, and it was lined with all kinds of shells. That's it."

Lance threw his hands in the air. "Tosh! Do you know how many secluded beaches there are here? Hundreds or maybe thousands. We're going back there, and you'll have to stay in there until you can tell me where Kate is! And you too, old man. I don't believe you didn't see anything in that place. I've noticed that only the blood relatives of the original Kelsall clan see images, so, what happened to you in there and what are you covering up?"

Leo stood up. "That's enough! Forget about me. You made a deal with Kaleigh, and as I see it, a deal is a deal. That's what she saw. Let it be. Now tell her where her parents are staying. Besides that, there is no firm evidence to convince me that the mobsters have Kate. Other circumstances may be involved in her disappearance. For example, another sailor could have found her and could be helping her out, or she may have drowned, and her body is yet to be found. Just chill down until we get more details from the police."

Lance's face darkened. "All that gibberish may sound logical, but there's no way in hell that I will reveal the location of her parents until Kate is found."

Kayleigh implored Lance to be reasonable. "I trusted you enough to lend you money for your bail, why can't you do the same for me and tell me where they are hiding? It's no secret that you know. Besides I'm not going to harm them. Look at it this way—you're concerned about Kate like I am about my parents."

She could see the hardness in his face, and she watched him as he seemed to struggle to conceal the anger—or was it fear—simmering just below the surface. "Then why didn't the spirts in that house reveal their location to you? You want to know why? It's because they are safe. They led you to us because you would find that out. But somehow, I don't know how, I just know that's not the case with Kate!"

CHAPTER FORTY-FIVE

R usso dropped Sebbie off at the shuttle dock then pulled his boat away and floated among the disabled boats strewn about the harbor and waited.

Before opening the door to the Peace and Plenty, Sebbie pulled his hood over his head to hide his cap and adjusted his dark glasses.

Roberta stood behind the reception desk, and Sebbie took large steps as he approached her. With the envelope extended from his hand, he mumbled, "Give this to the Kelsalls." Then he turned quickly and hurried out the door before Roberta could reply. She was startled by the unexpected and sudden arrival of the stranger. She examined the envelope in her hands. It didn't appear to have anything odd about it and set it aside.

***

Brett and Mac worked together like a well-oiled team and managed to assemble the engine into the seaplane by the end of the day.

"Mac, I need to take her for a ride to see how she runs."

Mac shook his head. "You better wait for that A and P mechanic to check our work first. I'd hate for something to go wrong, and we'd lose everything we accomplished so far. I found this guy who works out by the airport, and he has a good reputation. He'll be here early in the morning."

Brett felt disappointed but managed to smile. "Good idea. I'll see you in the morning."

He left the marina and walked along the shore on his way back to the hotel. He was consumed by a feeling of euphoria. They had finally accomplished the job he'd been wanting to do for weeks.

He entered the hotel and walked through the lobby. Roberta had anticipated his arrival and was relieved when he appeared. She waved the envelope in her hand. "Mr. Kelsall, I have a message for you."

He flinched with surprise as he moved toward her. "Something new, Roberta?"

187

"Yes, it was quite odd though."

Brett wrinkled his forehead. "Odd, what's odd about it?"

"Not the envelope but the man who dropped it off. He seemed to be hiding himself under his hooded sweatshirt, and he acted suspicious."

Brett grunted. "What's next? Tell me, what's the message say?"

She handed him the envelope. "Sir, I would never read your mail. The man didn't say anything, other than just give it to the Kelsalls, and you're the first one I've seen all day."

Brett tore open the back flap and read the message. He growled. "That witch is at it again!" He paused to gather his thoughts. "Thanks, Roberta." He sprinted out the door, leaving Roberta in a state of wonder with her mouth wide open.

He jogged up the steps of the Government Building, right past Diane and planted himself in front of Mrs. Albury. "I'm here to see the detective!"

She tried to get more information from him. "What's your concern now, Mr. Kelsall?"

Brett refused to say. "Is he here?"

She recognized the anger in his face and rose. "I'll let him know that you're here."

Brett was not about to wait and followed her through the station to the detective's office. Detective Stevens was surprised by the interruption and rolled his eyes. "Brett, what's on your mind?"

He handed the letter to the detective. "This is on my mind, and now it's time for you and the Royal Bahamian Police to do something about these corrupt mobsters that have overtaken this island. We've been here too long without any obvious support from your department or the police. Meanwhile, my family continues to be subjected to constant abuse while you give us lip service on how you're investigating our complaints."

The detective stood. "Brett, please calm down."

"No, I'm not finished. These mobsters will not stop their tactics until they have the property they don't own. I want to know when it will end?"

"Brett, we are dealing with the results of a major storm and are involved in providing safety for those isolated here."

"What about murder, attempted murder, kidnapping, and missing people? All this has been overlooked while you clean up the mess the storm caused. Tell me if you're going to disregard this ransom note too?"

"No, I won't. You may be right; it's time to enlist the Royal Bahamian Defense Force. We'll need help from Nassau to capture the crime syndicate that has taken over our island."

Brett gritted his teeth; he was not familiar with the Defense Force, but they had to be better than the local police force. Turning away was not an option for him. "I'm not leaving this island until our issues are resolved. So, keep me informed."

***

Lance drove along the Queen's Highway heading back to George Town. No one had uttered a word since they'd left Santana's. The atmosphere in the car was still and distant. They inhaled the stale scent of the weathered seats and felt every bump in the road.

When the car stopped in front of the Peace and Plenty, Kayleigh and Leo flew out of the car. The stress of their visit to the Hermitage House and Lance's berating anger had them on edge. They watched with frustration as he sped away. Looking at each other they sighed.

"Hey, you two, wait up!" They heard Brett's voice and turned to see him walking toward them. Kayleigh ran to greet him and held him tight.

Brett could see the fright in her dark eyes. "Was it that bad?"

She gasped and filled her lungs with fresh air. He could feel the tension in her body. "Yes, but Lance's behavior was even worse. It was horrible!" She paused. "Brett, I'm sick of chasing ghosts, and I never want to go back in that house again."

"Kayleigh, slow down, what happened?"

Her brown eyes were as big as saucers. "You know the routine, I was emersed with a cloud of white, and I saw an image of an SOS sign dug in the sand on a deserted beach, but Lance insisted I give him more information than what I saw. He kept pumping me for more details, and he threatened to take us back to the Hermitage House until we came up with something he wanted to hear."

She stopped for a moment to calm herself. "I know he's upset about Kate's disappearance, and he blames us, because all this started when my parents arrived to claim their property."

Brett reached for her hand. "Let's go inside." He turned to his grandfather. "Gramps, are you alright? You haven't said a word."

189

Leo shook his head. "Nothing to add except that twerp should mind his manners."

Once inside Brett explained what happened at the police station.

Kayleigh moaned. "Poor Kate, it's all my fault that she was captured. She told me to stay away from her, but I didn't listen."

He drew her close. "Kayleigh, don't go there; my plane will be ready to fly in the morning, and together we'll search for that SOS sign. Don't fret, we'll find her."

CHAPTER FORTY-SIX

Kate lay on the recliner and looked at her feet that were still wrapped with ice packs and moaned. She bent forward and opened the towels so she could see her feet. "Darn it, they're still puffy." She lifted them out of the melting ice that was left in the towels. They didn't look as bad as yesterday. She grabbed the towel and slid off the recliner. Making her way to the sink, she emptied the remaining ice cubes and refilled the towel with fresh ice.

The swelling of her feet was less which gave her ankles some relief from the venomous pain she'd endured through the night. She climbed back into the recliner and rewrapped her feet in ice. Looking out the windows, she watched Gina who paced back and forth, watching and waiting for the men to return from George Town.

Kate gazed out beyond Gina at the calm aqua-blue sea thinking of how she was set off from the rest of the world; if only she could fly away from this madness.

***

Brett met Mac early in the morning and was surprised to see the A and P mechanic already inspecting his plane. "Mac, how long has he been here?"

"Not long, but he's taking his time inspecting every bolt, making sure everything works as it should, and she's fit to fly. There's not much we can do until he's finished; let's have a cup of coffee."

He walked over to his desk and picked up a piece of paper. "I have a list of the equipment I need you to pick up in Nassau so I can repair those sailboats."

Brett scanned the items on the list and took a sip of the hot brew. "This is gonna be quite a haul; let's see, stainless steel nuts and bolts, fittings, haloids, spreaders, and lumber. I'll do the best I can to find them."

The mechanic emerged from the plane's engine compartment. He was a large man with a serious demeanor and looked at Brett. "You the owner?"

"Yes, I am."

"It looks to be in good shape, nice job; there's no sign of corrosion that can easily build up on seaplanes. Your plane and engines are in good shape." A smile spread across his face. "Let's go for a ride."

"Sure thing." He looked at Mac. "Would you like to join us?"

"Sorry, man, I'm not a fan of flying. You two take her up. I'll stick to watercraft."

They moved the plane out into the cove and settled into the cockpit. Brett finished his check list drill and was anxious to take off. He felt like a kid who had his favorite toy back. He started the engines, and the plane skimmed over the water as it lifted one pontoon and then the other one and then they were airborne. The engines hummed as they rose above the sea and headed into the sky.

Brett circled over Stocking Island and flew along the coast looking for signs of a SOS but saw nothing. He then returned the mechanic to the marina and made good on his promise to help Mac when he returned from Nassau.

On his way back to the hotel he stopped at the clinic and arranged to take two patients and a nurse with him on his way to Nassau.

Leaving there he continued his walk back to the hotel when someone approached him from behind and stuck a gun under his ribs. He jerked when the gun pressed further into his body. "What the hell?" Adrenaline kicked into his veins, and he swung around trying to distance himself from the predator.

To his surprise Lance stood there pointing the gun at him. "Don't move; I'm in control here."

"What do you want from me?" Brett could tell Lance was in an agitated state and capable of being irrational, and he knew he best keep calm.

"I want you, Mr. Fly Boy, to take me for a plane ride. I saw you buzzing around earlier, and now it's time for us to go find Kate. I just left the police station, and they showed me the ransom note. Now there's no doubt in anyone's mind that she's been captured just like I suspected."

Brett watched Lance's eyes dart from side to side; he was frantic. "Lance what do you have in mind; where would you like me to take you?"

Lance raised his gun. "Don't be coy with me. Kayleigh said she saw a SOS on a beach; we need to find that beach!"

"Yes, in an ideal world, that's what needs to be done, but your one gun is no match for the Mob. Let's talk it over and offer our help to the police who are coordinating their men with the Bahamian Defense Force to form a man hunt to find Kate."

Lance frowned and put his gun down. "Mate, I think I am going off me trolly. An organized search makes sense, doesn't it? I don't want to put Kate in more danger."

Brett took a few steps away. "So, let's utilize their professional training, because I don't have a better idea at this time."

Lance put his gun aside and backed away.

"Lance, why don't you go back and talk with the police, then get yourself some rest. That might help you clear your mind."

He sighed. "I'll be in touch, mate." He turned and walked away.

Brett wiped his brow, thinking everything that happens in life is at the mercy of what is happening in the present. This place was trying his patience, but he refused to give in.

CHAPTER FORTY-SEVEN

B rett was weary from the complexity of his day and just wanted to relax. He entered the hotel lobby when he heard Roberta's familiar voice. "Mr. Kelsall, I have a message for you from the nurse at the clinic."

He blew out a few breaths and looked at her. "What's up?"

"She just asked that you give her a call back."

His lips curled slightly. "Thanks, I'll call her from the room."

Leo and Kayleigh were on the balcony when Brett walked in the room. Kayleigh's dark eyes were intense and beamed with joy. "You've done it! I watched you fly by. How great!!"

He cuddled her within his arms. "Yes, it feels great, but I've got a busy schedule tomorrow. Maybe we can find some private time for each other." He winked. "But first I must call the nurse at the clinic."

He punched the number on his phone. When it rang, it was answered immediately. "Hi, this is Brett Kelsall I'm returning the nurse's call." There was silence while he waited, and his nerves had been on edge since Lance had shoved the gun in his ribs, and he jolted the phone when the nurse spoke.

"Mr. Kelsall, we are all set for the transfer of two patients to Nassau in the morning, but I can't find anyone here who will be able to provide the medical coverage they need."

Brett hesitated. "Sorry to hear that; maybe someone on your staff will come through."

"I'm afraid not; they have been working their tails off taking care of the injured. I couldn't ask them to do more." Brett s disappointment was evident. "All right, I'll be leaving early. If you need me, let me know."

He looked at Kayleigh, and she quizzed him. "What was that about?" She paused and brushed her hands over the tiny bristles on his face.

He frowned. "Seems I've had one of your days."

"Oh, why's that?"

"I arranged to take a couple of the sickest patients at the clinic with me to Nassau. All the plans were final, but now they can't find staff to cover the transfer."

Kyleigh didn't miss a beat. "I'll go with them; my stewardess training should suffice. I can do CPR and take vital signs."

Brett considered the proposal. "That's a great idea. I'll call her back."

***

They arrived at Port Nassau and were met by an ambulance and assisted with the transfer of the patients; then they hailed a cab and collected all the parts needed for Mac and within a few hours they were on their way back to Exuma.

Brett marveled at his plane's performance and got lost in his own thoughts.

Kayleigh sat in silence, listening to the drone of the engines but soon got bored; she broke the silence. "Hey, instructor, how about teaching me to fly?"

Her question brought him back to the present. He looked at her mischievous smile. "Are you serious?"

She nodded. "Why of course I am. I'm used of being in the air, just not sure how to get up here."

Brett searched for an open area of the sea and dropped the plane into the water. "I'll give you a condensed version of the take off. If you think you could handle it, I'll walk you through the procedure, and if you're serious, I'll help you get your pilot's license, then teach you to fly a seaplane."

The lesson was brief, and they continued with their flight. The view from the sky was panoramic and looking down, it was easy to see the sandy beaches. "Brett, you know we should be looking for the SOS."

You're right; we're close enough to George Town to start our search. I'll bring her down a bit. It could be somewhere around here." Their hunt was uneventful, and as they glided over George Town, they noticed an increase of official watercraft in the water.

"Brett, what's going on down there?"

"Looks like those boats have artillery aboard, must be the arrival of the Royal Bahamian Defense Force. Maybe we'll get some results soon.

***

Leo was in the hotel alone getting ready to go out when he felt pain radiate up his left arm into his chest. Drops of perspiration formed on his forehead, so he sat down. "Not this again, and not now! I guess I better take one of those tranquilizers I have in the other room." He went to his room, reached for a tablet, and put it in his mouth. "Doc Eric told me I might have spells like this from time to time." He rested on his bed, and the pain subsided.

It was the damn stress in this place; first the bullet wound, then the kidnapping and the fall during the storm, but nothing was worse than that haunted house. That was too spooky. He wasn't sure if he'd really seen his ancestor or if he was losing his mind. Just thinking about it gave him goose bumps.

Leo relaxed and dosed off; when he awoke, he started jotting things down. He was satisfied with his notes and set the paper aside. Then he reached for the gun he had confiscated from Luigi and checked it. It was fully loaded, and the safety was intact. He placed the gun in the center of his back and slid it under his belt.

He'd keep it there until he returned. He needed it for safety precautions in case those thugs had any more ideas. He left the room and walked along the harbor seeking a place to eat. A restaurant called Freda's looked inviting. He asked for a seat by the window and ordered his lunch, then scanned the water, thinking about his home in the mountains. This place wasn't so bad. He was glad the deed had made Brett and Kayleigh happy. But once he completed his business here, he'd head back to where he belonged. He might come back for a visit now and then though. Gotta keep in touch with the young'uns.

"Rise above the Storm and you will find Sunshine."
Mario Fernandez

CHAPTER FORTY-EIGHT

G ina wanted more action; she thought it might have been wrong to go it alone, because she sensed things were changing. Killing men, blowing up buildings, and kidnapping people hadn't altered anything. Her dreams of making millions or even billions of dollars by building a casino on the Kelsall property seem to be fading. She could make more money with her drug trafficking operation, without all the hassle, plus she admitted she didn't like being isolated on this small island. She made up her mind to return to Exuma. She'd contact the guy that runs the bar at the Cellar; he had a close relationship with the crime syndicate in Nassau.

***

Kate watched the Chris Craft pull into the Marina and wondered what would happen next. She didn't have to wait long for an answer when Gina came through the door.

"Let me see your feet!" Gina demanded.

Kate raised them up off the recliner.

"Looks like the swelling has lessened; get ready, we are moving back to Exuma."

Kate thought about the SOS outlined in the sand. "Why's that? Where are you taking me now? And what about these ties around my ankles? Don't you think people will be suspicious when they see me struggling to walk?"

Gina grumbled. "Well, my British lassie, I guess I'll have to release them until we get to the Cellar. Then I might have to lock you in a box until I get the deed to the property."

Kate felt a wave of relief but knew better than to show Gina any sign of her new hope of escaping.

Gina pulled out a pair of scissors from her pocket and moved closer to the recliner. "Don't try anything funny or you might get a bullet through your pretty little head." She cut the ties that held Kate's ankles together. "Go put on your own clothes. I'll be back to collect you."

Kate exhaled. "I'll be ready"

Gina walked out, slamming the door behind her.

Kate looked at her feet and wiggled her toes. It felt so good to be out of those shackles. She couldn't wait to put on her own clothes and sandals, but she knew better than to get too excited. Who knows what they had instore for her. Just in case someone discovers the SOS, she'd better leave a note about going to the Cellar, wherever that was.

She put her clothes on while awaiting her next move. Her heart started to pound. No telling when they'd return. The more she thought about it, the more anxious she got. Soon she got herself so riled up that she began to hyperventilate. She closed her eyes and tried to slow her breathing, hoping it would help her calm down.

She found a notepad sitting on the counter and grabbed the pen alongside it, then scribbled a note that said, "Look in the cellar," and signed her initials. Next, she had to hide it in plain sight. She glanced at the gray uniform lying on the floor and slid it underneath, praying that someone would search the room and discover it.

She was having a hard time coping with her situation. She peered out the window at the marina and the large house, but there was no movement. She began to pace while she watched and waited for the creepy men to come for her. The day grew long, and when the sky turned into a shade of dusky gray, Sebbie arrived. "Sweetheart, it's time for us to leave."

He grabbed her and led her out. "Don't try anything that you'll regret."

He pushed her along the path to the marina. When she stumbled, her heart began to pound again. "Take it easy, my ankles are all torn up, and it hurts to walk. No thanks to you."

Russo stood behind the wheel of the Chris Craft, and the twin motors roared to life. With everyone aboard, he drove it though the Hog Cay Cut and headed north. By the time they reached the dock in George Town the last rays of light were dipping into the sea. Russo noticed the Defense Forces armored boats lined up outside the Government Building. "Looks like we better lay low. I'll leave you off here and slip away before anyone gets suspicious."

The threesome swiftly made their way past the market and slipped behind the Cellar. The gray color of twilight blended in with the concrete building. The bartender was waiting for them and led them to a door in the rear of the building. He opened it, revealing a furnished apartment reeking of smoke.

Kate swallowed hard. The flat was dimly lit, and the furnishings were tattered, giving the place a menacing feeling. The cold barren walls reminded her of a dungeon hiding some deranged creature who lived there and could jump out and murder someone at any moment. Not unlike the creatures who held her captive.

Gina pushed her aside. "Seems no one is interested in saving your ass, sweety, but we'll keep you around for a while. Come with me, I'll show you your new accommodations."

She led Kate to a dark windowless room which held a cot and a card table. "Out of the kindness of my heart, I'm not going to bind your ankles, but I'm locking you in this room."

Kate shuddered. "This is worse! It's like being in solitary confinement. It's inhumane! I haven't done anything wrong, and I'm not a Kelsall, so let me out of here! I can't give you what you want!"

Gina turned and walked out, locking the door behind her.

***

Gina wrote a new ransom note and gave it to Russo. "Take this to the to the Pease and Plenty". This one demanded the deeds be left by the Banyan Tree in the park and threated that if it wasn't delivered by noon the next day, Kate would be killed.

Dark glasses covered Russo's face but otherwise he looked inconspicuous and blended in with the people gathered in the lobby. He sat down in a plush chair, waiting until the receptionist stepped away, then he left the note on the desk and walked out.

Brett took the new ransom note to the police who reviewed the note and regarded the threat as a prank. But because the mobsters threatened to kill Kate, they decided to place a manila envelope by the tree and a surveillance detail in the park and waited.

Meanwhile, the Defense Force patrol ships and two of their helicopters were scouring the beaches along the main island and the multiple cays surrounding the area in search of the SOS signal.

Brett and Kayleigh were in his seaplane covering the Little Exuma sector. After flying over the expansive beach that lined the shore of the island, Brett circled his plane over the ocean and banked it over Hog Cay. Kayleigh practically jumped out of her seat. "Brett, there it is! I saw the SOS on that deserted beach!"

He swung his plane around, lowering it to 50 feet and made a pass over the beach while Kayleigh took a picture.

"That a girl," Brett smiled. "Now it's time for the big guns to take charge!"

CHAPTER FORTY-NINE

The Royal Bahamian Defense Force surrounded Hog Cay. They cautioned the Kelsalls not to interfere with their operation, but after seeing the search end abruptly, the three of them decided to do some snooping on their own. Brett taxied his plane up to the beach, and they prowled around the grounds. "I don't think we're going to find much here. Let's check out the main house."

The door was left open, so they entered. The awe-inspiring structure was tainted by an array of dirty dishes that filled the kitchen sink. Dirty towels were strewn on the bathroom floors, and empty liquor bottles were piled up everywhere.

Kayleigh shook her head at the mess. "This trash looks recent. Whoever owns this place won't like all the garbage cluttering up their mansion."

After searching the house for a while Brett said, "Let's see what's in the small house. It looks like the kind that could be for the staff."

They marched together down the path to the less formal building which was less elegant but not as trashed. They looked around and found the plastic ties lying on the floor by the recliner. Kayleigh picked them up. "What are these? Look, Brett, they're covered with dried blood."

"Let me see." He took them from her. "They're attached together like a chain. I bet they shackled them to Kate's legs and were cut off when they left."

Kayleigh shuddered. "How cruel, poor Kate. Let's see what else we can find."

In the bathroom they found wet towels in the shower. Kayleigh picked one up. "This towel is dripping wet, and it too has blood stains on it."

Leo almost tripped over a gray dress and kicked it out of his way. "Did they have a maid here?"

"I doubt it, Gramps, this place is too much of a mess."

Kayleigh saw a piece of paper peeking out from under the uniform on the floor. "What's that?'

She picked it up and gasped in surprise. "It's a note from Kate!"

"Let me see! What does it say?"

"It's brief and says look in the cellar. KR"

Brett shook his head. "I don't get it. These houses don't have cellars, and I didn't see a wine cellar anywhere. We'd better go back and see if we can find one in the manor house."

"Wait a minute, Sonny." Leo's lips were pursed, and he waved his hands. "Isn't that the name of the place you took me to for hot dogs when that mafia brut kidnapped me?"

Kayleigh burst out. "That's it! They moved there because it is a hangout for the type of creepy people that the police tend to ignore."

"Get a grip." Brett pointed out, "Before we play any more detective games, we better take this note to the police. The Defense Force has special training, and they'll know what to do. Let's go, we're done here."

***

Lance walked through the heavily guarded park with a manila envelope in his hands. Russo and Sebbie stood in the shadows and watched. "Seb, I don't like this. It's too easy; something ain't right, Let's get out of here."

Lance reached the tree and looked around before dropping the envelope on the ground, then he backed away and waited. After an hour passed and no movement was seen, the surveillance was cancelled.

The hit men escaped the trap and alerted Gina of the fleet of armed vessels in Elizabeth Harbor. Gina knew it was time to leave Exuma and made up her mind to rethink her approach of taking over the Kelsall land for another day. The three of them slid into the front seat of the banged up green pickup and left town, leaving Kate locked in the dark isolated room.

Russo asked, "Where to?"

Gina contemplated their next move. "We can't go to the airport; let's head north to the town of Barretarre, it's a small island known for being an ideal spot for those that like to go bone fishing. We'll rent a boat and head north."

They reached the town which lies off the northwestern tip of Great Exuma in less than an hour and drove through the community with its colorful painted houses. "Look for a marina that rents boats."

Sebbie pointed. "There's a shell flag waving at the end of a dock; let's stop there; they'll know where we can get a boat."

Russo parked the truck then sauntered up the dock to a man standing by the fuel pump. "Hey, buddy, I'd like to rent a boat to go bone fishing this afternoon."

The man looked Russo over. "You don't look the type; you a fisherman?"

Russo nodded. "I've done my share of bone fishing. Just want to take it out for a couple of hours."

"We got boats to rent. Gonna cost you a couple hundred dollars."

Russo wrinkled his brow. "That's a bit steep. What'll I get for the Benjamins?"

The man looked at him with a straight face. "If you don't damage my boat, I'll give you some back. The fee is $25.00 an hour; that includes rods, bait, and fuel, and we have a guide if you want, but that'll be extra. The rest is for insurance in case you damage our vessel."

Russo reached in his pocket, pulled out some cash, and counted out $200.00. "Here you go, and I'm leaving my truck, so don't worry; I'll be back."

The man busied himself preparing the boat while the others waited on the dock. When the boat was fully loaded, they left the dock and followed the channel which hugged the shoreline until they reached deeper water where Russo opened her up and sped away.

***

The Kelsall group returned to George Town, and Brett brought the note to the police station. By late afternoon the Bahamian Defense Force team surrounded the Cellar and stormed into the bar with their weapons raised. "Hands up, don't anyone move."

The bartender yelled, "What's the meaning of this?"

The Commander shouted, "Come out here, barkeep, and keep your hands raised. We have firsthand information indicating that you are harboring criminals here."

Two of the Force Sergeants grabbed him, and one placed his weapon under the barkeep's chin. "Where are they?"

The man didn't respond, so a sergeant shoved him. "Show us around your establishment."

203

The bartender didn't move. "I don't have any idea what you're talking about." He twisted and attempted to push the man holding the gun. "Get off."

That move called for force. "Have it your way." The Commander called for his men to storm the building. Meanwhile, they arrested the bartender. Outside, the men located the door to the apartment and broke in, but the room was vacant.

Kate heard the commotion, but not knowing what was happening, she remained silent.

The men checked the locked door to the room where Kate was held. "Anyone in there?"

Kate froze; fearing that imminent danger lay on the other side.

The bold orders continued. "We're breaking in!"

Kate screamed! "Stop, don't shoot! Help me! Please!"

"Stand back from the door!"

A gun shot blew the lock off the door which swung open. Men in uniform filled the room.

Kate was in shock and tears welled up in her eyes.

In an intimidating tone, one of the Force soldiers asked, "Who are you?"

She looked at him through her tears. "I'm Kate Robinson."

CHAPTER FIFTY

The Commander of the Defense Force escorted Kate to the police station. The detective invited them to use his office for the interview. "Miss, please try to relax. I know you've been through a traumatic ordeal, but we need you to start from the time you were abducted and explain to us what happened."

The crowded room was a suffocating environment, and Kate felt overwhelmed. She looked at the men and slowly sipped the tea they had offered which helped to calm her nerves. She tried her best to give a detailed account of her captivity. She stressed that she was unaware of where her kidnappers had disappeared.

The men in the room were satisfied with her testimony, and the next thing she knew, she was reunited with Lance who had waited patiently for her in the reception area.

He embraced her, holding her tight. "I know you've been through a great deal, and I promise you, it will all end soon. All this will be over soon, and we will be happier than ever before in our lives."

"Lance, I have collywobbles, and I'm knackered, but you were right to warn me about befriending Kayleigh. None of this would have happened if I'd listened. I'm sorry, love."

"You need to get some rest. While you go back to the sailboat, I must fulfill my obligation to take Kayleigh to her parents."

She smiled tenderly. "I'm so happy to be here with you. When the Kellsals are reunited, things will go back to normal, and everyone will be able to move on." They walked to the dock, and Kate boarded the shuttle boat to Stocking Island. She gave Lance a big hug. "Hurry back."

**

Lance waited for the dock to clear, then as prearranged, Brett taxied his seaplane up to the dock, and Lance climbed aboard. They headed for Cave Cay.

During the flight Lance explained to Brett and Kayleigh why he helped move Ted and Carole onto the houseboat.

Kayleigh was both irritated and pleased. "I guess I owe you an apology, but I still don't understand why you wouldn't tell me all that. It would have been so simple."

When they reached the cay, Brett circled above, trying to determine the best place to land. "This place looks deserted, and where is the houseboat?"

Lance was baffled by the absence of the houseboat. "This is incredible." He shook his head. "Something is drastically wrong."

Kayleigh was having difficulty controlling herself. "Drastically wrong! Where are they? Where did they go? What's happened to them? You just left them here alone and never checked on them again?"

She dabbed a tear that rolled down her cheek, biting her lip as she stared at Lance. "This is crazy, first you said your intent was to protect them, but they're gone. For all we know, they could be dead."

Lance was embarrassed. "Let's talk with the man who maintains this place."

Brett landed his plane in the marina basin and taxied over to the dock where the caretaker ran out to meet them. The plane bobbed around in the water as Brett emerged from the hatch. The man on the dock called out to him. "Mister, you having trouble? We don't get many seaplanes here."

Lance joined Brett on the rear of the plane. "Hi, there mate, I escorted a couple in a houseboat here a while back, and they rented one of the slips from you. You're Ed, right?"

"Yes, of course, I remember you, you're a Brit."

"They were supposed to remain here until I returned. Where'd they go?"

Ed had a weather-beaten complexion like an old salt and hesitated for an instant. "We had a break in. Some guys were looking for money; they robbed the little I had and shot me. The couple left shortly after that incident. I guess it upset the woman, and the next thing I knew, they were gone. Skipped out during the night, they did. Never said where they were going."

"Are you sure?"

His face darkened. "Yeah, I'm sure!"

"Sorry, it's just that the guy didn't know much about running a houseboat in these waters."

Ed sighed. "I don't get involved, not my business." Brett leaned forward. "Can you tell us if there are any other marinas close by where they may have gone?"

"Exuma to the south and Staniel Cay to the north; they both have facilities like marinas, stores, and restaurants. You should fly around the area and see if you can spot them. Don't see many houseboats that colorful around here."

"Thanks, we'll do that."

They scrambled back inside the plane. Brett checked his GPS for the location of Staniel Cay and flew the plane in that direction. The flight was brief. "We're here, folks, look for the houseboat."

The plane glided over the Staniel Cay Yacht Club with many mega sized luxury vessels lining the slips.

"I don't see any yet. Lance, can you see? You're the one who knows what it looks like."

Exasperated, he moaned. "Yes, Kayleigh, I'm looking."

Brett reduced the plane's altitude as they scanned the area. Lance shouted, "I see it, it's that colorful boat at that marina."

Brett could clearly see the reefs and sandbars and splashed the seaplane in an open area away from the congestion of the many boats. There wasn't enough space to move his plane closer. Staniel Cay Creek was home to several transient yachtsmen. Before long a few curious boaters approached them in their dinghies. "Hey, captain, do you need any help?"

Brett waved and smiled. "We'd apricate a lift to the marina, we need to contact the people staying on the houseboat."

Kayleigh and Brett jumped in the dinghy. "Lance, hold the fort, we won't be long."

The dinghy skipped along the water and drew close to the dock, then the sailor said, "I'll tie up here and wait for you in the bar. Just let me know when you want to get back to the plane."

Kayleigh smiled at him. "You're kind, thanks." She grabbed Brett's hand, and they bounced along the dock and jumped on the front deck of the houseboat.

The commotion startled Carole. "Ted, come quick; someone's on the boat!"

Kayleigh ran to the door and entered. Ted yelled, "What's the meaning of...Oh, my! Kayleigh, it's you!"

She bounded into his arms, and he hugged her. "Carole, come quick!" Tears of joy tumbled down their cheeks.

Kayleigh kissed Carole. "Mom, I missed you so much! You look great. I was so worried about your safety."

After sharing their stories, they quickly decided to leave, and Lance volunteered to help drive them back to Exuma.

Brett waited until they were on their way, then took off in his plane.

***

Leo opted to remain in the hotel while the others went to find Ted and Carole. He was concerned about the recent bouts of chest pain he was experiencing and thought about how his life had changed being with Brett and Kayleigh. He enjoyed being involved in their adventure and felt his life was more fulfilled with the laughter and comradery he experienced by being with them. It would make him happy if they chose to make a life for themselves together. He pulled out the recent note he had written and added to it. "I need to make this legal just in case something unforeseen happens to me," he muttered.

He slipped through the lobby and strolled down the sidewalk along the harbor and noticed that the disabled sailboats were slowly disappearing. He climbed the stairs and opened the door to the Government Building and approached the receptionist. Her smile and beautiful blue eyes seem to welcome him. Suddenly, the paper in his hand was shaking, and his knees felt weak.

Diane noticed his nervousness. "Sir, how may I help you?"

"I have just completed this document, and I need to have someone make it legal."

"I'll be glad to help you, Mister…?"

"Oh, I'm sorry, Miss, my name is Leo Kelsall."

She grinned and took the paper from his trembling hands. "It's not an everyday occurrence that one writes their last will and testament, but if it helps, I know Miss Jones and Mr. Brett, so you're in good hands."

Leo proudly said, "He's my grandson."

"Yes, sir. I'll be just a moment, if you wish, have a seat and make yourself comfortable."

Diane returned with a completed government form signed and sealed and placed it along with his handwritten note in an envelope. "Here you go, Mr. Kelsall, now you can relax; everything is legal."

Leo glanced in the envelope. "Thanks, dear."

She helped Leo up and escorted him to the door. "See, it wasn't all that bad. Watch your step on the stairs."

He turned, briefly closed his eyes, and sighed.

CHAPTER FIFTY-ONE

The Kelsall family was finally reunited and made their departure plans. Ted and Carole booked a flight from Exuma International Airport to Florida. Brett, Kayleigh, and Leo would be returning to the states on the seaplane.

They were all gathered on the dock waiting for Lance and Kate. Kayleigh's eyes glistened as she stood between Ted and Carole. "Mom, it was such a great idea to say our final goodbyes to Little Exuma with a picnic lunch on our own special beach."

"I want to savor the splendor of our property until we get a chance to return."

Brett reached for Kayleigh and embraced her, then planted a kiss on her forehead. "This is a joyous occasion for all of us to be able celebrate the results of the unforeseen trouble everyone has endured; somehow now seems it might have been worth it."

He turned to Leo. "And thanks, Gramps, for letting us enjoy our own piece of paradise."

"I never anticipated that an ancient piece of paper could have caused such turmoil to all of you. I'm sorry for that, but it united us in such a way that has made me a happy man."

The sound of the approaching shuttle boat disrupted their conversation. Lance jumped on the dock, but to everyone's surprise he was alone. "Where's Kate?"

"She doesn't feel well. Everything she's been through lately has gotten her down." Kayleigh noted that he was avoiding making eye contact with her, and she sensed that something wasn't right. "That's too bad; I'll miss her."

Ted was anxious to leave. "Is everyone ready? Carole and Kayleigh packed our lunch, so everyone get in the rental jeep."

This time the trip to Little Exuma flew by, and the bumpy ride on the unpaved landscape went unnoticed. Ted stopped the jeep when the terrain became unpassable. Everyone jumped out and weaved their way through the lush vegetation which opened onto the most magnificent beach on the island.

Carole opened the picnic basket. "Come on, everyone, don't be shy; it's loaded with food and drink."

Kayleigh sat by the water and shared her dreams of the future. "I'm building a cute bungalow right over there where I can run out and jump in the water, then frolic for the rest of the day."

The others joined in, each presenting their grandiose plans. The day seemed to end much too soon. Ted gathered the clan together. "I don't mean to be a kill joy, but it's time we leave. I don't want to drive in the dark."

They all seemed happy as they piled back in the jeep. Lance, who hadn't offered much throughout the day, spoke up from the back as they passed the salt pond. "Ted, wouldn't you like to stop at the Hermitage House to say goodbye to your friendly family ghosts."

There was little response. Kayleigh frowned, "Lance, that's not even funny."

"It wasn't meant to be." He held up his gun and pointed it at them and demanded, "Ted, park the jeep by the front of the building; then you're all going inside."

Ted, Leo, and Brett hesitated. Lance continued. "Get going up the hill, then inside, all of you now!"

Kayleigh tried to control herself not wanting to escalate the situation. "Can you share what's bothering you, Lance, so we can understand what's on your mind?"

"Get inside, and I'll explain."

They filed into the dark, gloomy building with its suffocating scent of mold and clung to each other.

Lance's gun was a high-powered fully automatic gun that he pointed at the Kelsalls. "Let me explain why I'm here in Exuma. I was hired by a group of lawyers in Devonshire, England, who represent the Kelsall's holdings. The remaining distant descendants have no interest in the land here in Exuma, but there is a trust the lawyers must review periodically. During a recent appraisal, it was noted that members of an underworld organization were actively pursuing a plan to confiscate the Kelsall property and build a massive casino. I was summoned to prevent that from happening."

Carole was frantic and terrified and clutched Ted's arm. "Lance, you were so nice to us and kept us safe. What changed?"

"All of you changed it."

Kayleigh scoffed, "What do you mean, we changed it?"

211

"The lawyers instructed me to make sure this land stays in the right hands, and after being involved with you people, I have concluded you are not the right fit for this land. You are a bunch of Yanks. This land belongs to the British descendants. You people come from the states that supported the American Revolution against England. You don't deserve this beautiful place. So, I thought this would be an appropriate place for all of you to meet your demise."

Kayleigh's heart pounded, but she stood tall beside Brett. "I get it; your unscrupulous plan to claim our land in the name of some lawyers from England is in fact to cover your own maleficence, and your nonchalant attitude about killing us is totally obnoxious."

"That doesn't matter now, does it? Take your time to get to know the ghosts that haunt this place, because soon you will be one of them."

Brett was at his wits end and took a step forward. "We are all Kelsalls and are granted all the rights to this land. Your plan will never work."

Lance's mouth formed a sinister grin. "We will see who wins in the end, won't we? A high powdered automatic weapon against folklore and a piece of paper. Don't try anything clever. Now get back."

He looked beyond the group. "Where are those ghosts today? They seem to be hiding."

Within moments Kayleigh began to feel a weird tingling creep over her. She shivered and held Brett tight. Soon white clouds surrounded each couple, obscuring Lance's vision.

Leo stood alone when John Kelsall reappeared. "It's you again," Leo gasped.

"Yes, Leo, I'm here to remind you of our prior conversation. You do remember it, don't you?"

"Sure. You warned me about evil forces."

"That's right; now you can see there is a devil in this room who isn't confined to hell yet."

Lance was startled. "Old man, are you talking to yourself?"

"No, I'm having a conversation with John."

"John who? Where is he?"

Leo saw the unmistakable panic in Lance's movements. "He was right here."

Lance diverted his attention and looked beyond Leo, giving Leo the chance to grab Luigi's gun from under his belt. He took aim and pulled the trigger, hitting Lance in the chest.

"Take that, you abominable maggot."

Lance's crumpled body lay still, and his cold eyes could no longer see.

***

The white curtain of clouds sheltering the others slowly dissipated, and they emerged from their safe harbor. Kayleigh was still entwined with Brett, and her eyes searched the room looking for her mother and father. Everyone was accountable, but confusion covered their faces.

Kayleigh sighed with relief. "That was a mystical moment. I felt so warm and serene and overwhelmed with contentment. I've never felt like that before in my life."

They all agreed they had encountered similar experiences. Once their bewilderment passed, they looked through their dusky surroundings and were astonished to see two bodies lying on the floor. Gasping, Kayleigh exclaimed, "What could have happened to them?"

They rushed to where the fallen bodies of both men lay. Lance was dead, but Leo reached for Brett.

In a whisper, he said, "Sonny, I did my best to protect my family." Clutching his chest, his labored voice was barely audible. "Thank you for helping me realize that there's more to life than gold. It's my time; please let me go and carry on." He closed his eyes and expelled his last breath.

Kayleigh rushed to his side. "We have to save him. I'll start compressions."

Brett stopped her. "No, Kayleigh, please honor his dying words."

Streams of tears ran down her cheeks, and she looked at her parents. "He gave his all because he loved us."

***

Another glorious sunrise accompanied by a soft sea breeze spread it's light over the Hermitage House and Plantation. The Kelsalls stood together while the preacher spoke. A new tomb joined the others that had been there for centuries, and it was covered with a blanket of flowers. Detective Stevens, Mr. Nichols, Diane, and Mrs. Albury were joined by the many other George Town people that were gathered there to give their condolences to the Kelsall family for the loss of Leo.

Earlier in the week, the police had been called to the scene of the crime and had disposed of Lance's body. It was revealed that Kate was unaware of the wicked plans that Lance had devised, but she was shocked and currently grieved over her loss.

Gina and her companions had run out of fuel and were adrift when the Royal Bahama Defense Force discovered them while returning to their base in Nassau. The trio was now sitting in jail.

***

Later the two couples stood outside the Peace and Plenty saying their goodbyes. Kayleigh hugged her parents. "Have a safe flight home. I'll be in touch.

Carole kissed Kayleigh. "When will you be returning to work, dear?"

Kayleigh hesitated, then a wide grin covered her face. "Mom, I'm not going back to work as a stewardess anytime soon."

"You're not? You have such a fascinating job that takes you all over the world, and maybe you could meet another nice pilot."

"Mom, I have a nice pilot right here! I'm going to join Brett in California. He promised to teach me how to fly a seaplane. Plus, he's hired me to help him with his business and manage Uncle Leo's estate."

Carole looked at Ted. "What do you think about that, Ted?"

He comforted her. "Carole, Kayleigh has a good head on her shoulders and is capable of making her own decisions; besides, Brett is a fine young man."

As they turned to go, Kate came running up to them. "I'm so glad I didn't miss you. Just wanted to tell you I'm moving my sailboat back to Little Exuma. Thanks for leasing me a spot of land that I can call my own. I'll have to start a new life, but I know I can do it. I've finished my article about the resemblances between the Hermitage House and the Henock House, the one in Devon, so I'll receive a salary for my work. Meanwhile, I'll look for work around here. I'm not worried though, for I have your Uncle Leo to watch over me."

The rental jeep sped away toward the airport while Brett lifted the seaplane above Elizabeth Harbor. Kayleigh was full of enthusiasm and planted a kiss on Brett's check. "We're off on a new adventure, and my heart is full of joy!"

Brett turned to smile at her. "You're beautiful, and you make me so happy."

He banked his plane so they could see Elizabeth Harbor, giving them the last glimpse of the beautiful island of Exuma, then soared into the sky.

"Everything in life is an experience
Whether you walked a dark path
Or an easy road, every journey on
Our course comes to an end or a
Beautiful beginning."

Soul ink'n Quill
Tony Perrtge

THE END

215

AUTHOR' S NOTE

A History of the Exumas

Isles where Columbus first unfurled
The Spanish Flag in the western world.
Isles where the pirates once held sway
And scuttled ships off many a cay.
Isles of summer and endless June,
Velvet nights and a golden moon,
Waters of turquoise and lazuli,
Whitest of beaches and sapphire sea.
Isles of romance, story, and song,
Of gallant deeds and bitter wrong.

Anonymous
Printed in *Postage Stamps And
Postal History of the Bahamas*
by Harold C.D. Gisburn

The Exuma Guide 3rd Edition
By Stephen J. Pavlidis

ABOUT THE AUTHOR

SUSANN ELIZABETH RICHARDS is a Registered Nurse with a master's degree in Human Resource Development and Administration from Barry University in Miami Shores, Florida. She has published articles in the Journal for Healthcare Quality. She is the author of *Below the Glow, The Swashbuckler's Odyssey,* and *The Baleful Beads.*

Susann and her husband have sailed extensively throughout Long Island Sound, down the east coast of the United States, spending time on the Chesapeake Bay, then to Florida and the Bahama Islands. They have also sailed through the American and British Virgin Islands.

Other adventures took them to some of the Caribbean Islands including Jamacia, The Cayman Islands, Cancun, plus Bimini, Grand Bahama Island, the Abaco Islands, Eleuthera, and The Exuma Island Chain, all within the Bahamas

She holds an advanced Scuba diver certificate and lives in Sebastian, Florida with her husband Dan and two Persian cats. *The Exuma Enigma* is her fourth book.

Pamela Goldstein

Made in United States
Orlando, FL
05 March 2023